Reflections: Samantha's Story

An Ash Train Time Travel Story

GK Bird

Dedication

Thank you to everyone who has read my stories and
commented positively on them.
Your encouragement keeps me pulling words out of
thin air and fitting them together until they form a
mostly cohesive tale.
I appreciate each and every one of you.

Author's Notes

This story is set in Australia so the spelling, grammar,
and punctuation used throughout the book follows
Australian English rules.

The Ash Train stories can be read in any order.

The Ash Train concept grew out of my original short
story, **The Ash Man**, which was included in my **Saving
the Scarlet Macaw & Other Stories** collection.

Contents

1. Your Secret Admirer   1

2. Fourteen   9

3. Not So Secret Admirer   17

4. Empty   21

5. The Ash Man   28

6. Choices   48

7. Second Chances   63

8. Fourteen Again   74

9. Not So Secret Admirer   79

10. Waiting   84

11. Gone   90

12. Aftermath   94

13. Staying   101

14. Awake   105

15. Worthless   111

16. Alone   118

17. Stories   126

18. Variables   136

19. Attention   143

20. Reminiscences   153

21. Companions   162

22. Thinking   171

23. Missing   173

24. Connections   185

25. Where   196

26. Mistakes   204

27. Frustration   207

28. Planning   214

29. Searching   229

30. Watching   239

31. Witnesses   250

32. Angry   261

33. Melbourne   266

34. Ex   275

35. Paranoia   289

36. Options   305

37. Chase   314

38. Keep Going   324

39. Hiding   332

40. Found   336

41. Confession   344

42. Together   353

43. Escape   363

44. Fixing Mistakes   370

45. Promises   381

46. The Ash Train   387

47. Beginnings   391

1

Your Secret Admirer

Mon, 19 March 1984 – Samantha

"LOVELY SAMANTHA, JUST SEEING your stunning eyes makes my day worthwhile."

Samantha quickly folded the note in half and glanced over her shoulder to make sure no one was nearby. As usual, no one was taking any notice of her, so she smoothed the paper open again and read the rest of the short note, feeling the heat rise in her cheeks as she read.

Lovely Samantha, just seeing your stunning eyes makes my day worthwhile.

The contrast of your perfect green eyes against your jet-black hair takes my breath away every time I gaze upon you. The way the light twinkles in your hair reminds me of starlight on the deepest, darkest night.

I hope you don't mind me saying this, but I wish you would push your hair off your face, so people can see how truly beautiful you are. It's a shame to hide such beauty behind a curtain, even when that curtain is your magnificent hair.

When I look at you, I see our future, so bright and overflowing with love that I sometimes feel like I'm drowning. But I don't want to be saved.

It doesn't seem fair that I know you so well, when you don't even know who I am. I want you to know me in the same way that I know you. Better even. I've almost built up the courage to reveal who I am. I just hope you're not disappointed. It won't be long now.

Love always, YSA (Your Secret Admirer)

She hated that she'd always been a blusher, and she looked at her feet, making her long hair fall in front of her face. She read the note through again, then stood up straight. Tucking her hair back behind her ears, she stared defiantly around the bustling school corridor. *Is he watching me now?* She felt a small thrill in the pit of her stomach at the thought before she turned back to her locker.

This was the fifth note YSA had pushed through the air vents in her locker over the past few weeks for her to find.

When she'd found the first note, she'd assumed it was a joke, probably orchestrated by her sister. She didn't recognise the handwriting, so she knew Suzanna had not written it herself, but she wouldn't put it past her twin to have dared someone to do it. Determined not to give her sister the satisfaction of seeing any sort of reaction, she'd screwed that first note up, tossed it in her bag, and didn't mention it to anyone.

When the second note came, she'd skimmed it with the same scepticism, crumpled it up, and tossed it in her bag with the first.

But, after the third note arrived, and Suzanna still hadn't said anything, Samantha started to believe – hope, really – that it was no joke. There was no way Suzanna could have kept a secret for that long. If it had been her prank, she would have blurted it out by now, just to get the laughs from her cronies at her sister's expense.

After the fourth note, Samantha finally, truly, believed she really did have a secret admirer. She'd pulled the other three notes out of her bag, uncrumpled them, and read all four of them slowly, word by wonderful word. She now believed, with all her heart, that one person in this world genuinely saw her for who she truly was, not just as the loner twin sister of the most popular girl in school.

Samantha folded the latest note carefully and placed it in her history textbook with the other four. She didn't want her sister to find them, and a history book was somewhere she knew her sister would never look.

Suzanna and Samantha may have looked almost identical on the outside, almost reflections of each other, but they were very different personalities on the inside. Suzanna was outgoing and confident and always had a gaggle of followers, male and female, hanging on her every word. Whereas Samantha was more introverted and had no close friends. Not since Tina had moved away just before the start of high school last year. Samantha did not make friends easily. She felt awkward with people she didn't know and struggled to find common interests to talk about. Instead of socialising after Tina left, Samantha had put her head down and studied, which was something her sister rarely did.

Someone suddenly collided into her, slamming her against her open locker with a bang, and knocking the history book out of her hand.

"What are you looking so chuffed about, Sammie? Did you ace another history test?"

The book thumped to the floor, falling open and threatening to release the precious cargo it held. Samantha crouched down and grabbed it, hastily stuffing the notes back inside. This was her secret, and she wouldn't share it with anyone, especially her sister.

She stood up and glared at Suzanna, clutching the book to her chest, while her sister's friends fake-laughed as if Suzanna's words were the funniest words they'd ever heard.

"Wouldn't you like to know," Samantha mumbled, dropping her gaze to her feet so her hair hid her face again. Suzanna knew Samantha hated her calling her Sammie because the way she said it made her sound like a baby. It was only a week until they both turned fourteen, but Suzanna always found a way to make her sister feel inferior, especially at school.

"Actually, I *would* like to know. That's why I asked."

Suzanna turned to Becca, Catherine, and Andrew who were standing behind her. "How often have you seen my downer sister looking happy at school?"

"Um, probably never," Becca said as Catherine snorted.

"Oh, actually there was that one time," Suzanna said, mock-seriously, holding her finger up to make a point. "Remember, a couple of months ago, when Mr Beresford called that surprise history test? She did look pretty happy about that!"

Becca, Catherine, and Andrew laughed loudly as Samantha turned back to her locker, her face red again but not from the same emotion as before. She swept textbooks into her bag, not even checking to see whether they were ones she needed, slammed the locker door closed, and spun the combination lock.

She pushed past her sister and, as she walked away, she heard Suzanna say to her friends, "What did I do?"

Later that afternoon, Samantha was deep in thought, hunched over her maths homework. She sat at the kitchen table and assumed her sister was lounging on the couch, sketching scenes from her day, as she always did. Suzanna was lucky in that she didn't have to study to get good grades, so she didn't. Instead, she spent most of her spare time observing the world around her and recording it in charcoal pencil drawings in her sketchbook.

Neither Mum nor Dad was home from work yet, so they had the house to themselves.

Samantha didn't hear Suzanna sneak up behind her and she jumped, inhaling sharply, when her sister pounced on her bent-over back.

"You're such a jerk," Samantha said, pushing her off.

"Sorry for what I said today," Suzanna said, pulling out the chair next to Samantha and sitting down. "But you know I've got a reputation to protect."

"Why do you have to make me the butt of every joke?" Samantha questioned, staring seriously at her sister. "It's not much fun on this end, you know."

"I know. I know. I'm sorry, OK? I'll try to leave you alone at school from now on."

But they both knew she wouldn't because Samantha was such an easy target.

Suzanna stood up and moved to stand behind Samantha. She pulled her sister's hair back and started to braid it, pulling out tangles with her fingers. "Anyway, our birthday's only a week away. I'm so looking forward to the party. We haven't had a proper birthday party since we turned ten."

"I'm not," Samantha said, trying to concentrate on the algebra in front of her as Suzanna's braiding joggled her head. "I would have been happy to just go out to dinner with the family like we always do."

Suzanna groaned and continued to play with her sister's hair. "Don't be such a downer. It's gonna be great. All that room at the park down by the lake. Mum's organised a live band, and there'll be cake, heaps of presents, games, friends, all the good stuff. Don't expect to get home too early. This party's going until late."

"No one would even miss me if I wasn't there," Samantha said, turning to face her sister.

Suzanna stared at her. "*I* would miss you," she said. "This is not a party for *me*. It's a party for *us*. We'll never turn fourteen again, you know."

"But it will be all *your* friends," Samantha said, turning back to her homework. "We all know how many of *my* friends will turn up."

"You never know," Suzanna said. She looked down at her sister, raising an eyebrow as a mysterious smile played on her lips. "Maybe you'll be surprised."

Samantha looked up at Suzanna, wondering what she meant by that, but Suzanna had already turned away and headed back to the lounge room.

2

Fourteen

Sat, 24 March 1984 – Samantha

"TODAY WE SHOULD LOOK identical," Suzanna declared, turning her head left, then right, as she looked in the mirror. "No one will know which of us they're talking to."

"Why?" Samantha asked, sitting on the bed behind her, stroking Arabella, their tortoiseshell cat. "That used to be funny, but we're not kids anymore."

"Exactly. This might be the last chance we get," Suzanna said, staring at the mirror and running her hands down the length of her long black hair. "I think I'll cut my hair short after this party. I'm getting sick of it always getting in the way and shorter hair looks more grown up. What do you think? Doesn't your hair annoy you?"

Samantha thought of what YSA had written about her hair and smiled to herself as her stomach tingled slightly. She wouldn't be cutting her own hair any time soon.

"Do we even have matching outfits anymore?" Samantha asked.

"We can make something work," Suzanna said, sliding pale pink lipstick across her lips, then smearing it with her fingertips. "Come here. I'll do your makeup to look like mine."

Samantha didn't normally wear makeup, but despite her initial apprehension about this birthday party, the closer it got, the more excited she felt and wanted to look her best.

I wonder if YSA will know which one is me, she wondered, thinking about the sixth note she'd received a couple of days ago. Today was the day he would reveal himself. *Of course, he'll know.*

Suzanna decided they'd both wear white t-shirts, with pale pink button-up shirts over the top, with the top three buttons undone, of course. These would be tucked into high-waisted light blue denim jeans, pulled tight with a chunky black belt. They stood next to each other and inspected themselves in the mirror. The only difference between them was the belt buckle.

"Hang on," said Samantha. She ran to her room and returned with two pale pink satin ribbons. She tied one around Suzanna's hair and put the other in her own, before turning to examine their reflections again.

"Perfect," said Suzanna, throwing her arms around Samantha and squeezing her tightly. "Even I can't tell us apart. Ooh, I'm so excited. This is going to be the best birthday ever."

"The best birthday *so far*," Samantha corrected her, and they both laughed and headed downstairs.

Mum had already headed to the park to make sure everything was set up and ready for when they arrived, and to greet any early guests.

Dad was waiting in the lounge room holding a camera and had a huge smile plastered across his face.

"Oh my," he exclaimed, holding his arms out. "Who's this? Have you two beautiful women seen my little girls? They were here a little while ago." He pretended to look behind them, then smiled as he looked at them again. "Seriously, though, I'd better start watching out for boys now, because none of them will be able to keep away from you. The truth is, I'm a little jealous of you both, right now."

"Why? Do you want the boys to be looking at you?" Suzanna teased.

"No, silly. Because you have your whole lives ahead of you," he said. "At fourteen, you can still be anything you want to be. There's plenty of time to make your dreams happen. Promise me you'll do what you want to do, not what other people tell you to do. Promise me you'll live happy, for me?"

They both smiled and hugged him tight. He pretended he couldn't breathe but he held onto them, reluctantly letting them go when they finally pulled away.

He posed them together in front of the dark blue curtains and took several photographs, pretending to be a paparazzo, telling them to smile and 'look here'.

"Can you tell who's who?" Suzanna teased.

He brought his finger to his lip as he studied Suzanna closely, then did the same with Samantha. "I'm your father. Of course, I can."

"Okay, then, who am I?" Suzanna asked, raising an eyebrow.

Dad smiled and changed the subject. "We'd better get going. You don't want to be late for your own party, do you?"

By 5 PM, the party was in full swing.

It looked like the whole town had turned out, young and old, including families from nearby farms and smaller towns. Miranda Springs was big enough to have a hospital, police station, and primary and high schools, but small enough that everyone knew everyone, and everyone's business. Typical of small Australian country towns, no one wanted to miss out on the chance to celebrate at someone else's expense.

People stood in groups in the park picnic area, chatting and drinking from paper cups. Even some of the teachers from school were there.

Samantha sat on a seat at a wooden picnic table helping her mother who was fussing about with salads and bread, tomato sauce and mayonnaise. She watched Suzanna who was in the middle of a group of people dancing to the loud covers of popular songs played by a local rock band. It seemed as if no one could get enough of her and everyone wanted her attention.

"Why don't you go and join them?" her mother said, glancing up. "Go have fun like your sister."

"Nah, I don't want to," Samantha said, standing up to hand some plastic cutlery to Mr Beresford, her history teacher, who'd just filled his plate with bread.

He took it with a smile and winked at her. It felt a bit weird seeing him outside the school environment. Even though she'd walked his dog for him last school holidays, she hadn't really paid much attention to him, being more focused on the small white Maltese terrier at the time. She realised he wasn't as old as she'd thought he was. He couldn't have been much more than forty, but even that seems old when you've just turned fourteen.

He suddenly bent down, fiddled with something, then stood up again. "Is this yours? It was on the ground."

"Thank you." She hadn't realised her small black leather bag had fallen onto the ground, and she took it from him with a smile.

She sat down again as he wandered off to talk with a group of other teachers.

She pulled her bag onto her lap and felt around inside it for the six notes from YSA. Her heart fluttered and her stomach tingled as she felt them crinkle under her fingertips. She desperately wanted to pull them out and read them, over and over, but she also didn't want anyone else to know about them. They were for her and her alone. Something that she didn't have to share with her twin.

She looked around but couldn't see anyone looking at her. She was starting to think that YSA had chickened out. The party had been going for hours, and no one had come up to her, except for the odd person who thought she was Suzanna. It was awkward when that happened, but also slightly amusing to see the moment when it twigged as to who they were talking to.

She watched her father for a while. He was in his element, manning the barbeque. While the long line of meat-seeking partygoers held their plates out like Oliver Twist, he expertly doled out steak, sausages, rissoles, and potatoes wrapped in tin foil. With each offering, he regaled the party people with embarrassing stories of the twins growing up.

Occasionally one of the people would look over at her and laugh, which made her feel cringey. But Dad was Dad. There was nothing she could do about that, and she knew he was just having fun.

She frowned when her father called Suzanna over and handed the metal tongs to her to take over. More surprising was that Suzanna didn't seem to mind.

"Just got to go get something," he called, waving as he headed for the car.

The light was starting to dim when Dad got back. The passenger side door swung open before the car had even fully stopped, and Tina practically fell out. She looked around and waved wildly when she spotted Samantha.

Samantha stood up and waved back, just as wildly. Her bag slipped to the ground again, completely forgotten, as she ran across the grass towards her former best friend.

3

Not So Secret Admirer

Sat, 24 March 1984 – Suzanna

SUZANNA SMILED AS SHE watched Samantha and Tina walking towards the swing set, talking ten to the dozen. Samantha and Tina used to spend a lot of time here and, since Tina had moved away, Samantha sometimes came here and swung slowly, silently, lost in thought. She looked so sad, it broke Suzanna's heart to see her here alone.

It had taken a bit of detective work, but seeing Samantha's reaction, Suzanna was glad she'd made the effort to track Tina down. She'd been expecting Tina's parents to say no, since it was such a long way to travel, but she needn't have worried. Dad had said he'd pay for her plane ticket and convinced them that Tina would be safe. He'd pick her up from the airport, and drop her back a few days later, making sure she got on her return flight safely.

Dad took his place again at the barbeque and Suzanna headed over to the table where Samantha had been sitting. She sat and watched her sister and her friend as they caught up with what had happened in their lives since they'd last seen each other more than eighteen months ago.

She moved and her foot kicked something. Glancing down, she bent over and picked up Samantha's bag. However, she grabbed it from the bottom, it tipped up, and some papers fell out. The breeze caught the pages, and they fluttered away, but Suzanna chased them and quickly caught them.

She was about to shove them back in the bag when a couple of words caught her eye in the fading light. 'Stunning', 'beautiful', 'perfect'.

Curious, she moved under a park light to read them. They were all dated, so she put them in order and started at the beginning.

There were seven notes, the last of which was dated today.

"What the hell?" she muttered as she read. "Why didn't you tell me about this, sis?"

She got to the last note.

My perfect Samantha, today is the day.

I didn't think this day would ever come, but we can finally be together. From this day forth, we'll never be apart. Nothing will ever come between us.

They'll be talking about us until our story becomes a legend, a myth lost in time. We'll be that family everyone aspires to but never achieves.

There's so much I want to say to you but today I will say these things in person, so this note can be short.

Come to the children's playground on the far side of the lake at 9 PM. I'll be waiting.

Love always, from YSNTBSSA (Your Soon Not To Be So Secret Admirer)

"This is so creepy," Suzanna said to herself, shaking her head. Surely Samantha couldn't believe this was real.

Suzanna checked her watch. 8:55 PM. She considered showing the notes to Dad or Mum, but she didn't want to embarrass her sister. Although it was almost dark now, she could see Samantha still with Tina, and she looked happy. So much happier than she had for a very long time.

"Alright," Suzanna said to herself. "I'll deal with this. This needs to stop, right now."

She slipped away from the party, walking down to the water and then along the dimly-lit footpath that led to the children's playground on the other side of the lake.

4

Empty

Sun, 24 March 2024 – Samantha

SAMANTHA FELT EMPTY AS she stared at the granite headstone.

For forty years, her mother truly believed Suzanna was coming home. Every night the front porch light had to be left on, the front door left unlocked, because that might be the night she came home. And what if she couldn't get in? What then?

For forty years, Samantha never believed her sister was coming home. She knew it in her heart, knew it was her fault that Suzanna was gone and there was nothing anyone could do to change that. She tried *being* Suzanna for a while, but it was just too hard, so she gave up.

And giving up became a part of who Samantha was. She gave up on her dreams, her studies, her belief that life was something you could control. For forty years, she let life happen *to* her rather than make it happen *for* her. It was so much easier to give control away so whatever happened would be someone else's fault.

"Did you truly believe she was coming home?" Samantha asked her mother's grave.

She remembered her mother's hysterics when, around five years after Suzanna's disappearance, her father suggested they consider moving somewhere that wasn't so full of memories. Samantha had sat on her bed with her hands over her ears, trying to block out her mother's high-pitched screams that accused him of wanting to forget their daughter, to erase her for good.

She looked around the cemetery, marvelling that the sky was clear blue, the sun was glaringly hot, and only a slight breeze stirred the petals of the flowers that were propped against other gravestones. In the movies, it always rained during funerals and people stood around with large black umbrellas, comforting each other and dabbing away tears with clean white handkerchiefs. This wasn't that, at all.

She watched the retreating backs of the three other people who'd come to her mother's funeral and wondered if they wondered why she wasn't crying. She looked back at the grave.

"I'm curious. What did you think would happen if she *did* come home, Mum? Did you think we'd all be magically transported back to 1984 to live our lives over, the way we were supposed to? Did you think that having Suzanna home would allow us to go back to playing happy families? I hate to tell you, but it doesn't work like that."

She sighed, wishing she'd asked her mother these questions while she was still capable of answering, but it was too late now. Maybe she'd ask her in the afterlife that she didn't believe in.

Samantha took a step and laid her hand on the headstone that had yet to have her mother's details added underneath her father's. "Love you, Dad."

She pulled her cap low over her face and walked home, sweating under the hot sun, but with eyes as dry as the brown summer grass along the side of the tarmac.

Forty years had made little difference to the size of the town. Children were born, adults left, seniors stayed until they ended up in the ground, the one place they could no longer escape from, like her parents.

She barely noticed the scenery as she walked. The same houses sat on the same blocks, only now the paint was faded, the boards warped, the windows dirty. Stringy yellow grass forced its way between the concrete slabs of the driveways and footpaths, growing up around the carcasses of rusty old cars and bikes.

She glared at the lake and the neglected picnic grounds as she passed them, refusing to let them intimidate her into walking faster. A couple of kids were aimlessly kicking a soccer ball on what was once a well-kept green grassy area but was now just red and grey dirt. A rusty metal goal post, flecked with old white paint flakes, lay abandoned on the ground, and she thought that was a fitting symbol of the story of this town and of her own life. Faded, worn out, and no one cared.

She stopped at the front door of the place she'd once called home, hesitating for a second before grabbing the handle and twisting it. Of course, the door was unlocked. She smiled to herself. If she'd done that in the city, she'd come home to an empty flat. Not that she had much to steal anyway. Her last boyfriend had seen to that.

She briefly wondered if she should have visited her mother more often, especially after her father's death two years ago. She knew her mother's mental and physical health was declining – the local priest had reached out to her a couple of times – but she couldn't bring herself to come back here.

The last time she'd visited, her mother kept calling her Suzanna. She'd gritted her teeth and corrected her the first few times, but she could only stand it for a couple of days before she gave up and made an excuse, saying she had to get back home to her job. Her non-existent job, but her mother didn't know that.

She wandered into the kitchen, filled the kettle, and switched it on. She dug a dusty teabag out of a warped brown pottery container that either she or Suzanna had made at school and leaned down to get a mug out of the cupboard. Standing up, she leaned back against the bench waiting for the water to boil.

She let her gaze drift over the photo wall in the open dining area next to the kitchen. She lingered on the old sepia-toned pictures of her parents' parents, her parents as children, and her parents during their early years of being together. Next to these, taking up the most space, were colourful photos of her and Suzanna, from when they were babies, and their whole family from a time when they'd actually been happy.

One particular photo caught her eye. She walked over and stared at the photo her father had taken on the morning of their fourteenth birthday. The kettle clicked off behind her, but she didn't notice. This photo had not been here the last time she'd been in this house. It looked crinkled and worn, as if someone had held it and carried it and caressed it over and over and over for years.

Reaching out, she ran her finger over Suzanna and then herself. *We look so happy.*

It was the pale pink ribbon tacked to the corner of the photo that finally brought the tears to Samantha's eyes. The only remnant of Suzanna that had been found that day.

Samantha just stood there and finally let the tears out.

Samantha sat in the living room, listening to the sounds of the house as it creaked and groaned its way through the outside temperature change as the dark of night replaced the light of day. A flock of galahs screeched their way overhead as they headed to the gum trees at the park where they'd spend the night.

"Happy birthday to me," she murmured, raising her mug in a salute.

Their fourteenth birthday was the last real birthday she'd had. Sure, the day still came around every year, but there was no celebrating. Dad always remembered to send her a card, always signing it as from him and Mum, although Samantha knew Mum knew nothing about it. Whenever she spoke to him on the phone or visited, he'd ask if she'd received it, and she'd always said yes, even though she often hadn't because she'd moved or, in some cases, given him a false address.

The darkness brought some relief from the heat of the day, and she knew she should get up and close the curtains, get herself some dinner, maybe even turn on a light or the TV. But she just sat there cloaked in her lethargy, listening. Listening to the absence; the absence now from her life of anyone who'd ever meant anything to her.

Everyone had given up.

Maybe it was time for her to give up, too.

5

The Ash Man

Samantha

SAMANTHA WOKE SUDDENLY, HER body swaying violently left, then right, as the train carriage squealed over imperfections in the tracks.

She blinked rapidly, trying to clear her bleary eyes, and shook her head, trying to clear the fog from her mind. *Why am I on a train? I don't remember getting on a train.*

But the faded blue seat under her legs felt real and the rhythmic chack-chack-chack of the train's wheels sounded real. She felt the train speed up slightly.

She looked around, cringing at the thought that she'd fallen asleep in public. Not that it would have been the first time. She was seated near a window, about halfway down the carriage, facing forward.

It was quiet, except for the sound of the moving train and the wind whooshing by the windows. Checking behind and in front of her, she counted six other people – a man and a woman in front and two women and two men behind. None of them were sitting next to each other and she frowned as she noticed that they all had the same posture: sitting straight-backed, staring down at their hands which were resting in their laps.

All the windows in the carriage had dark blinds pulled down, and there were a number of empty seats that appeared to have piles of ashes on them. *When was the last time this carriage was cleaned?* She looked closer and realised the piles were too large to have come from cigarettes. They were more like the amount you'd expect to come out of an urn when you were releasing your loved one's cremated ashes into the air.

Samantha lifted a corner of the blind next to her but all she could see outside was a white fog. Or was it smoke? Flakes of what looked like dark ash particles pirouetted and danced as the train rushed along. Maybe another scorching Australian summer had produced another Australian bushfire?

For a moment, she thought she saw blurry, shadowy figures reaching out toward the train, but they were quickly left behind, and they seemed to blow apart in the train's wake.

She stood up and walked towards the front of the carriage. She stopped beside the woman who was sitting by the window on the lefthand side. The woman was younger than herself, and her tight-fitting navy-blue suit, her heavy makeup, and her blonde hair, pulled into a tight bun, made her look like an air stewardess.

"Excuse me, where is this train going?" Samantha asked.

"Sshh," the woman hissed, not looking up. "You have to wait for the Ash Man. Are you stupid?"

"What?" Samantha felt like she'd missed an important memo.

"Sshh," the woman repeated but wouldn't say anything more.

Samantha turned and tried to catch the eye of the man sitting opposite. He was in the aisle seat on the righthand side of the carriage. His hair was greasy, as if it hadn't been washed for weeks, and he wore a dirty grey knit jumper above drab brown cotton trousers so loose that they looked like they'd fall down if he stood up. He looked at his hands and his lips were moving, but he wasn't speaking out loud. Was he praying? She stared, willing him to look at her, but he just sat there, mumbling to himself.

She walked towards the rear of the carriage and stopped near a woman sitting in an aisle seat. The wrinkles etched deep into her face marked her as most likely being in her seventies or eighties, possibly even older. Her short curly grey hair was neat, and she wore a floral dress with thick stockings and orthopaedic sandals. A wooden cane rested beside her, and she was smiling as she sat there looking down at her arthritic hands.

"Excuse me," Samantha said.

The woman looked up. "Yes, dear?"

Samantha sat on the aisle seat opposite her. "Could you please tell me where this train is going?"

"Well, that depends," responded the woman. "You need to wait for the Ash Man. He'll let you know where you're headed."

"Who's the Ash Man?" asked Samantha. "Is he the conductor? I don't know if I've got a ticket."

The woman reached out and patted Samantha's hand. "Just go back to your seat and wait for the Ash Man, dear. He'll explain everything."

Samantha felt a sudden change in pressure and awoke out of her doze.

The rhythmic sound of the train indicated that it had sped up again. Turning in her seat, she saw that the rear carriage door was wide open, and a man was silhouetted in the blinding light that was visible behind him.

Her eyes watered from the glare, even though she shielded her eyes against it. She couldn't quite make out what the man looked like even after he stepped inside and the door closed behind him.

She quickly changed seats, so she was facing the rear of the carriage. Blinking and rubbing her stinging eyes, she watched the man walk slowly down the aisle. He looked like a gunslinger out of an old American western movie, but without the guns on his hips.

This had to be the Ash Man.

The Ash Man strolled, radiating authority, pausing beside each person and, each time he did, the train sped up a bit more. He didn't say anything, and none of them, except the older woman she'd spoken to, looked up. No one else was eager to meet his gaze.

As he got closer, Samantha saw peppery grey hair peeking out from under a grey cowboy hat. His hair matched the colour of his handlebar moustache and the myriad whiskers sprouting from his weatherworn cheeks and chin. His most striking feature, his arctic blue eyes, nestled under bushy iron-grey eyebrows and his forehead was crinkled as if he frowned a lot. He wore grey boots, grey jeans, and a grey shirt under a long loose grey leather coat that reached almost to the floor.

He paused beside her and the train sped up. She looked up at him, almost in defiance of everyone else's fear. The authority emanating off him was almost palpable and he met her gaze. She couldn't read his expression, and she looked away before he did, then she slipped back into her original seat, and watched him as he continued on his way.

The Ash Man stopped beside the woman and the man near the front of the carriage.

"Please," the woman moaned, refusing to look at him. "Please, do him first! I'm not ready."

The Ash Man sat down next to her, twisted slightly, and touched a finger gently to her lips. The woman became still and quiet. He just looked at her for a few seconds before leaning across and pulling up the blind on the window.

The woman shook her head from side to side, refusing to look out. But the Ash Man cupped her chin and turned her head, so she had no choice. She kept her eyes squeezed shut until the Ash Man leaned in and whispered something that only she could hear. She reluctantly opened her eyes and stared out at the same white fog, or smoke, that Samantha had seen when she'd peeked behind the blind on her own window.

"No, that's not what happened," the woman moaned, trying to turn her head away but the Ash Man wouldn't let her. Obviously, the woman was seeing something that Samantha wasn't. "I already told you, that wasn't my fault."

"I don't believe that's true, and I don't believe you do, either," the Ash Man murmured as he drew the blind back down over the window. "If you don't take responsibility for your actions, you don't get to move on. I already told you this."

The Ash Man placed his right hand on top of the woman's shaking head, and she dissolved as if she'd suddenly dried up and crumbled into dust. All that was left on the seat was a pile of ashes, like the ones Samantha saw on other seats throughout the carriage.

The Ash Man sighed, stood up, and turned to the man in the seat opposite. The man looked relieved but scared and he shuffled over to the seat by the window.

A wobbly smile appeared on his lips as he watched the Ash Man sit beside him.

The Ash Man leaned over and raised the blind next to the man. The man looked out and started to cry. Samantha leaned forward, trying to see what the man was seeing, but all she could see was the fog.

"Yes," the man sobbed. "I did that. I was so heartbroken when my mother died. She was my last living relative, you know. For the few months before her death, she never even remembered who I was. I knew it was stupid to drink and drive, but I did it anyway. I felt like I'd lost everything when she died. I was so alone, and nothing mattered anymore. I didn't care about anything or anyone. It was dark and it was wet, and everything seemed to be happening in fast motion. I put my foot down, trying to beat the red light, but instead Amanda had to swerve to miss me. She slid sideways into the light pole and flipped down the embankment. I didn't even stop to check whether she needed help."

The man looked at the Ash Man before looking back out the window. His breath hitched and he sniffed, but the tears continued to fall.

"I know it's no excuse and I take full responsibility for Amanda's death. I regret the pain I caused her family, especially by not coming forward and taking responsibility while I was still alive. I've lived with that regret every day for over thirty years. I thought creating a scholarship in her name would help ease my conscience, make everything right, but it didn't. I could never bring myself to tell her family that it was me who'd killed their daughter. They thought I was being kind and generous and, rather than despising me, they thanked me. They thanked me every year on the anniversary of her death. I'm glad I can now finally admit it and take what's coming to me. Thank you."

The Ash Man leaned over and pulled down the blind, then settled back in his seat. He sat for a couple of minutes just looking at the man, before standing up and pointing to the door that led to the next carriage. "I think that's true. You can move on."

The man shook his head but stood up anyway. "I don't deserve it. I deserve to be nothing but a pile of ashes."

The Ash Man moved out of the way and said, "What happens next for you is not my call. I believe you're genuine about your regret, so my job here is done."

The man held out his hand and shook the Ash Man's hand before moving slowly toward the door at the front of the carriage. He glanced back once after opening the door, then he stepped through and was gone.

Samantha slumped in her seat as she thought about what the man and the Ash Man had said. *Is this some sort of death train?* she wondered. *If so, I must be dead,* her logical mind told her. That thought was strangely calming, and all she felt was relief as she sat up straight and watched the Ash Man approach.

The seat next to her creaked as he sat and she smelled sweet cigar smoke as he turned towards her.

Before he could say anything, she blurted out, "Am I dead?"

The Ash Man's voice was deep and raspy and sounded almost apologetic as he replied. "Yes."

She took a deep breath and closed her eyes. "How did I die? The last thing I remember is sitting in my mother's house on my own in the dark."

"I can show you," the Ash Man said, reaching across her for the blind. "If you really want to see."

He waited for her answer, while she sat there with her eyes closed and thought about it. *Did it matter? Would it change anything?*

"No," she eventually murmured, opening her eyes and looking at the creases criss-crossing the back of the Ash Man's hand as he held the bottom of the blind.

"It doesn't really matter. I had nothing anyway, and no one's going to miss me."

The Ash Man let go of the blind and sat back in his seat, not saying anything.

"Where is this train going?" Samantha asked. She turned her head and looked at the Ash Man's face, taking in every wrinkle and crevice before meeting the gaze of his blue eyes. "How does this work?"

"This is your transportation to the afterlife," the Ash Man said. "This is the first judgement point, where you'll be found either worthy of moving on to the next stage or not."

"And if I'm not, I end up as a pile of ashes, just like all these other people?" she said, indicating to the ash piles on the surrounding seats. "Every one of these piles was once a person?"

"Yes," the Ash Man confirmed.

"Why doesn't someone clean the carriage, remove all these ash people?" she asked. She knew it was irrelevant, but her mind was grasping at random things, so it didn't have to deal with the reality of her death.

"The ashes stay until someone else needs the seat," the Ash Man said. "Then they'll blow away and join the others outside."

Samantha had a sudden thought. "Do you judge me on the life I lived overall or on individual things I did, the harm I caused?"

The Ash Man smiled and shook his head. "I don't judge you at all. You judge yourself. I ask you some questions and you answer with your own truth. Some people never tell themselves the real truth even when they're dead. When a soul knows deep down that they're still lying to themselves, that they will never accept their flaws and failings, they burn up under the weight of their conscience."

Samantha turned away and they sat in silence as she thought about what he'd said.

"OK, hit me with the questions."

"You get two chances," said the Ash Man. "We watch a summary of your life, the important points as determined by you, then I ask you the first question. If you miss that one, I leave and give you time to reflect and think about your truth. When I come back, I ask you the second question. If your soul judges you worthy, you move on to the next carriage. If not, well … you've seen what happens."

"What happens in the next carriage?"

"It's the second judgement point."

"Yeah, but what happens?"

"I can't tell you that."

Samantha sat for a few more minutes, then took a deep breath. She looked straight ahead, focussing on the back of the seat opposite her. "OK, let's do this."

The Ash Man leaned across and pulled up the blind next to her. She looked out and watched her life start to play out in front of her as if the white fog was a cinema screen and she was watching a movie.

She watched herself and Suzanna born to a loving couple, who raised them both with love and kindness. She found herself smiling as she watched herself and her sister toddling across the floor as they learned to walk, leaning on each other for support. They moved on to learning to ride bikes, and she felt the pain of skinned knees and elbows, but it was a good pain. A shared pain.

They grew older and started school, feeling brave but scared as they rode their bikes to school by themselves for the first time. She watched herself cry as another girl bullied her in the playground until Suzanna got up in the girl's face, telling her to back off or she'd have deal with her.

She listened to Suzanna insisting that they needed their own friends; they couldn't just be each other's best friend forever. She remembered feeling discarded by her sister and unimportant as she ate lunch on her own, while Suzanna had a group of followers who she mucked about with and who hung on her every word.

Then she and Tina were put together on a school assignment, and they discovered they had a lot of the same interests and dreams for the future. She remembered feeling special when Tina invited just *her* over, not her sister, not anyone else, for a sleepover on Tina's eleventh birthday.

She watched herself cry quietly in bed the night Tina had told her she was moving away and wouldn't be attending the same high school as her. Tina's father was in the Royal Australian Air Force, and he'd been reassigned to a base on the opposite side of the country.

Samantha watched her first day at high school. The way Suzanna walked as if she owned the place, while she herself slunk along the unfamiliar maze of corridors, trying not to be noticed, carrying an armload of books, with no friends beside her.

She felt pathetic as she watched herself reading and believing in the notes she'd found in her locker during the second year of high school. She wasn't even aware of the thin line of tears running down her cheeks as she realised just how pitiful she'd been even before Suzanna disappeared.

She turned to the Ash Man to say something, but he was watching her life movie too, so she turned back, knowing what was coming next. She didn't want to watch, but she also couldn't look away.

It was their fourteenth birthday party. They dressed identically and Dad took photos, beaming with pride over 'his girls'. She sobbed out loud as she remembered his words, about living happy and that they had their whole lives ahead of them. *How wrong you were, Dad.*

The movie setting changed, and she and Tina were now sitting on the swing set at the party, and she remembered how happy she'd been to have someone to talk to again, so she didn't feel so alone anymore. Tina had told her that it was Suzanna who'd arranged everything, and Samantha had been determined to thank her sister, but she'd never had the chance.

There were a lot of things she'd wanted to say to her sister over the forty years she'd lived without her, but the time for that never arose again.

One of Suzanna's friends asked Mum where Suzanna was, and she watched Mum and Dad moving around the groups of people at the party, trying to find Suzanna, asking if anyone had seen her. She remembered how scared she'd felt when she realised this was serious, that it wasn't just Suzanna playing a prank. Something had happened to her sister, and no one had seen anything. *How could she have just disappeared with all those people around?*

The rest of that night and the following days blurred, and the movie seemed to speed up, hurtling through the next forty years matching the speed of the train.

She watched herself sitting in her room, staring at herself in the mirror, night after night. She watched herself sneak into Suzanna's room late at night and get into her bed, curling up and quietly weeping into the fur of Suzanna's blue teddy bear, wondering why she couldn't feel her sister reaching out to her. They were twins; they were supposed to be able to feel the other and know when something was wrong. Was she just defective or had Suzanna died and broken their connection?

She relived the morning when Mum found her in Suzanna's bed and thought Suzanna had come home in the night. Mum left deep bloody gouges in Dad's face when he pulled her away, telling her it was Samantha, before he forced her to swallow the pills that would calm her down.

Did you forget you had another daughter? she wondered. *Why couldn't you see* me, *Mum? See that I was lost and grieving as much as you? I missed her too and it was my fault she was gone.*

Samantha hadn't told anyone about the notes. They'd been in her bag, and her bag had never been found, so she didn't have them anyway. She had never received a final note, and no one had approached her at the party, so she couldn't be sure YSA had even been there or wanted to follow through with what he'd started. Maybe it really had been a prank and whoever had done it got cold feet at the last moment. At least, that's what she'd told herself at the time.

She fooled herself for a long time, telling herself the notes had nothing to do with Suzanna's disappearance. She'd been selfish and scared of being judged. By the time she'd realised that a little bit of embarrassment would have been a small price to pay to get her sister back, it was way too late. She'd already accepted that her twin was never coming home, and she couldn't stand the thought of how Dad would look at her if she told him. He wouldn't say it out loud, but his eyes would shout it for the world to hear: *it's your fault she's gone.*

After Suzanna's disappearance, Samantha's life had spiralled out of control. As she watched her life movie, she relived the feelings of uselessness, guilt, and depression that she'd carried with her since that day.

She watched herself ostracised at school, as if losing your sister might be contagious. Catherine had physically recoiled when Mr Michaels made her work with Samantha on a science assignment where they had to build a volcano using a soft drink bottle, baking soda, and vinegar. When no one was paying attention, Catherine passed her a note that she couldn't disagree with:

It should have been you. No one would have missed you, but everyone misses Suzanna.

She stopped studying, couldn't make herself focus, and didn't bother to try on exams, anymore. After graduating high school, her low marks meant she had no chance of going to university, not that she wanted to by that point. The only jobs she could get were menial, low-paid ones. And in a small country town, there weren't many of those.

Her mother's insistence that Suzanna was going to walk through the door at any moment started to grind at her until she knew she had to get out of the house before she said or did something she'd regret. So, she moved to Melbourne. *A change is as good as a holiday, right?* But, again, she could only manage to get casual low-paying jobs, mainly bartending and waitressing, that barely kept her above the poverty line.

Loser boyfriend after loser boyfriend paraded in front of her, manipulating and controlling her, stealing from her, treating her like a servant rather than someone they cared about. And she just let it happen. She knew she wasn't worthy of love.

She watched herself sleeping on a park bench, or under cardboard in a dark alley, when she was 'between apartments' or had no one that she could hit up for a few nights of sleeping on a couch. She hadn't even cared that something might happen to her. In fact, she almost wished it would. Then it would be over.

She couldn't end it herself, though, even at her lowest points. She could not do that to Dad. She'd done everything she could to make sure he never knew the full extent of what she'd done or what she'd had to do to get by and it had almost been a relief when he died. She wouldn't have to pretend anymore.

Even though she wanted to close her eyes and forget all of her life after she'd turned fourteen, she forced herself to watch until the end.

The last thing she saw was herself sitting in an armchair in the dark in her mother's house, before the Ash Man leaned across and pulled down the blind. He sat back in his seat and appeared to reflect on what they'd both just watched, glancing at her on and off as if trying to decide the best question to ask.

After a few minutes, the Ash Man turned and whispered into Samantha's ear.

"Tell me about your biggest regret, a time when something you did, or didn't do, changed the course of other people's lives for the worse."

6

Choices

Samantha

ONCE SAMANTHA STARTED TALKING, she couldn't stop. She didn't even wipe the tears away as a flood of words and emotions poured directly out of her soul.

The Ash Man just sat and listened. He didn't comfort her in any way or make any sound while she spoke. Not even a sigh or a word of encouragement as she faltered several times, stopping to catch her hitching breath before forging on with her story.

When she finished speaking, she felt empty and so, so tired, but there was no sense of relief. She'd thought finally telling someone about how she'd been responsible for ruining her family's lives would be cathartic, but she felt no sense of a lifting burden. The emotional boulder she'd been carrying since she was fourteen still weighed heavy on her back.

The Ash Man sat beside her and closed his eyes. She wondered if he'd fallen asleep, but he opened them again a few minutes later, turned his head, and looked at her. She couldn't read the expression on his face, but she felt his ice blue eyes pierce right through to the centre of her being.

"I think that's true. You can move on," he said, standing up and pointing to the door that led to the next carriage.

Samantha stayed where she was. The thought of being turned into a pile of ashes and never having to think about anything ever again strangely appealed to her. "Are you ever wrong?"

"Sometimes, but not often," the Ash Man smiled down at her.

"What happens if you're wrong? What happens in the next carriage?" she asked, still reluctant to stand up.

The Ash Man continued to look at her. "I can't tell you that. My job is here, not there. Now, it's time for you to go."

Samantha finally stood up, her hands automatically smoothing the creases in her jeans. Stepping out into the aisle, she moved towards the door at the front of the carriage.

She glanced back as she pulled open the door and saw the Ash Man moving down the aisle to the next person, the older woman she'd spoken to earlier.

Samantha took a deep breath and stepped through the doorway onto the next leg of her journey.

The second carriage was nothing like the first. It was still a train carriage, but this one was more spacious, opulent, and clean. There were no piles of ash here.

Samantha stood just inside the door, taking in the plush navy-blue carpeted aisle, and the heavy green damask curtains, woven with intricate gold and silver patterns, covering the windows. The dark maroon leather seats were like high-backed armchairs, each pair facing another pair with a polished mahogany dinner table between each set. She felt incredibly underdressed in her dusty black jeans and faded grey t-shirt with its barely legible heavy metal band logo.

The sounds of a dinner party – people talking and laughing, and the clink of cutlery on fine bone china plates – came from the front of the carriage, from the last row of seats on the right.

She jumped as a man dressed all in black, like a waiter in a fancy restaurant, appeared by her side.

"Welcome," he said, gesturing to the front of the carriage. "Please, follow me."

She followed him without a word.

Halfway down the carriage, she passed the man who'd entered this carriage before her. He was sitting at one of the tables on his own. His table was set with a white linen tablecloth, silver cutlery, and a crystal wine glass. He stared at the untouched meal in front of him, and Samantha heard him muttering as she passed, "I don't know. I don't know. What do I do?"

They reached the last row, and the waiter indicated to an empty aisle seat on the left. "Please, sit."

Samantha sat and the two women and two men sitting at the table across the aisle stopped their light-hearted banter, put down their forks, and turned to inspect her.

"What now?" she said after a few minutes when none of them spoke. "What happens now?"

"Now, Samantha, you have a choice to make," the blonde woman answered. "What happens next is up to you."

"What do you mean? I'm dead, what choice could possibly be left for me?"

The black-haired man picked up his fork, stabbed it into a chunk of meat, then pointed it at her as he spoke.

"You essentially have two choices. Do you want to be reborn, have another go round as it were, as someone completely new? Or have you had enough of the tedium of living and prefer to move straight on to your eternal afterlife?"

The man put the meat into his mouth and began to chew slowly. The other three also turned back to their meals. The brunette woman sipped a pale honey-coloured liquid from her wine glass, the red-haired man pushed julienned carrots around his plate, and the blonde woman dabbed at her mouth with a clean white linen napkin.

Samantha sat still, staring at the seat in front of her as the man's words sunk in. The waiter suddenly appeared beside her again and she watched him blankly as he put a crystal wine glass in front of her.

"Water or wine?" he asked. "Or another beverage of your choice?"

"Nothing, thank you," she muttered automatically, waving him away as her mind turned over and over what the black-haired man had said. The waiter bowed and seemed to glide back down the aisle.

"I need to know more," she finally said, turning her head to look across the aisle. "I need more information."

The four people turned to look at her again. The blonde woman raised her eyebrows expectantly.

"What is the afterlife?" Samantha asked. "What happens?"

"Well," said the blonde woman. "That depends on your beliefs and what you, deep down, think you deserve. Say you truly believe that you deserve to go to a place called Heaven and be reunited with your loved ones to live eternally in peace and happiness, then that's what you'll experience. If you believe you deserve to go to a place called Hell and be tortured for eternity in brimstone and hellfire, then that's what you'll experience. If you or your religion has other beliefs of what happens to a soul after death, then that's what you'll experience."

"What if I don't have any expectations of what an afterlife might be like?" Samantha said. "I'm not religious. I figured that once you're dead, you're dead. That's it. No more thinking, no more existing at all, just an absolute nothingness that you're not even aware of.

I didn't think there'd be a train involved, or choices to make."

"An absolute nothingness is an expectation in itself," said the brunette woman with a nod. "That can be accommodated and, truthfully, often is, more than ever nowadays."

Samantha took a deep breath, realising how attractive that option sounded. It sounded just like giving up, which she was very good at.

"You say I can be reborn and live another life?"

The red-haired man smiled at her as he answered. "Yes, you can. You can choose to live a new life, but you won't remember any of your old life. You won't even remember the Ash Train until you end up back here again. You'll be a brand new person starting over in your own brand new universe."

"What do you mean, my own universe?" Samantha felt like she was failing to grasp an important concept. "How do human lives actually work?"

The red-haired man looked at the black-haired man, who gave an almost imperceptible nod, then looked at her again as he answered.

"Every soul lives in their own universe. New universes are being created all the time as new souls are brought into being and old souls choose to live again. Your mind creates your universe, and your thoughts shape it. Your universe evolves with you, through things that happen, through things you think and do. When you died, your universe essentially winked out of existence, leaving space for a new one to begin."

"Are you telling me that everything that happened to me was my own doing, my own choice?" Samantha was trying to get her head around this concept of a private universe. "I think you're saying that everyone in my universe was made up by my mind and put there by me to do things that I made them do? If I got sick or hurt, was that me making a choice to get sick or hurt? Are you saying *I* decided my sister should go missing, that she would never be found, and *I* decided how my family would react to it?"

"Not exactly," the man said with a sigh. "Universes bump and jostle each other all the time. That's real people interacting. The people you met, communicated with, or even read about, in your life were other real individuals, but how *you* saw and interpreted those interactions were from *your* perspective and that's how they were incorporated into *your* universe." He turned and pointed to the man sitting halfway back down the carriage. "He lived in his own universe. If you had interacted, your universe would only have experienced it and incorporated it from your perspective, and his would have done the same, only from his perspective."

The blonde woman chimed in. "Negative experiences, such as sickness or injury, are just a part of life, things that happen. You can't control everything, but how you see it and experience it and react to it is unique to you."

Samantha sat back. She felt like she was still missing an important point. She reached out and picked up the empty crystal glass in front of her and studied it while she thought.

"You said that my universe died when I died," she eventually said, turning back to look across the aisle at the four people sitting there. "Then, where am I now? What is this place? Who are you and who makes the rules?"

The black-haired man sighed before answering. "The Ash Train is like a way station, outside of time and space. It's one of many. We're here to offer you a way forward, if you choose to accept it. That's all I can say. Your mind cannot fully grasp the intricacies of life and death, so there's no point even trying to explain it."

Samantha was frustrated, but she realised this was the only explanation she was going to get, and it would be useless to keep pushing the point.

"How come people in the previous carriage seemed to know what was going on, when I didn't?" she asked, stalling for time.

"This was your first life," the brunette woman said, putting her wine glass down. "If you've only lived one life, you wake up on the Ash Train after you die, but you don't know what's happening. If you've lived more than one life, that is you chose rebirth, you wake up on the Ash Train after you die, and you remember the Ash Train and know what's coming. Also, some of those people failed at their first encounter with the Ash Man and are onto their second chance at judgement."

"What about children? How can a baby, or even a four-year-old, make any sort of choice let alone understand what's happening?"

The brunette woman sighed as if Samantha's questions were taking time away from the dinner party they'd been enjoying before she came along. "If a soul dies before the age of eight, they don't catch the train. They are automatically put on the rebirth cycle."

"I can see that you're a restless soul, but you now have all the information we can give you," the black-haired man said, sounding slightly irritated. "You can have time to think about it, if you need it. It's an important decision that shouldn't be rushed." He gestured back down the carriage. "Go and sit, enjoy a meal, while you mull over your options."

Samantha still had questions, though, and thought there was something she wasn't being told. She stayed seated but turned so her legs were in the aisle. She leaned forward, resting her forearms on her thighs as she looked at the red-haired man again. "When universes 'bump into each other', as you say, can one person influence someone else's universe by what they say and do, the decisions they make?"

"It's complicated, but yes, that's exactly what happens," he answered. "The interaction is *experienced* by both, but the *outcomes* may be different in each universe. For example, one might just move on and forget all about it. But the other person might continue to think about it and make life-changing decisions based on that interaction."

"What if I killed someone?" Samantha asked, glancing at the man halfway down the carriage. She could see that he'd perked up and was listening to their conversation. "Would they only be dead in my universe?"

"If you kill someone, you kill their universe," the black-haired man said curtly. "That's it for them. They then come here and, if they pass the Ash Man, they make the same choice you're making now."

Samantha took a deep breath and sat back in her seat again. A thought occurred to her. "Can I change my mind if I choose the wrong way?"

"No," the brunette woman said. "If you choose rebirth, you won't remember even having made the choice. You won't remember any of this until you die again and end up back here." She gestured around the carriage with her fork. "If you choose the afterlife, well, that's a one-way ticket. You'll remember the life you just lived, but no one will hear you call if you decide it's not for you."

"What if I don't choose? What happens then?"

"If you do not choose, we will choose for you."

Samantha sat for a bit longer, thinking.

"Can I be reborn and live the same life again?" she finally asked. "Can I recreate my personal universe and remember my previous life?"

"No," said the black-haired man. "If you're reborn, you start from scratch, with no memories of any other previous lives. How a universe plays out is not preset, not set in stone."

"But…," Samantha said, her mind working harder and faster than it had since she'd been thirteen years old with dreams and ambitions and a whole life ahead of her. She stared at the black-haired man. "But, what if … what if, I combine my two options and truly believe my afterlife should be the recreation of my universe starting from a specific point in my life to allow me to change the outcome of a momentary lapse of judgement? Not to save myself, but to save someone else."

The four people exchanged glances, and no one spoke.

Samantha forged on as her brain ticked over the implications of what she was asking. "Because it's my afterlife, all my memories would be intact, wouldn't they? And, because I could change something I did or didn't do, my new universe would then evolve and change accordingly because my perspective would be different. Could my choices change the outcome for someone else? Could I live in that universe until I die again, when I would return here? Is that against the rules?"

The black-haired man sighed and put down his knife and fork. "You're not the first to think of it. Some very restless souls have asked similar questions, wanting to go back and rectify a mistake that left a hole in their soul. You cannot relive the exact same timeline. That one is done and dusted for you."

He closed his eyes and tilted his head, looking like he was listening to a voice in his head that only he could hear. When he reopened his eyes, he sighed again before continuing to speak.

"However, it is possible to create a new timeline, along the lines of what you described. It's difficult to achieve and uses a lot of resources, which is why it's not generally offered as an option. One soul going back can affect so many different universes, which means all those universes have to be recreated and then started again from a particular point on the timeline. It's messy and complicated."

He sighed again, pushed his plate away, and wiped his mouth with his napkin, before staring at Samantha so intensely that she couldn't look away.

"We have to get permission to do it, and there are technicalities to be dealt with, but it's not completely impossible. But be aware that you only get one try. If you don't get the outcome you want, then too bad. When you come back, you have to go through the Ash Man again, and if you manage to pass him, you will *have* to choose either proper rebirth or eternal afterlife."

"Then that's my choice," Samantha said. "That's what I want. I need to go back and give my sister a chance at the life she deserved."

7

Second Chances

Sat, 24 March 1984 – Samantha

SAMANTHA WOKE UP WITH a massive headache. She was lying on her stomach, and she groaned as she lifted her hand, searching for her phone on the bedside table. She felt around and heard the thump of a book falling to the floor, but she couldn't find her phone.

She didn't remember drinking last night, but she must have. Her mouth was dry, her head pounded, and her stomach felt queasy. Without opening her eyes, she felt around again, this time for the ibuprofen that lived beside her bed, but it seemed to be missing too.

The bedroom door suddenly flung open, and she heard footsteps walking over to the window. Someone yanked the curtains open, and Samantha turned onto her side, burying her head under the blankets to block out the glare that invaded the room.

"Why are you still in bed, lazy bones? Get up, this is our day, and we can't waste a minute of it."

It took her brain a few minutes to recognise a voice she hadn't heard in over forty years. The blankets slid down off her face, and she lay there staring at Suzanna, hangover symptoms completely forgotten.

"You look like you've seen a ghost," Suzanna said, flopping down on her back on the bed next to Samantha. She turned to face her and pushed a strand of long dark hair off her sister's face. "What's the matter, Sammie?"

Warm tears flowed freely down Samantha's face, soaking the pillow. She reached out and ran her hand over the contours of Suzanna's face. She felt real. This wasn't a dream. She didn't even care what Suzanna called her. The only thing that mattered was that she was here and she was alive.

"It worked," she said, laughing through her tears as she reached out and pulled her sister into a tight embrace.

Suzanna hugged her back, then sat up. "You're weird. Did anyone ever tell you that?"

"All the time, sis," Samantha replied, unable to tear her gaze away from her sister. "More often than you know."

"Hurry up, girls," Mum shouted from the kitchen. "If you want these blueberry pancakes for your birthday breakfast, you need to come now. I've got a lot to organise today to get the park set up for the party."

Suzanna went to stand up, and Samantha gripped her forearm to stop her. "Happy birthday, Suzanna. I love you. We'll get through this day together, and there'll be many more this time around."

Suzanna looked at her, a quizzical expression on her face, before smiling at her and heading for the door. "Same to you, Sams. Now come on. Aren't you curious about what we got?"

As Suzanna disappeared through the doorway, Samantha whispered, "I already got what I want. I don't need anything else."

Samantha got out of bed and looked at herself in the mirror. She ran her hands over her flat stomach. It had been a long time since she'd been this slim. She moved her arms and legs and flexed her fingers, marvelling at the absence of pain. She stared at her reflection. She hadn't worn her hair this long in almost forty years, and there were no signs of the strands of grey she'd become accustomed to.

"Hurry up, Samantha," Mum called again. "I need to get going. Your father's already gone, but he'll be back by midday to pick you girls up."

Samantha headed to the kitchen and came up behind her mother, surprising her by wrapping her arms around her and kissing her cheek as buttery blueberry pancakes slid from the pan onto their plates. "Hi, Mum. I don't think I tell you enough, but I love you. Thank you for everything you do for us."

Her mother smiled, only half serious as she shrugged her off. "What's gotten into you today? Maybe you should have a birthday every day."

While they were eating, Mum gave them both a small present, neatly wrapped in green paper with gold and silver patterns, reminding Samantha of the curtains on the Ash Train. Much to Suzanna's disappointment, the rest of the presents had been loaded into Mum's car, ready to be taken to the party to be added to the pile for opening later.

Suzanna tore open the wrapping on hers and pulled out a small square black box. She lifted the lid and gasped when she saw the silver necklace, bracelet, and earrings. All three pieces of jewellery had a matching green leaf-shaped charm attached, almost the same colour as the twins' eyes. Her bracelet also had other silver charms of varying shapes, including a cat, a sunflower, a castle, and an 'S'.

Samantha opened hers and found the same jewellery, the only difference being the charms on the bracelet. Hers also had the 'S' and the leaf, but these were accompanied by a horse, a rose, and a book.

Samantha spent the rest of the morning of her second fourteenth birthday shadowing her sister. Wherever Suzanna went, Samantha went. She knew it was irrational, but she felt that if she took her eyes off her for even a second, her sister would vanish and the whole universe would crumble into ashes.

"Why are you following me everywhere?" Suzanna groaned, trying to push Samantha away and close her bedroom door. "You're like one of those dogs whose owner goes away to war, then comes back after five years and the dog won't let them out of their sight and ends up sleeping on their grave when they die. Would you sleep on my grave if I was dead?"

"Don't say that," Samantha said with a frown. "That's not funny."

"Well, give me some space. I need to get ready, and you do too."

"I need to tell you something," Samantha said, putting her foot in the doorway to stop Suzanna from closing it. "Something important."

"Well, it will have to wait," Suzanna said, kicking Samantha's foot out of the way and closing the door in her face. "It can't be more important than this party. Tell me later."

Samantha stood and stared at the door for a couple of minutes, before walking away. She wandered around the house, running her fingers over books and photos, furniture and knick-knacks, marvelling at how she'd forgotten most of this.

She picked up a small glass horse family: stallion, mare, and foal. They all had toffee-coloured swirls through them and were linked by a gold chain. She studied them with a smile on her face, remembering when she'd bought it at a school fair years ago. She'd felt so grown up when she pulled her own coins out of her own pocket and counted them out carefully before solemnly exchanging them with the lady behind the table.

"Hey, shouldn't you be getting ready?"

Dad put his hand on her shoulder, interrupting her thoughts. She turned to him and felt the tears prickling her eyes as she pulled him into a tight hug. She blinked them away before he could see them, then pulled back from him.

"Just thinking, remembering," she said, smiling at him as she put the horse family back on the bookshelf. "It's good to see you, Dad."

Dad smiled back. "It's good to see you too, Sammie."

She'd never minded Dad calling her Sammie. The way he said it didn't make her feel like a child; it made her feel loved. He turned to walk away.

"I need to tell you something, Dad," she said, reaching out but not quite touching his shoulder. "There's something you need to know."

"OK, but can you tell me later?" he said, glancing back at her. "You really should be getting ready. It's nearly midday and I need to get photos of the two of you before we go."

Samantha was sitting on Suzanna's bed stroking Arabella as she watched her sister applying makeup.

The cat's silky fur was calming as she tried to work out how to bring up the YSA notes in a way that sounded natural. Even though mentally she was fifty-four years old and thought she'd given up caring what people thought years ago, she still cringed at the thought of what her twin would think. She didn't want Suzanna to think she was weak for believing the notes just because she was a pathetic lonely loser.

"Today we should look identical," Suzanna declared, turning her head left, then right, as she looked in the mirror. "No one will know which of us they're talking to."

"I don't know if I want to," Samantha said.

"Why not," pouted Suzanna, leaning into the mirror to examine a freckle on her nose. "Don't be a party-pooper."

Over the years, Samantha had wondered if them looking identical today had been the cause of Suzanna's disappearance. Maybe whoever took her thought they were taking Samantha? *Were they disappointed or elated when they discovered they'd got the wrong twin?*

"It feels childish. We're not children anymore."

"This might be the last chance we get to do it." Suzanna ran her hands through her long dark hair. "I'm thinking I might cut my hair soon. Short hair looks more grown up, don't you think?"

"Maybe," sighed Samantha. "Anyway, I need to tell you something."

"We don't have time right now," Suzanna said, sliding pale pink lipstick across her lips, then smearing it with her fingertips. "You need to get dressed, then I'll do your makeup to look like mine."

Suzanna went over to her closet and rummaged through her clothes. She pulled out a white t-shirt and a pair of light blue jeans.

"Yes, this is what we'll wear. Those pale pink button-up shirts we got for Christmas last year will look nice over the white t-shirts. They might be a little tight now but should still fit well enough if we leave the top few buttons undone. Here." She tossed a chunky black belt at Samantha. "With a belt over the top, this will be perfect."

Samantha reluctantly took the belt and headed back to her room to get dressed. She was annoyed with herself for giving in so easily and for not just telling Suzanna about the notes, but she figured she still had time.

Instead of light blue jeans, she decided to wear dark blue ones. *That should be enough to tell us apart*, she thought as she pulled on her white t-shirt, then the pink shirt. She tucked the bottom of the pink shirt into her jeans, threaded the belt through the jeans' belt loops, and cinched it tight. She looked at herself in the mirror, then took a dark blue ribbon out of her top dresser drawer, before heading back to Suzanna's room.

As soon as Suzanna saw Samantha's jeans, she smiled and said, "Oh, you're right. The dark jeans look much better than the light ones. Give me a second."

Samantha sighed as Suzanna changed her jeans to match.

They stood next to each other and looked at themselves in the mirror.

Samantha moved behind her sister, pulled Suzanna's hair back, and tied the blue ribbon around it. "Perfect."

"I like the ribbon," Suzanna said, nodding, as Samantha stood beside her again. "Have you got another one like that?"

"No," Samantha lied. "I'm going to leave my hair loose."

"Why are you so against us looking identical?" Suzanna frowned, making Samantha sit so she could apply her makeup. "It will be fun. Here's what we'll do: at some point tonight, we'll change places, and you can be me, and I can be you for a while. See how the other half lives. Actually, me starting off wearing the ribbon is a good idea. I'll give it to you later, and everyone will think you're me."

"Aren't we too old for those sorts of pranks, now?" Samantha sighed, closing her eyes as Suzanna dabbed at her eyelids with blue eyeshadow. "I don't think your friends will appreciate it if they talk to me, thinking they're talking to you. What if they say stuff you don't want me to know?"

"It's our birthday," Suzanna said, pulling the mascara brush out of the bottle. "We can do what we want today. I don't have any secrets from you and my friends will be fine with it. They know how to take a joke."

They looked at their reflections.

"Perfect," said Suzanna, throwing her arms around Samantha and squeezing her tightly. "Except for the ribbon, even I can't tell us apart. Ooh, I'm so excited. This is going to be the best birthday ever."

"The best birthday *so far*," Samantha corrected her, and they both laughed and headed downstairs for Dad's photo shoot.

8

Fourteen Again

Sat, 24 March 1984 – Samantha

SAMANTHA ENJOYED SEEING ALL the townsfolk again. She'd forgotten a lot of them and many of the ones she did remember, both young and old in 1984, had died or moved away over the years since.

She smiled at Mrs Corcoran and handed her two slices of bread. Mrs Corcoran was her mother's boss, the owner of the Bluebird Café where her mother cooked and waitressed, and one of the only three people to attend her mother's funeral in 2024.

"Thank you, Samantha. I'll be back for the sauce once I've managed to wrangle some steak away from your father. That's if he doesn't talk my ear off, first."

"You're welcome," Samantha replied.

She looked over at the group of young people dancing to the music being played by the local rock band. Suzanna was right in the thick of the crowd, enjoying the attention. She looked up and met Samantha's gaze, motioning for her to come over and join in.

Samantha shook her head with a smile. She'd never been a joiner, more an observer, happy to watch from the sidelines. As she watched, it dawned on her that this was what she'd done all her life: watched things happen to other people, rather than experiencing those things herself. *That all changes after we get through today*, she thought.

"Penny for your thoughts."

Samantha pulled her gaze away from her sister and looked at Mr Beresford, her history teacher, who was standing next to her holding a paper plate loaded up with salads. He glanced over at the dancing crowd, then looked back at Samantha.

"My thoughts aren't worth that much," she said with a smile as she handed him a white plastic knife and fork.

"Don't underestimate the value of your mind," he replied with a wink. He suddenly bent down, fiddled with something, then stood up again. "Is this yours? It was on the ground."

"Thank you." She hadn't realised her small black leather bag had fallen onto the ground, and she took it from him with a smile.

She watched him walk away, heading for a group of teachers who were standing around talking. He wasn't as old as she'd always thought, maybe in his forties, maybe even late thirties. She might have been attracted to him if her current body had been the same age as her mind. His dark shoulder-length hair with small streaks of grey and his close-shaven beard was similar to what she would describe as her 'type'. She shook her head. He was her teacher. *What am I thinking?*

"Go and join Suzannah," her mother urged, interrupting her thoughts. "Parties are supposed to be fun, especially at your age."

"I'm fine, I want to be here with you," Samantha replied. She turned to her mother. "Mum, can I tell you something? Something important?"

Her mother started to answer, but the band decided right then to take a break, and suddenly Suzanna was front and centre with her crowd of followers. Everyone started grabbing at the food and soft drinks on the table. A plate of potato chips was knocked onto the grass, and a fizzy bottle of lemonade sprayed its contents into the air as teenagers laughed and pushed each other.

"Tell me later, love," her mother said, putting a hand on Samantha's forearm.

Samantha turned her attention to her father. He was manning the barbeque, doling out steak and sausages and rissoles onto paper plates, each serving accompanied by a, typically embarrassing, story about 'his girls'.

She looked at her watch. It was almost time for him to go and pick Tina up from the airport, not that she was supposed to know that. She put her bag on the flat wooden seat and headed over to him.

He was surprised when she appeared next to him and even more surprised when she prised the barbeque tongs from his hand.

"Let me do it for a while, Dad," she said. "Go and have something to eat."

"Oh, thanks, Sammie," he said. "That's really good timing. I need to go and get something, and I was just about to ask your sister to take over for me."

He pulled out his car keys and Samantha watched him head towards the car. The band suddenly started up again, and she turned her attention back to her sister who was leading her boisterous crowd back onto the grassy dancefloor in a conga line.

9

Not So Secret Admirer

Sat, 24 March 1984 – Suzanna

SUZANNA WATCHED SAMANTHA AND Tina swinging together, laughing and chatting. Her sister's hair flowed like a dark river behind her as she swung higher and higher.

She was glad her sister was happy, although she'd definitely been weird today. Weirder than normal, anyway. Samantha had seemed both happy and sad all day and had hardly let Suzanna out of her sight, almost like she'd never see her again if she took her eyes off her.

It was a little bit suffocating but, when Suzanna thought about it, she realised they hadn't been spending much time together lately. She silently promised her sister to do something about that once

Tina had gone home again. She felt bad when she thought about her own behaviour towards Samantha at school, and she decided she'd pull her into her own friend group. If anyone didn't like it, they could just leave. Samantha shouldn't have to be lonely, when Suzanna had enough friends to go around.

Samantha looked up, caught her eye, and waved. Even though the light was fading, Suzanna read the 'thank you' on her lips and she smiled and waved back. Tina must have told her of Suzanna's efforts to get her here for this party.

Everyone was starting to get tired, so Suzanna didn't have quite as many followers as she'd had earlier in the night. She was glad, though, because it was exhausting being the centre of attention all the time. Sometimes she envied her sister's aloneness.

The band was taking another break, and the night was cooling down, so a lot of people started moving over to the forty-four-gallon drums with the fires in them that her father and Mick, her father's business partner, had set out around the area.

"Give me a few minutes," she said to her friends. "I just need some time out."

She turned away and headed over to the table where her mother was setting out the desserts.

"Anything I can do?" Suzanna asked her mother, watching her fuss with the two-tiered rectangular birthday cake.

The pale pink cake was huge, decorated with small green flowers around the edges. Her mother was setting out candles on the top layer, spelling out two lots of the number fourteen on either side of a large green 'S'.

"No," her mother said with a laugh. "Have a rest while they're all leaving you alone. You've hardly stopped all day."

Suzanna hugged her mother. "Thanks, Mum, but you haven't stopped all day, either. You're the one who needs a rest. What would we do without you?"

"I don't know," her mother said, concentrating on the candles again. "Starve?"

Suzanna didn't notice Samantha's bag on the seat, and she knocked it onto the ground as she sat down. Leaning over, she picked it up, but the bag tipped and some loose papers fell out. She quickly stood up and stamped on them to stop the breeze from catching them.

She was about to shove them back in the bag when a couple of words caught her eye in the fading light. 'Stunning', 'beautiful', 'perfect', 'overflowing with love'.

She glanced at her mother, then moved away to stand under a park light to read the notes. They were all dated, so she put them in order and started at the beginning. There were seven notes, the last of which was dated today.

"What the hell?" she muttered as she read. She looked up, feeling guilty for invading her sister's privacy, but Samantha and Tina were walking away, heading towards the public bathroom, still deep in conversation and not taking any notice of anyone else. "Was this what you wanted to tell me this morning, Sammie? I'm so sorry I didn't have time for you."

She got to the last note.

My perfect Samantha, today is the day.

I didn't think this day would ever come, but we can finally be together. From this day forth, we'll never be apart. Nothing will ever come between us.

They'll be talking about us until our story becomes a legend, a myth lost in time. We'll be that family everyone aspires to but never achieves.

There's so much I want to say to you but today I will say these things in person, so this note can be short.

Come to the children's playground on the far side of the lake at 9 PM. I'll be waiting.

Love always, from YSNTBSSA (Your Soon Not To Be So Secret Admirer)

"This is so creepy," Suzanna muttered, shaking her head. Surely Samantha couldn't believe this was real. "This is a joke, right? A prank?"

Suzanna checked her watch: 8:55 PM. She considered showing the notes to Dad or Mum, but she didn't want to embarrass her sister.

"Alright," Suzanna said. "I'll deal with this. This needs to stop, now."

She looked around. No one was watching her as she shoved the notes into the bag. She walked down to the water and headed along the dimly-lit footpath that led to the children's playground on the other side of the lake.

10

Waiting

Sat, 24 March 1984 – Suzanna

SUZANNA REACHED THE CHILDREN'S playground but there was no one there, so she sat on the swing to wait, fiddling with her new bracelet. She held Samantha's bag in her lap and checked her watch: 9:20 PM. She'd give this creep, or creeps if there was more than one in on this prank, another twenty minutes or so, then head back to the party.

She doubted anyone would show up, but she really hoped they would. They needed to know they couldn't mess with her sister like this. They needed to learn that messing with Samantha was the same as messing with Suzanna, and that was not something you wanted to do.

It was quiet. The only sounds of the night were the slight creak of the swing as it moved under her weight, the rustle of a few leaves as a light breeze drifted past, and a slight thumping bass noise she could feel more than hear coming from the party across the lake. The lights around the playground barely lit up the play equipment, and the nearby dirt carpark had no lights, so she couldn't tell if there were any cars there.

She pulled Samantha's ribbon out of her hair – it was starting to come loose anyway – and ran her fingers along it, enjoying the feel of the satin texture, while she moved the swing slightly backwards and forwards. She thought about how she would sketch today's events and her fingers itched to get started.

About five more minutes passed, then a small white dog ran up and snuffled around her shoes. She leaned over to pat it and realised she knew this dog. Samantha had fed and walked it a few times during the last school holidays for pocket money. It belonged to their history teacher, Mr Beresford, who lived across the road and a couple of doors down from them.

Samantha had droned on about Maltese terriers and how well trained this dog was, but Suzanna had zoned out so she couldn't remember much of what she'd said, let alone the dog's name. Her sister was like that. She'd research every little thing to the bone and then wonder why no one wanted to hear every little detail.

"Oh, hey, can you grab him?" someone called, sounding like they were out of breath.

She picked up the lead that was dragging on the ground behind the dog, then looked up.

"Thank you, Samantha," Mr Beresford said, standing with his hands on his hips and breathing heavily. "I didn't think I was going to catch him." He looked around. "Are you here on your own?" He glanced across the lake. "Your party looks like it's still going strong."

Suzanna didn't correct his mistaken identity and handed him the dog's lead. "I'm waiting for someone."

"Do you want me to wait with you?" he asked, sitting on the swing next to her. He watched her hand stroking the ribbon. "You shouldn't be out here in the dark by yourself."

She shook her head. "You don't have to. I'm sure they'll be along soon." She looked at her watch: 9:30 PM. "I'll wait another ten minutes, then if they don't show up, I'll head back. I'll be fine."

Mr Beresford nodded and started to get to his feet, but he stumbled as the swing swung backwards. He fell to his knees, grunting as his hands slapped the tan bark under the swing. He let go of the dog's lead and the dog bounded off towards the carpark.

"Damn," he said. "Would you mind helping me catch him again? I don't think I can chase him around the park again. I'm not as young as I used to be."

As Suzanna slipped easily off the swing to run after the dog, the ribbon slipped out of her hand and Samantha's bag fell off her lap onto the ground. The blue ribbon was hard to see against the dark tan bark and she hesitated, almost stopping to pick up the bag, but then kept going. She'd get them when she came back.

She caught up to the dog near a dark-coloured car at the very back of the dirt carpark. The car was parked in the very last park, behind a row of bushes where it couldn't be seen from the playground. The dog was looking eagerly between her and the car. He looked like he was smiling, and he wagged his tail as if he wanted to get in.

"Is this your car?" she murmured to the dog as she bent over and picked up the lead. She patted the dog's head as she stood up.

"It is."

Mr Beresford was right behind her, and she suddenly felt his arms wrap around her. One hand slid up and over her mouth, muffling her slight scream, while his other arm held her own arms tight against her sides. Samantha's small black bag hung from the arm he had around her, and it banged against her leg.

"I'm sorry, it has to be like this," he said into her ear. "But I need time to explain, so we can't do it here."

Suzanna thrashed wildly from side to side, desperately trying to get her arms up but he was too strong. She didn't feel her new bracelet break and slip off her wrist as she dropped the dog's lead. The dog thought it was a game and bounded around them, making small, happy, yipping sounds.

She tried to remember what they'd been taught years ago when she and Samantha had taken some self-defence lessons. She raked her heels down his shins, but it made no difference.

She relaxed for a minute and leaned forward. When she felt his weight shift with hers, she suddenly swung her head backwards, hearing a satisfying crunch as the back of her head hit him in the nose.

"Damn," he muttered, sniffing and loosening his grip slightly, but not enough for her to get away. "Settle down. Why is it always like this? I don't want to hurt you. Why don't you ever understand that?"

He pulled his hand away from her mouth and she heard him rub his face. She tried to scream, but it got caught in her throat and only a low moan managed to escape.

He was still behind her with one arm holding her tightly, and he clamped his other, now bloody, hand over her nose and mouth. Within seconds, she was dizzy, and she tried desperately to stay conscious, but then everything went black.

11

Gone

Sat, 24 March 1984 – Samantha

SAMANTHA WAITED FOR TINA outside the bathroom. The party was still in full swing around her, even though some of the older folk had left. Tina had eaten something on the flight that hadn't agreed with her, so she was still in the bathroom. Samantha didn't remember this from the first time this birthday happened, but she'd promised Tina she'd wait for her.

She'd also promised herself that she'd continue to watch Suzanna, so she'd see the exact moment that she slipped away or when someone grabbed her. She not only wanted to make sure Suzanna didn't disappear this time, but she also wanted the person responsible to be held accountable. She knew it was dangerous, but if they could catch him in the act, or if she could be the bait rather than Suzanna, he wouldn't be able to try again or do it to anyone else.

But, talking to Tina again, the only friend she'd ever really had, she'd become distracted. She pushed her hair off her face and looked at her watch: 9:30 PM.

She tried to find Suzanna but couldn't see her anywhere. The band had started up again, and she assumed her sister was still in the middle of the crowd. She smiled to herself as she watched teenagers gyrating crazily on the now flattened grass to music she now thought of as golden oldies. *If this is what these kids are like on soft drink, what will they be like when they're old enough to drink alcohol?*

Her father had finished cooking and was now at the table with her mother. She watched them talking and she thought her heart would break when she saw her father reach out, take her mother's hand, and kiss the back of it. Her mother smiled, leaned towards him, and tenderly brushed his hair off his forehead before kissing him there. They were still so in love. Samantha had to make sure that didn't change this time around.

She wiped happy tears from her eyes and took a deep breath, turning her gaze back to the dancing crowd. She moved slightly left, then right, then stood on tiptoes, trying to see over people to see Suzanna, but she couldn't spot her. Her heart skipped a beat, and she suddenly found it hard to breathe.

"Tina, is anyone else in there?" she called. *Maybe Suzanna was in there?*

"No, just me," Tina answered, her voice muffled by the thick concrete bricks of the building.

"I'm just going to find Suzanna. I'll be back in a minute."

"OK."

She waded into the melee of dancers, calling, "Suzanna! Suzanna!"

She shoved her way past people she normally wouldn't have gone anywhere near at school, but she wasn't a scared schoolkid anymore. A couple of them pushed her back and she copped a few elbows in the ribs, but she gave as good as she got and kept going.

A niggling fear started to work its way up her back and crawl across her shoulders when she couldn't find her sister. She saw Catherine and grabbed her arm, pulling her away from the group. Catherine tried to jerk her arm away, but Samantha held tight and dragged her to a clear spot on the grass.

"Where's Suzanna?" Samantha demanded, getting right up in Catherine's face. "Where is she?"

"I don't know," Catherine snapped. She yanked her arm out of Samantha's grip and took a step back. "I'm not her keeper. Last I saw she was with your mother. She said she needed a break."

Catherine headed back to the group, rubbing her arm and muttering to herself as she glanced back over her shoulder at Samantha. "Crazy bitch."

Samantha turned to look at the table where her mother and father were standing. They were both smiling, standing side-by-side, one arm around the other, watching the party.

Samantha suddenly felt cold, her mind went numb, she couldn't breathe, and she couldn't feel her heart beating.

Someone knocked into her, and she could have sworn she felt her heart start again, and her brain kick back into life.

She ran over to the table, gesturing frantically at her parents as she called. "Where's Suzanna? Where is she? She can't be gone again! This is bullshit. This is the only chance I get to make this right."

12

Aftermath

Sat, 24 March 1984 – Samantha

THIS TIME AROUND, SAMANTHA refused to leave the park.

The first time she'd lived this day, she'd allowed Senior Constable Atkins to bundle her, and her hysterical mother, into Mick's battered white Holden ute and let him take them home. Even though the policeman had said it was in case Suzanna had returned there for some reason, she knew now that it was to get them out of the way, in a similar way to how doctors wouldn't let relatives watch an emergency operation. She was also sure the young constable didn't know how to handle females, let alone a situation like this.

But not this time. She was not leaving this time.

Her parents didn't believe her at first and they moved around the partygoers, looking for Suzanna, becoming increasingly agitated when no one had seen her. They were now back standing near the table with the cake, numb with shock, unable to move or think clearly. They were holding hands as if the connection was a physical conduit that allowed them to share their fear.

Tina was also standing near them, looking scared, unsure of what she should do.

Everyone else was milling around like sheep in a saleyard, not knowing what to do. The band had stopped playing as more and more people realised something was terribly wrong.

So, until the police arrived, Samantha took control. She knew from watching future true crime shows that the first forty-eight hours were crucial in missing persons cases, and she was damned if she was going to waste a precious second of this second chance she'd been given.

This was the first time since she'd returned that she missed having a phone in her pocket, but mobile phones were unheard of in small town Australia in 1984. She couldn't just call up the local policeman and tell him to get down here.

She went over to Mick. "Go and get the constable, get him down here immediately," she ordered.

Surprisingly, he didn't argue. He ran to his ute and peeled out of the carpark, spinning the wheels in a spray of gravel in his haste.

"Everybody look for Suzanna," Samantha yelled. "She's got to be here somewhere. She can't have just disappeared."

She went over to her parents.

"We'll find her," Samantha reassured them, putting a gentle hand on each of their forearms before turning back to watch people tramping around the area.

They were checking the carpark, the bushes, the trees, the bathrooms, everywhere they could think of. They were possibly destroying evidence, but Samantha didn't care right now. All she wanted was to find her sister.

She thought about the first time Suzanna had gone missing and remembered the pale pink ribbon that had been found on the ground near the playground on the other side of the lake. Samantha started in that direction, reaching into her pocket and, again, realised she had no phone, no convenient source of light.

"Has anyone got a torch? We need more light."

A couple of older people put their hands up, then went and retrieved torches from their cars.

"Please search the other playground," she pleaded, pointing across the lake. They nodded and headed to the footpath that wound around the lake. She was pretty sure Suzanna wouldn't still be there, and she knew she needed to stay here for now, at least until the police arrived. People needed to be told what to do.

"Someone search the lake, especially the reeds along the banks," she called, even though she knew they wouldn't find anything. There was always that chance that enough had changed for there to be a clue this time that hadn't been there the first time around. "Check right around the lake, not just this side."

Mick came back about thirty minutes later, followed closely by a police car with its lights flashing but no siren blaring.

Senior Constable Atkins started to head over to her parents, but Samantha stepped in front of him, making him stop.

"My sister has been abducted," she told him.

"I highly doubt that," he responded, managing to sound both dismissive and incredulous at the same time. He was maybe fifteen years older than her, and this town was his first solo appointment after completing his training and mandatory time on the streets. "Things like that don't happen in nice towns like this."

"Well, she hasn't just fallen asleep under a bush!" she snapped, but he pushed past her and went over to her parents.

She followed him and heard him say to her father, "Don't worry. Teenagers do this sort of thing all the time. She probably got bored and headed home. Have you checked there?"

Her father shook his head, unable to speak, and her mother started to weep uncontrollably, becoming more and more hysterical as time wore on.

"She *hasn't* gone home," Samantha stated. "Someone has taken her!"

The constable sighed. He ignored her and spoke directly to her father again. "Your wife and daughter should head home. Being here is not going to help. Someone should be at home in case…" He glanced at writing on the cake. "Samantha, is it? In case she's there or on her way there. Is there someone who can take them?"

"It's Suzanna," Samantha said, trying to control her temper. "Suzanna has been taken by someone. She hasn't just decided to go home. The sooner you take this seriously, the more chance we have of finding her."

Mick, who had been standing nearby listening, stepped forward, putting a hand on Samantha's shoulder. "I'll take them."

Samantha pushed his hand off and addressed the constable. "I'm not going anywhere. I know Suzanna is not there. What if she's lying dead in a ditch or something? Hell, she could be drowning in the lake, for all we know. We don't know what this person has done with her. We have to find her tonight."

Her words made her mother wail even louder, but she didn't care at this point. She wasn't going to let an inexperienced police officer be the reason they didn't find Suzanna. She had to be found this time around, and found alive.

"We normally wait twenty-four hours before taking a missing person report," the constable started to say. "It's..."

"This is a fourteen-year-old girl," Samantha snapped, interrupting his next words. "She was here, and now she's not. Someone has taken her. Do you want it on your record – or your conscience – that you could have stopped something bad from happening to her, but your hesitation impeded the investigation?

The longer we wait, the more likely it is that she won't be coming home alive."

Senior Constable Atkins looked unsure of what to do, of how serious to take this.

"You need to call in your superiors," Samantha said, moving closer to the constable and getting in his face. "We need to set up a proper, organised, search party, and we need people who have experience with this kind of thing."

He stepped back, hesitating at her aggressive manner, then looked at her father again. "Sir, what do you think has happened?"

Samantha's father looked between her and Senior Constable Atkins, and Samantha saw the moment his mind unfroze.

"She's right. Do what she says. Get some proper help down here. This is urgent." He turned to his friend. "Mick, please take my wife home and, if you wouldn't mind, wait there with her."

13

Staying

Sat, 24 March / Sun, 25 March 1984 – Samantha

BY THE TIME SUNDAY morning rolled around, everyone was snapping at each other. No one had slept and, true to her word, Samantha had refused to leave the park.

The people who'd searched the playground across the lake had found the dark blue ribbon Suzanna had been wearing underneath one of the swings, but there was no other sign of her. It was enough to convince Senior Constable Atkins to call in police from nearby towns, as well as the big guns from Melbourne, although it would be several hours before they arrived.

While they were waiting, Samantha told her father and the constable about the YSA notes. She looked at the ground as she told them, her cheeks hot and sweat beading on her forehead, but she pushed through the embarrassment. She told them what the notes had said, how she'd believed them, and how she was supposed to meet the note writer today at the party, but nobody had spoken to her, and she'd not received a seventh note. She'd read the six notes enough times that even now, with forty more years of memories layered on top, she could still recite them word for word.

"I doubt that has anything to do this. It sounds like a school kid prank, but show us anyway, if you feel you must," Senior Constable Atkins said.

Samantha wondered if he'd worked on how to sound arrogant and dismissive at the same time, or if it was something all police learned at police college.

She went to get her bag from where she'd left it on the picnic table seat, but it wasn't there. She hunted around on the ground and started to panic when she couldn't find it. Then, she remembered that the first time around, her bag had also gone missing with Suzanna and was also never found.

"Someone must have taken my bag. The notes were in there. Maybe Suzanna saw them and decided to confront this person. Or maybe the person who wrote them took it so there'd be no evidence."

Senior Constable Atkins didn't look convinced, but he jotted something in his notebook, then turned away, heading over to a police car that had just pulled into the carpark. An older sergeant from a nearby town got out and took charge, much to the younger policeman's obvious relief.

By now it was nearing midnight and the partygoers who hadn't already left were back to standing around in small groups, talking in hushed voices, occasionally glancing over at Samantha and her father. Every place anyone could think of had been searched but there was no sign of Suzanna, except for the ribbon.

The sergeant ordered Senior Constable Atkins to take everyone's names and send them all home. They would interview them later.

As more police arrived, they spread out with their powerful torches, searching the immediate vicinity, everywhere the partygoers had already searched, including the playground across the lake. Not surprisingly, they didn't find anything more and the night dragged on, as sluggish as molasses on a cold day.

The police tried to convince Samantha and her father to go home, but she dug in her heels and refused to leave. She sat on the picnic table, next to the birthday cake, staring into the dark, desperately hoping that just her presence here would be enough to change the timeline to give Suzanna the opportunity to get away from her abductor and come back.

She looked up at the starry night and thought about universes. She tried to force hers to give her what she wanted, tried to will Suzanna walking back along the track around the lake, but nothing changed.

The sky began to turn grey as morning approached and she barely heard her father taking the unopened presents and loading them into his car. She jumped when he put his arm around her and rested his head against hers.

"I'm going to go and check on Mum," he whispered. He tried to hide his tears, but Samantha heard them in his voice. "Won't you come with me? You need some sleep."

"How can I sleep, Dad?" she asked with a sigh. She hadn't cried for Suzanna yet, and her eyes felt grainy and dry as if she'd spent days in the desert. "How can you? I don't know if I'll ever sleep again if we don't find her this time."

14

Awake

Sun, 25 March 1984 – Suzanna

SUZANNA AWOKE SLOWLY, CURLED in a tight foetal ball. She rolled onto her back, wincing at the tightness and the ache in the muscles across her back and shoulders as she moved. It felt like the last school holidays when she'd spent five hours a day for a whole week at tennis camp.

The room was dim, with a soft blue glow coming from somewhere. She looked at her watch, but it had stopped with its glowing hands helpfully pointing out 3:24 AM. She must have forgotten to wind it up yesterday.

She started to stretch her legs and, when her feet hit the wooden baseboard of the bed, she realised this was not her bed, not her room. She sat up quickly and stared at the pinkest room she'd ever seen.

The bright pink doona, adorned with fairies sitting on mushrooms, crinkled as she pulled her legs up and wrapped her arms around her knees. At the end of the bed, three soft toys – a small pink cat, a pink elephant, and a round, white indeterminate creature that looked like a fluffy marshmallow – smiled at her.

On her right, she saw that the blue glow was coming from a small rectangular night light plugged into a socket low down on a wall between a bookshelf and a pale pink door that was closed. A small white three-drawer bedside table was pushed up hard against the bed on that side, and a circus merry-go-round lamp with smiling pink horses sat still and patient, waiting to begin their merry march around and around whenever she needed more light.

Even in the dull glow of the night light, she could see the walls and ceiling were painted a dark dusky pink, like the colour of chewed-up musk stick lollies. A multitude of glow-in-the-dark stars and planets were scattered across the ceiling, and it felt like she was looking up at a crowded night sky, although their luminescence was starting to fade, ready to be recharged by daylight again to be ready for the next night.

White short-pile carpet covered the floor, overlaid by a pink and blue rug with cavorting cats, dogs, and horses. Opposite the bed, a closed pale pink door separated two halves of a built-in closet that otherwise spanned that wall of the room.

On her left was a pale pink dressing table next to a window with curtains that matched the doona. Pink and silver tinsel wrapped around the edges of the mirror gave it a festive, although childish, feel.

She swung her legs over the left side of the bed and stood up. She drew in a sharp breath when she saw herself in the dressing table mirror. She was wearing a frilly pink and white nightdress – at least one size too small for her – over dark pink shorts. She wrapped her arms tightly around herself and closed her eyes, realising that he'd undressed her and dressed her again while she'd been unconscious.

She put her hand up to her throat, realising her new necklace, earrings, and bracelet were all gone, too. Her breath hitched in her throat, and she suppressed the feeling of loss of identity that threatened to overwhelm her.

She took a deep breath, forced her eyes open and her arms down by her sides, and stared at her reflection. "Keep it together, Suzanna," she admonished herself. "There's nothing you can do about it now. It's in the past. You need to get out of here, not stand around feeling sorry for yourself."

She stepped across to the curtains and yanked them open, fully expecting to see the sun and blue sky. However, all she saw was a shiny silver sheet of corrugated iron. The glass had been removed, and the window had been covered over on the outside. All that remained were the windowsill and the curtains inside the room. She turned away, disappointed, and went back to the dressing table.

She picked up a pink brush, pulled it through her hair once, then put it down again. She examined a plastic cup full of hair clips and rubber bands, some of which had strands of tightly wrapped dark hair caught in them. She sat down on the pink fuzzy chair and pulled open the top right drawer. It was empty.

Movement caught her eye in the mirror, and the door behind her started to slowly open. She jumped to her feet and spun around.

"Oh good, you're awake," Mr Beresford said with a smile as he leaned in, peering around the edge of the door. "I thought you were going to sleep all day. How are you feeling on this lovely Sunday afternoon?"

Suzanna stared at him, and her arms subconsciously came back up to wrap protectively around her upper body. She didn't answer, not sure what to say in this situation.

He stepped into the room and switched on the overhead light. He closed the door quietly, then leaned back against it as he just stared at her.

"You are so beautiful, Samantha," he said with a dreamy look on his face. "I knew you would be. I've always known it."

"I'm not Samantha," Suzanna said. "I'm Suzanna."

Mr Beresford frowned. "Why would you say that? Why would you lie to me?"

"I'm not lying," she said. "You got the wrong sister."

His demeanour suddenly changed, like a storm blowing up out of nowhere on a hot, sunny day. He stood up straight, crossed his arms, and narrowed his eyes at her.

"Stop it. Stop it now," he ordered. "You need to learn that lying is a sin, and that sin is bad. You should have been brought up better than that. Obviously, you've been allowed to get away with sinful things, so you don't know the proper way to behave. You're lucky I'm here now to set you straight. I'm going to let you think about what you've done wrong, and you can apologise to me later." He wrinkled his nose and pointed to the other door, the one in between the closets. "The bathroom is through there. You should have a shower. I can smell you from here. There are clean clothes in the closet."

With that he turned, yanked open the bedroom door, and left, shutting it forcefully behind himself. She heard him turn a key, but she rushed over to it anyway, gripping the handle and jiggling it, trying to make it turn, but it wouldn't budge.

"HELP," she called as loud as she could as she banged her fists against the door. "HELP ME!"

But no one came.

15

Worthless

Sun, 25 March 1984 – Samantha

IT WAS LATE AFTERNOON on Sunday, and Samantha was frustrated at how slow the police were being. They made her sit at the picnic table – assigning a young female constable to stay with her – and wouldn't let her join the search or hear their discussions.

Once the detective in charge had arrived and taken over the investigation, she'd tried to impress on him the importance of YSA and the notes. With forty years of hindsight, she recognised the pattern of grooming a lonely teenage girl to get her on her own. She was more convinced than ever, that Suzanna had been taken in her place.

Detective White was a bit more diplomatic about his opinion than Senior Constable Atkins had been.

He promised to look into it, but she could tell he also thought it was just a schoolkid prank and didn't give it much credence. Especially since there was no evidence now; just the word of a fourteen-year-old girl who'd just lost her sister and was now grasping at straws.

She sat there with her head in her hands, racking her brain, trying to remember every detail of the first time Suzanna went missing, but there wasn't much to remember. She'd been at home for most of it, so she hadn't seen what the police had done in the immediate aftermath here at the park.

The dry heat and the sound of flies buzzing hungrily around the abandoned pink birthday cake turned her stomach and made her head ache. She looked up at the female officer. Her name might have been Belinda, but Samantha hadn't really been listening when she'd introduced herself.

"I need to walk," Samantha said, standing up. "I can't just sit here doing nothing."

"Let me take you home," maybe-Belinda suggested, remaining seated. She looked up at Samantha, shielding her eyes from the glare of the sun. "There's nothing you can do here. There are protocols to follow, and we can't let you compromise the operation."

"What operation? You can hardly call standing around, looking out of your depth, an operation. This is not going to find my sister." Samantha hated how snarky she sounded. She knew the police were doing what they could, what they knew how to do, but she also knew it wasn't enough. Something new had to happen this time around.

She started to walk, heading for the footpath that would take her around the lake to the playground on the other side. She vaguely heard maybe-Belinda scramble to her feet and run after her. She shrugged the young constable's hand off her shoulder when she tried to stop her and kept walking.

When she reached the playground, she stood behind the blue and white checked police tape, just staring at the swing set. The dark blue ribbon Suzanna had been wearing had been found in the tan bark under the lefthand swing.

She ducked under the police tape, much to maybe-Belinda's consternation. She sat on the swing, listening to it creak as it moved slightly forward and backward under her weight. She closed her eyes, trying to see what Suzanna had seen. *Had Suzanna sat here waiting, or even talking to this person?* This man. She was sure it was a man.

How could anyone have taken her strong, independent, confident sister? The one who wasn't afraid to stand up for Samantha, or indeed anyone who needed an advocate. She imagined Suzanna fighting like a wildcat, spitting and screaming, when she realised what was happening.

The music at the party had been loud, so, even if she *had* screamed, most likely no one would have heard her unless they were nearby.

He must have knocked her out somehow. She played it out in her head, pictured a faceless man picking up an unconscious Suzanna and bundling her into a vehicle. It's the only way this could have worked.

Samantha opened her eyes. "Did they search the carpark?"

"Of course," replied maybe-Belinda, who was still standing behind the police tape.

Samantha stood up and walked across the tan bark, keeping her eyes peeled to the ground. She pushed the police tape up as she went underneath it and headed for the carpark. A small fluffy cloud of white dog fur rolled past her foot, encouraged on its way by the light breeze that had started up. She thought nothing of it. A lot of people walked their dogs around the lake. Hell, she'd walked Mr Beresford's dog around here plenty of times.

She stood by the pine log barrier that separated the playground area from the dirt carpark and narrowed her eyes. *If you wanted to abduct someone, where would you park?* There were no lights and a row of trees down the middle split the carpark into front and back areas.

If you didn't want anyone to see your car, you'd park it in the very back corner, she reasoned. It would be dark, and the centre trees would hide it from view so you wouldn't see it from the playground.

She walked around the middle row of trees, looking at the ground. It hadn't rained in weeks, so the dirt surface of the carpark was dusty. The back section of the carpark was covered with large round skid marks, from bored teenagers doing circles, faster and faster, probably in their parents' cars. Other tyre tracks overlaid the circles, and it was clear where people had driven around several large dust-filled potholes.

Then, over the top of the tyre tracks, were footprints. So many footprints, it was impossible to tell if any might have been from Suzanna or her attacker.

Samantha sighed and walked towards the back corner of the carpark. She stood with her hands on her hips, staring at the ground. It was just as scuffed and footprinted as the rest of the area. She bent down and thought she could see some small dog prints, almost erased by the human footprints.

She stood up again, imagining a car parked here. She didn't know what type of car it might have been, maybe it was a van, but she tried to gauge how long an average car would be, where its boot might be. *Would he have parked front in, or would he have reversed in?*

She walked around the imaginary car, imagining scenarios. *Had Suzanna come this far on her own? Why would she, unless she maybe knew him?* She saw Suzanna fighting, biting, kicking, frantically trying to get away from this maniac, until she was suddenly rendered unconscious, then shoved into the boot, with the lid slammed closed on top of her, leaving her in the dark.

She walked backwards and forwards, backwards and forwards, kicking up dust as the sun began to drop below the tree line. A shaft of yellow sunlight snuck through some leaves, dust motes dancing in the glare, and Samantha saw something glint near her foot.

She bent down and picked up Suzanna's broken birthday bracelet, blowing and rubbing the dust off the small charms – the leaf, the cat, the castle, the sunflower, the 'S'.

Tears trickled down her cheeks, and she finally cried. She cried for Suzanna. She cried for herself. She cried for blowing this second chance she'd been given and not making a damn bit of difference to anything. *I really am a worthless person who deserves to be nothing but a pile of ashes.*

16

Alone

Sun, 25 March 1984 – Suzanna

SUZANNA OPENED THE PALE pink door and stepped onto the cold tiles of the bathroom. She felt around on the wall next to her, found the light switch, and clicked it on. The light buzzed and flickered, then stabilised, bathing the room in glaring blue fluorescence.

She stood in the doorway, surveying the small room through swollen, red eyes. Her heart fluttered when she saw that there was no window in here either, and fresh tears beaded in the corners of her eyes. She angrily rubbed away the tears. *Get it together*, she told herself, sniffling and trying to take deep calming breaths.

The white floor tiles had a pink rainbow pattern through them. Where one ended, the next one started, but upside down, giving an illusion of pink waves rippling across the floor. On the wall to her right was a white toilet with a pink crocheted cover on the lid. On the wall to her left was a small basin with a cupboard underneath and a mirror above, pink and silver tinsel wrapped around the edges like the dressing table mirror in the bedroom.

A shower, with aluminium fittings and clear glass panels, took up the back left corner of the room, and a small tub sat to the right of it. Two large fluffy pink towels and a matching floor mat hung neatly on silver rails between the shower and the basin.

All this pink was starting to make her feel like she'd eaten too much fairy floss at the annual show. She hurried over to the toilet, threw the lid up with a bang, fell to her knees, and threw up. She sat there for a while with her head hanging, until she was sure her stomach was empty.

Standing up, she flushed the toilet and turned around. She looked at herself in the full-length mirror on the back of the partially-open door that led back to the bedroom. She wiped her mouth with the back of her hand and, despite her initial resistance to the idea of a shower in this place, she thought he had a point. She looked terrible, smelled worse, and felt dirty.

She put the pink floor mat down, opened the shower door and stepped inside. She was too scared to undress – scared he would come back when she was vulnerable. She turned the taps on hard, until the water was almost too hot for her to bear. Standing there with her eyes closed, she let the water wash over her, let the almost scalding water cleanse her of her tears and her shame at how easy it had been for him to have taken her, *stolen* her, and the thought of his hands on her, undressing and dressing her when she wasn't even aware of it. She didn't touch the pink bar of soap, the white face washer, or the shampoo bottle.

She didn't know how long she stood there with her eyes closed, picturing the filth running down her body, until it swirled away, down, down, down the drain beneath her feet. When the water started to cool down, she took a deep breath, opened her eyes, and turned the water off.

The sodden nightdress and shorts clung to her body and dripped pools of water when she stepped out onto the floor mat. She rubbed a towel over herself, but it didn't do much to dry the clothes she was wearing.

Grabbing the other towel, she wrapped it around her wet hair like a turban and went back into the bedroom, not caring that she left a watery trail on the carpet.

She slid open the door on the closet to the left of the bathroom door and found masses of pink dresses hanging neatly from a silver rail. They didn't look new, some of them looked crumpled and a couple had sweat stains under the arms. They were all too small for her, and she wasn't really a dress-wearer anyway.

The closet door on the other side hid drawers with underwear, shirts, shorts, and jeans. Only the larger size items seemed new, like they'd never been washed before. Some of the smaller ones had green and brown stains and were faded, as if they'd been washed a lot.

She found a white shirt with a picture of a pink cat on it and pink jeans that looked like the right size. She reluctantly took some underwear out of the bottom drawer. They looked new, at least, and, leaving the drawers open, she took the clothes back to the other side of the closet. She pushed the dresses to one side, stepped inside, closed the door, and got changed in the dark.

Leaving the wet clothes and the towel she'd had over her hair on the floor of the closet, and the closet doors open, she went back to the bed. She sat down and leaned back against the headboard again, with the pillow behind her shoulders soaking up the dampness from her hair, and her legs up, arms wrapped around her knees.

She still didn't know what her history teacher wanted with her … well, with Samantha, but she was glad he'd got the wrong twin. Samantha would not have been strong enough to cope with a situation like this.

She wasn't sure what time it was. There was no way of telling in this two-room pink prison. The covered-up window made sure she couldn't see the sun or the daylight, but she would wait. Wait for him to return. Wait for someone to come and rescue her.

As she sat there, she flexed her fingers. She needed to draw. It was almost a compulsion for her, something she had to do, a way to make sense of her day, a way to release pent up energy. She lifted her arm, concentrated hard, and sketched something in the air, trying to send a mental message to her twin, to her mother, to her father, to her friends, to anyone who was listening.

She didn't know if it went through, but she did it anyway. It made her feel like she was doing something, not just sitting and waiting for a madman to do whatever it was he intended to do with her.

Suzanna was dozing, still sitting on the bed, but slumped with her arms now relaxed at her sides. The sound of the key unlocking the bedroom door jolted her fully awake. She sat up straight, subconsciously hugging her knees again, feeling a dull ache in her neck.

The door opened slightly, just enough for Mr Beresford to lean his head in with a smile on his face, almost a carbon copy of the last time he'd done this. When he saw her sitting on the bed, he opened the door, stepped into the room, and shut the door behind himself again.

"That's better," he said, staring at her.

A dark look crossed his face when he noticed the water trail leading from the bathroom to the closet, and the open closet doors. He sighed and walked over to the first closet, closing the drawers and the door. He went to the other side, picked up the wet clothing and towel, and closed that door as well.

"I'll make allowances this one time, because you're confused and you obviously haven't been brought up properly," he grumbled, holding the damp items at arms length as he took them into the bathroom. "Mark my words, though, this will not become a habit."

As soon as he stepped into the bathroom, Suzanna leapt off the bed and had the bedroom door open in seconds. She ran blindly, heading left down the hallway, then turning right and finding herself in the living room at the front of the house. A brown and green couch and two armchairs faced a boxy TV and an archway led to the front door, next to which a beige push-button phone sat on a small wooden table.

She grabbed the front door handle and yanked. The handle turned easily, but the door wouldn't budge. Hammering her fists uselessly against the solid wooden door, sobbing at the futility of it, she noticed the three deadlocks fitted to the door above the handle, all of them engaged. She looked frantically around for the keys, yanking the small drawer out of the telephone table and spilling its contents all over the floor. She fell to her knees and scrabbled around in the papers and pens that were now lying on the floor, but there were no keys.

"Pick it all up and put it back," Mr Beresford said, standing over her as she stayed there on her knees. "Neatly, how it was."

"What do you want with me?" she sobbed, cowering away from him. "Please don't hurt me."

"Do as I say and you won't get hurt," he said. "You're not too old for a spanking. Only bad girls get hurt."

Weeping, she picked up everything, putting it all back in the drawer, then stood up and slotted the drawer back into the table.

"Now, we need to have a bit of a talk," he said, taking hold of her upper right arm and pulling her towards another doorway.

17

Stories

Sun, 25 March 1984 – Suzanna

MR BERESFORD MANOEUVRED SUZANNA through the door and into an open-plan kitchen/dining area.

A bench with overhead cupboards separated the kitchen from the small dining area and two stools sat next to the bench. A small round wooden dining table and four orange plastic chairs with metal frames took up most of the dining area. The chairs looked like the sort of chairs that were normally set out in the school gym for assemblies and events. Samantha's black leather bag was sitting on one of the chairs.

"You're hurting me," she said, focussing on Samantha's bag as he dragged her over to the table and forced her to sit, facing away from the kitchen.

"Well, don't make me," he said.

She rubbed her arm and tried to look around, but he stood right behind her blocking her view. He was just standing there, looking at her with a strange look on his face that made her uncomfortable.

"Can I please have some water?" she asked, squinting as she looked up at him.

"Of course," he said, turning away. "I'm not a monster."

He walked around the bench and into the kitchen, then bent down to get a glass out of a cupboard. While he was doing that, Suzanna stared at the window over the kitchen sink. The white curtains were closed. Fruit patterns – apples, oranges, bananas – were scattered haphazardly across the fabric. The dull grey light that filtered around the edges made her think it was early evening. She thought it must still be Sunday. *Surely, I haven't been here any longer than that?*

Mr Beresford filled the glass from the tap and brought it over to the table. He put it in front of her and then sat in the chair next to her.

He just looked at her in that strange way again, and she lifted the glass to her mouth and drank, not looking away from him at all. When the glass was empty, she set it down and took a deep breath. She heard a siren in the distance and hoped it was someone looking for her.

"What do you want with me?" she finally said when he didn't say anything. "I'm sure my parents and my sister are looking for me. If you let me go, I'll just say I went for a walk and got lost."

He laughed and said, "Your parents? They are not your parents, and you will not be going back there."

"What do you mean," she frowned.

"Those people are not your parents," he reiterated.

"I don't understand," she said.

"I need to tell you a story," he said with a big grin. "A story that will make you very happy. But first, are you hungry? You should eat. Keep your strength up."

Suzanna shook her head, annoyed at the tears that threatened to bubble up out of her eyes. "I just want to know what's going on and I want to go home."

"Let's cook pancakes while I tell you our story," he said, jumping up. He held his hand out and she reluctantly took it. She'd rather that than have him grab her arm again where it was already bruising.

He instructed her where to find the dry ingredients in the pantry, while he took a frying pan out of a cupboard under the stove. He lit a burner on the stove top and put the pan on it to heat up. He dug cooking utensils out of a drawer, and took eggs, butter, and milk out of the fridge.

He got her to mix the ingredients, laughing at her when the flour puffed up into her face when she stirred slightly too hard. Then he made her sit on one of the stools at the bench to watch him cook.

"So," he said, pouring the first lot of mixture into the heated pan and watching it bubble. "I never know quite where to start but just know that I've been looking for you for a very long time. There have been several times over the past few years when I thought I'd found you, but each time I was wrong. But I'm not wrong this time. I know I'm not. I knew it was you when I saw a certain look on your face in class one day, the way you were standing, the way you held yourself. You looked so lonely, as if you knew you didn't belong. Like you were living the wrong life. I'd seen that look before on your grandmother's face when I was young. That's when I knew."

"You know my grandmother?" Suzanna sat stiffly on the stool, scared and confused.

"Of course, I know your grandmother, she's my mother," he said, sliding a pancake onto a plate, then adding more bubbling mixture to the pan. "Grandparents are your parents parents."

"I know that," she said. "But I'm pretty sure I would have heard about an uncle. Dad's an only child and Mum's only got sisters."

"I wish you wouldn't call them that, and I'm not your uncle, but I'm getting ahead of myself," he said, sliding the second pancake ono the plate. "Let me finish making these, then we can discuss it while we're eating."

He cooked the rest of the pancakes in silence, while Suzanna tried to make sense of what he'd said. But it made no sense at all. Once the plate was full, he took it over to the table, coming back for two more plates, cutlery, and butter and honey.

He looked at her with raised eyebrows, indicating to the seat she'd been in earlier, and she moved from the stool to the table. Disappointingly, she noted that they were using white plastic knives and forks. She'd been hoping to get a proper knife that she could use either for self-defence or to try to jimmy the lock on the bedroom door later.

She wasn't hungry, but she cut slices off her pancake and pushed them around the plate while he spoke.

"The two most important things in the world are family and history," he started. "Years ago, I was married to a wonderful, beautiful woman. Her name was Margaret. We'd known each other through our school years, from primary right through to high school. We weren't close then, but we bumped into each other at a seminar one day a few years after we'd left school, and, well, one thing led to another, and we ended up married."

"Where is Margaret now, Mr Beresford?" Suzanna asked. She didn't see any sign that anyone but he lived here, but a brief hope flared in her chest that Margaret would come home, find out her husband had abducted a teenage girl, and would let her go.

He frowned and didn't answer her question. "Don't call me that. Call me Dad."

"Why would I do that," she asked, confused again.

"Be quiet for a minute and let me explain," he snapped. He sighed and continued his story. "I'm sorry, I keep forgetting that you don't already know all this. Anyway, Margaret and I tried for years to have a baby, but she kept miscarrying. We lost five babies, all around the same three-month mark. We didn't think we'd ever get the child we wanted. We considered adoption, but we wanted our baby to be made from us, a perfect combination of love. Then, Margaret got pregnant, again. For a sixth time. She stayed in the hospital for almost the whole pregnancy and our little girl managed to hang on, right through to eight months, when she couldn't hang on any longer."

Mr Beresford started to weep, but he dashed his tears away and stared at Suzanna. He reached out and put his hand over Suzanna's hand.

"That little baby was you. You are our Michelle. They told us you were stillborn, but I know you weren't. I know they took you. They wouldn't let us see you. They took you away from us and gave you to someone else. You are my baby and we're finally together again. Nothing can change that now."

Suzanna just stared at him. What do you say to a story like that? This man was obviously unhinged, driven mad from grief, but what should she do? She'd already seen how quickly his mood could change, turning from loving to violently angry in seconds, and she didn't want to antagonise him. But she also would not deny her own family.

"I'm really sorry, but I'm not your daughter, I'm not Michelle," Suzanna said softly, pulling her hand out from under his.

"You are my daughter," he responded, slamming his hands down on the table and making the plates, and Suzanna, jump.

"I'm a twin," Suzanna reasoned. "I have a twin sister. An identical twin sister. How could I be your daughter? Did your wife have twins?"

He closed his eyes, took a deep breath and let it out slowly, then he looked at her again. "That's what they want you to think. That girl is probably someone else's child that was also stolen at birth, probably from the same hospital on the same day by the same medical staff."

"But we're identical," she repeated, shaking her head. She pushed her chair back and stood up, backing away from him. "Why do we look alike if we're not related?"

"They've been lying to you, Michelle," he said, also standing. He moved closer to her, holding his arms out to the sides as if he wanted to pull her into an embrace. She moved back a step. She didn't want him to touch her. "They dressed you the same, gave you the same haircut, told you all your life that you're a twin. But it's just not true. Think about how different you are from that girl they tell you is your sister. I've seen it at school. You're intelligent, considerate, hardworking. She's lazy, bosses people around, and only thinks of herself."

Suzanna blinked, unexpectedly hurt by his description of her. Of course, he thought he was speaking to Samantha, so he didn't know he was actually insulting her. *Is that really what people think of me?*

"Why me?" she questioned, taking another step back. After his reaction to her saying she was not Samantha, she was reluctant to say it again. So, she'd keep up the pretence for now. "What makes you so sure I'm your daughter? How long ago did all this happen?"

"I told you," he said, moving towards her again. "I wrote it in the notes. I'd know you anywhere. I see my own mother in you, your expressions, your mannerisms, the way you stand, the way you walk, the way you look when you're thinking about a problem in class, the way your beautiful hair shines in the sun."

Suzanna turned away from him. "You're wrong," she said, shaking her head again. "You. Are. Wrong." Suddenly, she didn't care what he thought. "I'm not even the right twin. You thought you were taking Samantha, but I'm Suzanna. The lazy, bossy, selfish one."

He grabbed her arm, spun her around to face him, and slapped her hard across the face. Her head spun, her cheek burned, and she collapsed. His vice-like grip around her upper arm made it feel as if her shoulder was going to pop out of its socket.

"Stop lying," he yelled, dragging her towards the door as she tried and failed to get to her feet. "Stop it now, Michelle. That is not true. I will not have a liar for a daughter. You will go to your room and think about what you've said."

18

Variables

Sun, 25 March / Mon, 26 March 1984 – Samantha

AFTER THE POLICE EXTRICATED Suzanna's broken bracelet from Samantha's hand, they cordoned off the playground carpark, and the young female police constable drove her home. By this point, Samantha just let them tell her what to do. She'd shed all the tears she had in her, and she was numb.

When she walked in the door, her mother rushed over to her, sobbing and laughing while hugging her, thanking God that Suzanna had come home safely, that it had all been a terrible misunderstanding. Samantha stood motionless in the doorway, silent and tearless, while her father pulled her mother away, explaining that this was Samantha, that Suzanna was still missing.

Her mother slumped into a chair, all the fight gone out of her when she finally understood what he was saying.

Samantha went to her room, lay down on her bed, and stared at the ceiling. Even though she hadn't slept for almost two days, she couldn't sleep, couldn't think. She wondered briefly what had happened to Tina, then remembered that, last time this happened, the police had put her on an earlier flight home. In the forty years following Suzanna's disappearance, she and Tina had never spoken again.

At midnight, she could still hear her parents' voices in the kitchen. Every so often, her mother's voice would start to get louder, and her father's voice would stay steady, stoic, as he attempted to calm her down. A little while later, she heard them shuffling along the passageway towards their bedroom and she assumed her father had given her mother one of the sedatives the doctor had left for her.

Around 2 AM she got up and went to Suzanna's room, crawling into Suzanna's bed, pulling the blankets up around her neck, and cuddling Suzanna's blue teddy bear. She lay on her left side, staring at the INXS poster beside the slightly ajar door. Her gaze moved to the jar of coins and notes on the dressing table, and tears pricked the corners of her eyes even though she thought she was all cried out. She couldn't see the label in the dark, but she knew it said, 'Suzanna's Concert Fund', written in blue biro in her sister's scrawly handwriting. Suzanna was saving up to buy them both tickets to an INXS concert in Melbourne. The tears flowed stronger when she realised they would never attend that concert, or any concert, together, ever. Especially now that she'd failed for a second time to save her.

A short while later, she felt Arabella jump quietly onto the end of the bed, and step daintily as she made her way towards the pillow. Samantha moved the teddy bear and held the blankets up. The cat crept under the blankets, then turned and curled up with her head against Samantha's chest, purring loudly. Samantha stroked Arabella's head, and after a while the repetitive motion seemed to help her mind slip free from the bind it had been in since discovering Suzanna's bracelet, and she started thinking again.

She thought of the Ash Man and the Ash Train. Her previous life spooled out before her again, the same way it had when she'd stared out the window into the white fog, as she next to the Ash Man. She was appalled, again, at how pathetic she was, how useless, how she hadn't been able to change a single thing despite this second chance she'd been given.

How had this played out almost the same way as the first time around? She'd assumed changing minor things – or even just her presence here and knowing what was going to happen – would somehow magically change major things.

Did the Ash Train guardians know this would happen? That you couldn't change history? Is that why they only gave you one chance? Because they knew you'd keep going back for more when nothing changed, no matter how determined you claimed to be?

What was the point? She might as well give up, just like she'd been doing her whole life. Right now, she'd welcome the nothingness of being turned to ash. That's what her afterlife should be. She didn't deserve anything else. She was tired and didn't want to play this game anymore.

Her gaze wandered around the room again and came to rest on Suzanna's concert fund jar again. *This is not about me*, she realised. She could give up on herself – she'd been doing it her whole life – but she couldn't give up on Suzanna. Not this time. Suzanna needed to get to that concert. She needed to live the life she deserved, the one she'd missed out on because of Samantha's weakness and lack of character.

"I'm the only variable in this scenario," she murmured to Arabella, but the cat was snoring softly. She kept talking anyway. "I'm the only one who can change the outcome. This is my universe, but what I do and say also affects Suzanna's universe, not to mention everyone else's. Not that I've done much of a job, so far. I need to change more things, bigger things, otherwise this will all have been for nothing."

She wasn't aware of falling asleep. Her eyes drifted closed, and she nodded off into a dark land devoid of dreams and nightmares. She didn't feel Arabella crawl out from under the blankets sometime in the early morning hours, stretch, jump down off the bed, and leave the room.

Samantha slept the sleep of the dead, but her mind kept picking at the problem, turning it this way, then that, pulling at a thread here and there, trying to see a way out of this maze that she couldn't see while she was awake.

"Suzanna!"

The scream pulled Samatha out of an ashy fog and back into consciousness. The bed creaked and she fought to escape the smothering arms that pulled her into her mother's chest. She squirmed out of the tight embrace and tried to push her mother away.

"Stop it," she said, leaning back as she kept pushing her mother's arms away. "I'm Samantha."

Her mother kept trying to grab her, calling Suzanna's name, until her father came in and pulled her away. Her mother fought hard, gouging bloody trenches down his cheeks with her fingernails, but he kept hold of her, dragging her out the door and down the passageway towards the kitchen. She kept screaming until suddenly she went quiet.

Samantha got up and went back to her own room. She got clean clothes out of the cupboard and headed for the bathroom.

She stood under the shower with her eyes closed and her mind empty. The water was almost too hot, and her skin turned pink making it look like she'd got a light sunburn. But she stood there, letting it sluice down her body, washing off the physical and mental grime from the last few days.

"You need to find me, Sammie. I can't do this on my own. We need to do this together."

It was just a whisper, but her eyes flew open, and she looked around the steamy bathroom. There was no one there, but a certainty flowed through her, and she knew that Suzanna was still alive. It was not too late. This was not something she'd felt the first time this had happened.

"Where are you, Suze?" she whispered back, closing her eyes again, but there was no reply. A flash of pink darted through her mind, but she didn't know what, if anything, that might mean.

She turned the taps off and stepped out of the shower, grabbing the blue towel and rubbing her hair and face with it. When the steam cleared, she just stood there looking at the mirror. At the words someone had scrawled on there with their fingertip.

"HELP ME, SAMMIE!"

19

Attention

Mon, 26 March 1984 – Samantha

THE MEDIA HAD ARRIVED and brought the rain with them.

After months of hot, dry weather, dark swollen clouds had rolled in with the news vans and set up overhead just as the vans set up across the road. Rain was teeming down, puddling and running off into overflowing gutters as the water arrived faster than the thirsty ground could absorb it.

Samantha and her father stood at the front window, watching reporters and cameramen chatting and laughing under umbrellas on the front lawn. The rain running down the window distorted them all, making them look like they were melting, like the Wicked Witch of the West.

"How can they laugh?" Samantha's father asked softly, but Samantha had no answer.

Suzanna was today's story, but Samantha knew she wouldn't be for long. Especially, if the police had no updates, which she knew they didn't, and wouldn't ever. The media would move on, always chasing the next big thing in the news cycle, and a missing girl from a nondescript Australian town wouldn't hold their attention for too long.

Not long after the media moved on, the psychics would start up, offering to lead them to Suzanna's body, which was 'near a body of water' or 'somewhere related to the number 3 or the letter B', or telling them she was living on a sheep station in the outback where she didn't want to be found.

Samantha remembered Suzanna's story popping up again a couple of times in the future. On slow news days, television stations would rehash cold cases of missing persons, restating the same things that everyone already knew, baiting people with implications of new evidence. But there was never any new evidence; the programs were just trying to fill their timeslots, oblivious to how these stories brought fresh pain to loved ones who still had no answers. People on the Internet would ooh and aah and posit their theories, then something more interesting would come along and Suzanna would disappear again, forgotten again. Forgotten by everyone except the people closest to her, her family, all of whom would deal with it in their own way over the years.

A police car rolled slowly down the street and all the people on the front lawn turned and watched it pull into the driveway. As soon as it stopped, the reporters surged forward, pushing and shoving each other as if they were in a mosh pit at a heavy metal concert. Detective White and his partner got out of the car, ignoring the questions being yelled at them, and pushing away the cameras that were shoved in their faces.

"Are there any updates?"

"Have you found her?"

"How is the family doing?"

"Will this rain hinder the investigation?"

Sheltering under a big black umbrella, the detectives kept their heads down as they headed for the front door of the house. When they reached the front verandah, Detective White turned and held up his hands in a stop gesture.

"Please, stay back. We'll be holding a press conference later this afternoon at the town hall. You'll get your update then. Thank you."

He turned back towards the house and the reporters stopped following, but the cameras were aimed at the front door, hoping to catch a glimpse of the grieving family through the smallest gap. Samantha saw one camera turn towards the front window where she and her father were standing. The cameraman shouted something, and suddenly all the cameras were pointing at them.

Her father stayed there, his face as glum as the weather, while Samantha went to the front door and let the detectives in.

As soon as she opened the door, the reporters started yelling questions again and the cameras swung back to the door.

"Are you happy with how the police are handling this?"

"How are you coping?"

"Is there anything you want to say to Suzanna?"

"Do you believe someone took her?"

The two policemen stepped inside and shut the door quickly behind them, having left their dripping umbrella leaning against the wall outside.

She ushered them into the kitchen, then went to the living room and put her arm around her father's shoulders.

"Come on, Dad," she said, gently turning him and moving him towards the kitchen.

He walked beside her, offering no resistance, and he sat at the dining table next to her, opposite the detectives.

Detective White linked his hands together on the table and looked at Samantha's father. He winced at the red scratches on his cheeks. "How's your wife, Robert?"

"She's asleep," Samantha answered for him. Her mother was asleep in Suzanna's bed. "We have to keep her sedated, or she becomes hysterical. She insists on leaving the front door unlocked, in case Suzanna comes home and can't get in. But we've already had several reporters open the door and waltz on in, and they're harder to get rid of than mice, so it's better if she just sleeps."

Both detectives nodded and there was an awkward silence.

"You haven't found anything, have you?" Samantha asked, looking from one detective to the other.

"Unfortunately, no," Detective White said, looking down at his hands. "And this rain has washed away any evidence that might have still been there. So, we're trying to regroup, trying to work out what to do next."

"You had more than a day to gather evidence," Samantha snapped. She took a breath. There wasn't anything she could do about that now. "What about the notes I told you about? They've got to have something to do with this. This man was grooming me. Surely, you can see that."

Detective White frowned and looked at her. "I'm not sure what you mean."

Samantha realised that grooming was not a common word used in 1984 for this type of scenario, so she explained. "Grooming means establishing an emotional connection with a vulnerable person to make them compliant, make them suggestible, and encourage them to do something they wouldn't normally do."

Detective White sighed. "I haven't heard it called that before, but I see what you mean. I'm still not sure there's a connection there. These alleged notes were addressed to you, not your sister, and you said she didn't know about them. So, why would she go to meet someone she didn't know when she hadn't been 'groomed', as you call it?"

"There's got to be a connection," Samantha insisted. "It can't be a coincidence that I was supposed to meet this person on Saturday night, the very night Suzanna disappeared. I've written all the notes out again, so you can see what they say, see the pattern."

Samantha stood up, went to her room, and came back with six pieces of paper.

Detective White took them from her and glanced at them before putting them in the inside pocket of his jacket. "Are you sure this is what they said?"

"They're word for word," Samantha assured him. "I read them enough times to know exactly what each and every one of them said, down to the typos, the commas, and the full stops."

"Even if these notes *are* related to Suzanna's disappearance, we may not be able to use these as evidence, because they're not the originals," he said, standing up, which also prompted his partner to stand. "If you still had them, we could have tested them for fingerprints or had a handwriting analyst look them over."

"This is the best I can do," Samantha said. "They were in my bag, and I assume you haven't found that yet?"

"No, we have not."

"Have you found *anything* else? Any sort of clue, whatsoever?"

"No, we have not," Detective White repeated reluctantly.

Samantha leaned back in her chair. She already knew they hadn't, but she'd still had to ask, just in case enough variables had changed to loosen a pebble, a clue, set free a butterfly that hadn't been visible the first time around.

Her father just sat and watched their exchange. He was still in shock and had accepted, for now, that his remaining daughter was in charge, and he trusted her to do what was needed, to ask the right questions. He looked up, blinking rapidly, when Detective White moved over and put his hand on his shoulder.

"Robert, we're having a press conference this afternoon at the town hall. It would help if you, your wife, and your daughter were there to say something to the cameras. A plea to whoever might have her to let her go, or a plea to Suzanna to come home if she can."

Samantha remembered the press conference from the first time. It didn't go well. Her mother had been confused and upset by the insensitive questions the reporters shouted at them, especially the ones speculating about trouble at home or implying that Suzanna might have left on her own accord. Her mother had collapsed and had to be taken away in an ambulance.

"Mum's not up to it," Samantha said, standing up. She looked at her father. "Dad and I will discuss it and decide whether one or both of us should be there. What time is it?"

"2 PM," Detective White said, heading to the hallway, back to the front door, trailed by his partner and Samantha. "We'll send a car to pick you up at 1:30. I don't want you to have to run the gauntlet through that mob outside on your own."

As soon as the door was opened, the reporters surged forward again, shouting and elbowing each other to get the best vantage point. One blonde woman in high heels slipped in the mud, and her flailing hands also caught the man beside her. They both fell on their backsides with an oompf, and Samantha might have smiled were it not for the circumstances.

"What have you just told the family?"

"Are you any closer to finding her?"

"Do you have any suspects? Was it a local?"

"Are you sure she didn't leave on her own?"

The umbrella didn't do much of a job keeping the two burly detectives dry as they walked quickly back to their car. Detective White opened the back door and tossed the umbrella onto the floor. They both got in and reversed slowly down the driveway, making a cameraman trying to get a close-up jump quickly out of the way.

20

Reminiscences

Mon, 26 March 1984 – Samantha

BY THE TIME 11 AM rolled around, it was still pouring outside, and Samantha was stalking around the house like a caged lion. She couldn't stay cooped up here doing nothing. Doing nothing changed nothing.

She checked on her mother, but she was still asleep on Suzanna's bed. Arabella was curled up close to her mother's back, and she opened an eye to look at Samantha standing in the doorway, before closing it again and snuggling a bit closer. The cat was picking up the vibes in the house; she knew something was wrong, and she was keeping close to her people, comforting them, reminding them that they weren't alone. *We don't deserve pets*, Samantha thought with a sad smile.

Samantha returned to the kitchen where her father was still sitting at the table just staring at his hands. She made him a cup of tea and set it in front of him. Tears came to his eyes, and she pulled up a chair and sat next to him, putting her hand over his.

"What's up, Dad?" she asked gently.

He pointed to the writing on the side of the mug. "What a joke," he mumbled.

"No, it's not." She squeezed his hands. "You *are* the World's Greatest Dad. What's happened is not your fault. It's mine. I should have told you what was happening, and you would have dealt with it. Instead, pathetic loser over here just wanted to believe someone could love me for who I am, even when I knew better."

"*I* love you for who you are," he whispered, tears trickling down his cheeks. He put a hand up and pushed a strand of hair off her face. "I always have, Sammie. I'm so sorry you had to feel like that, that you felt so alone and unloved. I didn't know, and I should have. I'm your father and I'm ashamed you thought you couldn't come to me. You're not a loser. Never think of yourself like that."

Samantha dashed the tears out of her eyes and hugged her father. "It's not your fault. Nothing is your fault, Dad."

They stayed like that for several minutes, before her father spoke softly. "What are we going to do, Sammie? How do we get her back?" He then said out loud what they'd all been thinking. "What if she's dead? What if she's not coming back?"

She sat back, gripped his face and made him look at her. "Listen to me. She's not dead. I know she's not. I can't stay here doing nothing. I'm going out there to find her. When the police come at 1:30, go with them to the press conference, but don't take Mum. Don't leave her alone, though. Insist that the policewoman who was with me yesterday stay here with her. If they say no, dig your heels in and say you won't go, then, that it's not safe to leave Mum on her own."

Her father put his hand up and stroked her cheek. "Go get 'em, Sammie. If anyone can find her, it's you. Do what you have to do, but be careful. Please, be careful. We can't lose you, too."

The sound of the rain on the tin roofs masked any noise Samantha made as she snuck out the backdoor. Her purple bike was leaning up against the house, nice and dry under the pergola, where she knew she'd left it after school on Friday afternoon.

She looked at Suzanna's green bike, lying on the ground under the clothesline in the rain, where her sister had let it fall after coasting in late after tennis practice. It was scratched and the silver pedals were rusty, whereas her own bike looked new, like it had just come from the shop.

She smiled wryly. Suzanna had always been messy, and Samantha was always neat. Mum was always chiding Suzanna for leaving clothes around her bedroom, too lazy to put dirty ones in the laundry basket, too lazy to put clean ones away in drawers and closets. Ever since they were little, Suzanna had left her toys and sketches and pencils and colouring books all over the house, dumped her wet towel on the floor of the bathroom rather than hanging it on its rail, just laughing when she was told off but never changing her ways.

"I don't have time for that," she'd say with a wink to Samantha. "Life's too short to waste time on trivial things that don't matter."

The first time Suzanna went missing, Samantha had tried to be messy, too. She'd needed to feel what it was like to be her sister. She missed her and thought it would make her feel closer to her. Everybody missed her and her grieving brain told her that if she acted like Suzanna, maybe people wouldn't be so sad. They could all pretend that Samantha was the missing one and be happy again.

For about a week, she left wet towels on the floor in the bathroom, left plastic wrapping and empty cereal boxes on kitchen counters, dropped her jacket, and tramped mud onto the floor when she came in after school. But no one said anything. Mum barely noticed her, and Dad was busy looking after Mum, making sure she didn't hurt herself. No one at school would even look at Samantha unless they had to.

But it was just too hard, so Samantha gave up and went back to being her neat self, at least while she still lived at home. For a while, it made her feel like she had a smidgeon of control, and she went to the opposite end of the spectrum, becoming obsessed with cleanliness.

By that point, Dad was the only one keeping the household together. He did everything, shopping and cooking after work and looking after the yard on the weekends, while Mum just sat on the couch with the TV blaring mindlessly in the background. Every half hour or so, Mum would get up to check that the front door wasn't locked, and she'd walk out to the verandah and check the street, before heading back in and going back to her place on the couch.

So, Samantha had cleaned, and cleaned, and cleaned, determined not to be a burden on Dad. She'd whisk plates away almost before they finished eating and have them washed and dried and put away before Mum or Dad had even left the table. She ran the washing machine several times a week, washing clothes, bedding, towels, soft toys, whether they needed it or not. She vacuumed, and dusted, and wiped, and mopped, all of which helped her to not think of Suzanna for at least a few minutes at a time.

But, once she'd moved out of home, the depression and succession of toxic relationships overwhelmed the neat freak side of her, and she became worse than Suzanna had ever been. She grimaced when she remembered the black mould on walls and ceilings in houses that never had their windows opened, hair and dust accumulating in corners and hallways that were never vacuumed, and stacks of damp newspapers and empty bottles piled just outside the door, never quite making it to the bin.

She shook off her reminiscences. That would not happen this time.

She pulled the hood of her parka over her head, stepped out into the rain, picked up Suzanna's bike, and wheeled it out the back gate, into the lane. She slogged through the muddy lane, dragging the bike until she reached the bitumen road, then mounted and started pedalling towards the park.

There was no one at the park, which wasn't surprising in this weather. The rain hadn't let up at all, the wind had picked up, and everyone was staying indoors. The community was spooked.

The blue-checked police tape still surrounded the playground where the dark blue ribbon had been found, and another line flapped uselessly in the mud where it had originally roped off the entrance to the carpark. But there were no police. There wasn't much point, since the rain had already ruined any crime scene there might have been.

Samantha leaned Suzanna's bike up against a post, walked across the grass, and ducked under the tape. She sat on the swing where she knew Suzanna had sat. She closed her eyes and swung slowly, trying to channel her sister, trying to see what she saw when she was waiting here, see what she was seeing now.

"Help me, Suze," she murmured. "Help me to help you."

Her thoughts turned to the notes. They had to be the key to this. She recited them out loud as she swung, ignoring the dampness that seeped into her jeans and soaked through her parka, making her shiver.

Who could have written them? There was no way a kid could have composed those notes. It had to have been an adult, or an older kid at least, one nearing the end of their schooling. The wording, the way the phrasing had been arranged to manipulate her emotions. It had to be someone who knew her well, someone who'd watched her for a long time. It had to be someone who had access to the school, to her locker. Someone who wouldn't look out of place in the corridors.

She thought harder, and swung higher, putting her head back and letting the rain pelt her face. *Was it a teacher or a janitor or a parent or someone who worked in the canteen or library?* She discounted the canteen, since that was staffed mainly by volunteer mothers, and she was confident that the notes had been written by a man.

She slowed the swing and stopped it, sitting for a bit longer with her head down, listening to the patter of rain on her hood.

She had to go and check out the school.

The young policewoman had told her yesterday that school was cancelled for the week. She'd also said the school was offering onsite counselling to any students who felt they needed it, but Samantha knew no one would take them up on it. Therapy was not something Australian teenagers in small towns in 1984 would ever consider. Out here, counselling would consist of friends consoling friends, and townsfolk whispering and gossiping in the street, the shop, the pub, until eventually the attitude would change to 'shit happens, it didn't happen to you, there's nothing you can do about it, move on'.

She picked up Suzanna's bike and headed to the school.

21

Companions

Mon, 26 March 1984 – Samantha

AS EXPECTED, THE SCHOOL was empty and silent.

Normally on a Monday lunchtime, the grassy oval and bitumen courtyards would be overflowing with the colour and activity of boisterous younger students chasing each other, kicking or throwing balls, or older ones lounging around, talking and laughing in their cliques while they ate. But today, the usual hubbub was absent, and the dismal grey of the clouds and the sodden ground seemed to reflect the current sentiment in the community, giving the school an air of loneliness and abandonment.

As Samantha pedalled into the empty carpark, heading for the bike racks down the back, she thought she might be the only person left in the world. Maybe some sort of apocalypse had occurred while she'd slept, and everyone but her had died.

On more than one occasion, she and Tina had discussed that very scenario, and she sighed, wishing she had someone to talk to now. Someone she could tell the truth to, who would believe her strange tale of disappearances, death, ash trains, and second chances. Someone she could bounce ideas off rather than trying to organise the chaos in her head on her own.

She pushed the front wheel of Suzanna's bike through the metal bars of the bike rack, leaving it standing to attention in stark contrast to the sad rusty old bike slumped a few spots away. The old bike was a fixture here, like the physical manifestation of the ghost of a long-departed student. No one knew whose it was. It had just always been here, missing its rear wheel and seat, forever enslaved by a rusted chunky chain and padlock threaded through its flat front wheel, destined never to be freed.

She walked over to the front doors of the school and pulled on one of them, but it was locked. She headed around the left side of the main building, looking for a ground floor classroom with an open window. For now, she ignored the two standalone, demountable buildings that had been plonked at the back when the local pupil population had grown a few years ago.

Around the back, she spotted a slightly open window in a science lab. Standing on tiptoes in the mud close to the grey brick wall, she pushed the window up as high as she could. Digging her toes into the mortar between the bricks for leverage, she hauled herself up onto the windowsill. She sat for a second, breathing heavily, then pushed the window up higher, and climbed through onto a large black science desk. It was not lost on her that if she'd still been in her fifty-four-year-old body, she could never have done this.

Once inside, she stood there for a minute, then once her breathing slowed down, she crossed to the classroom door, opened it, and stepped out into the corridor.

She walked in the direction of the lockers, not knowing what she was looking for. She just hoped she'd recognise it when she saw it.

The silence of the school unnerved her, and she had a niggling sense of wrongdoing. In her previous life, after she'd left home, there were times when she'd broken into buildings, but it had been only abandoned ones, and only when she'd needed to get out of the weather. She'd never been alone in an active school building like this, and it felt eerie and wrong. She could almost hear the ghostly babble of students going about their school day, even though she was the only one here. *At least they didn't have twenty-four-hour surveillance cameras and intruder alarms in small town schools in 1984*, she thought.

The squeaking of her wet shoes on the lino floor echoed around the corridor, uncomfortably loud, and she kept looking behind, expecting to see a teacher or janitor about to clamp a hand on her shoulder and ask what she was doing here. If she got caught, she decided she'd say she was looking for the counsellor. No one would argue with that.

She stopped at her locker and looked at the next one over. Almost of its own volition, her arm rose up, and her fingertip traced over the hastily scrawled name on the square white label: Suzanna Buchanan. She smiled sadly, then turned back to her own locker.

She couldn't remember the combination, and she tried a few numbers before it finally clicked open. She was grateful that it wasn't a computer with a password that locked you out after three attempts. One-by-one, she pulled out the books, leafing through them for any loose papers. Maybe YSA had left a note that she hadn't found, that had been buried under books. But she didn't find anything except homework and test papers, most of them with an A grade circled in red pen.

Closing her locker again, she turned and leaned back against it as she contemplated the immediate area. She pictured a faceless man walking up and slipping a note through the air vent of her locker. He had to have done it when no one else was around, which meant it had to be someone who worked here, someone who had a reason to be here out of hours.

A crash from the direction of the science lab she'd come in through made her jump and her chest contracted with a sharp pain, making her wonder if she was having a heart attack. She cautiously headed back to the lab and stopped outside the door. She'd left it open, and she stayed off to the side so no one in the room would see her.

"Damn it all to bloody hell," a female voice muttered. "How the hell can you be that clumsy? You're an idiot."

Samantha leaned around the doorframe and peered into the room. A young woman was leaning over, trying to retrieve a Bunsen burner from the middle of a pile of shattered glass that looked like it used to be a beaker.

She looked to be in her mid-twenties, with bleached, wavy, strawberry blonde hair pulled up into a ponytail that sprouted from the top of her head like a fountain. She wore blue jeans with a white shirt and denim jacket over the top and clutched a beige canvas tote bag under her arm. Her large, round tortoiseshell glasses magnified her eyes, so she seemed to have a constant look of surprise on her face.

She saw Samantha and waved. She put the Bunsen burner on the desk and took a step towards the door, kicking a test tube along the floor. Another step and Samantha heard the crunch of glass as the woman stepped on the rolling test tube.

"Far out," the woman said with a sigh. She looked down, then back up at Samantha. "How can anyone be this unlucky?"

Samantha moved to stand properly in the doorway. She crossed her arms. "Who are you?"

"Toni Clayton," the woman introduced herself. "I'd come over and shake your hand, Samantha, but I'm worried I'll break something else. I'm sorry about what's happened to your sister."

Samantha narrowed her eyes and frowned. "Are you following me? Are you a reporter?"

"I wasn't technically following you at first. I was looking for a way in, too, and saw you climb through this window, so that's when I became a follower," Toni said, reaching up and pulling her ponytail tighter.

"Who exactly are you?" Samantha repeated.

Toni sighed. "Well, I *am* a reporter, but..."

Samantha turned and stalked away. She heard the glass stuck in Toni's shoes crunching after her down the corridor.

"I don't have time for this," Samantha said, waving her arm and keeping on walking. She had no plan of where she was going, just any direction away from this woman. "Leave me alone."

"Let me explain," Toni called, running to catch up. "You're going to want to hear this. Trust me."

"Why should I?" Samantha said, turning abruptly, causing Toni to stop just before she ran into her. "You people are leeches. You're not interested in me or my sister. All you want are views and tomorrow you'll have moved onto the next big thing. My sister is missing and the longer it takes to find her, the less chance that she'll still be alive when we do. *If* we do." She turned away again. "I'm not talking to a reporter."

"Please," Toni said, reaching out and touching Samantha's shoulder. "I do care about your sister. But

I believe this is bigger than just Suzanna. I think this man has done this before. I don't think Suzanna is his first."

Samantha spun around and stared at her for a few seconds before she spoke. "You're talking about a serial offender?"

"I am," said Toni. "I have no proof these girls are not still alive, but I don't believe they are."

"How many are we talking about?" Samantha asked.

"At least four others, before your sister."

"Why haven't the police said anything? Why haven't I heard about this on the news? Most of the people currently camped on our front lawn seem to think Suzanna just waltzed off down the road on her own. Apparently, that's just what teenagers do these days."

"The disappearances have happened across jurisdictions and about two years apart. If it's one thing Australian police don't want to do, it's talk to each other. And these girls were not all the same age when they were taken. He's been taking older girls each time, so anyone looking at these cases on the surface will not easily connect them."

"But you have?"

Toni nodded, then she tilted her head, thinking as she looked at Samantha. "Why are *you* here, Samantha?

What are you looking for? I don't think it's because you forgot to take your homework with you."

"I could ask you the same thing," Samantha said, crossing her arms. "Why are you here if, as you claim, you weren't following me?"

"I think this person works in a school. You?"

Samantha sighed. "I want to see what you've got before I tell you anything else. I still don't know if I can trust you."

22

Thinking

Mon, 26 March 1984 – Suzanna

SUZANNA LAY CURLED UP in the bed. Her stomach grumbled and she regretted not eating more of the pancakes when she'd had the chance.

After their 'talk' in the kitchen, Mr Beresford had dragged her back to the pink room and left her lying on the floor. He stood over her for a few minutes, glowering at her but didn't say anything. Then he'd gone, slamming the door behind him.

She'd rubbed her bruised arm and listened to the key turn in the lock, then his footsteps getting quieter before the only sound left was her soft weeping.

She didn't remember getting into bed and cringed at the thought of him touching her while she was asleep.

But she was still in the same clothes, so maybe she'd got in herself?

It was raining, hard by the sound of it, she could hear it pounding on the tin roof and gurgling down the downpipes. *How much time has passed since the birthday party?* she wondered. *Is it night or day, Monday or Tuesday, maybe even Wednesday?*

She just lay there, listening to the water and thinking of her family. *How are they coping?* She smiled as she thought of Dad, being stoic and taking charge, driving around town looking for her. Mum would be worried, but she'd be taking care of Samantha, making sure she didn't forget to eat. Samantha would be numb, unable to think as depression lowered over her like the storm clouds outside.

She sent her sister another mental message, hoping to kick her out of her funk. Samantha was smart. If anyone could work this out, it would be her.

"Help me, Sammie, I can't do this on my own. Beresford. It's Beresford."

23

Missing

Mon, 26 March 1984 – Samantha

SAMANTHA AND TONI CLIMBED back out the science lab window and walked around to the front of the school.

"My research is back at my motel room," Toni said, slipping her arms out of her jacket and pulling it over her head to protect her hair from the rain. "I'll drive."

She pointed across the street to a little blue Toyota Corona which had definitely seen better days. Yellow electrical tape held the driver's side mirror on, and the dented front bumper was hanging onto the lefthand side by nothing more than sliver of sweat and hope.

"I can't leave Suzanna's bike here," Samantha said, shaking her head. "Someone will find it, and I don't want anyone to think she left it here. Where are you staying? I'll meet you there."

"The Sundown Motel, Room 4," Toni said, and they both went their separate ways.

It only took Samantha ten minutes, but by the time she pedalled into the motel parking area, Toni was standing in the doorway of Room 4, waving her over. She leaned the bike on the wall under the canvas awning that covered the door and front window of the room.

As soon as she walked into the room, Samantha thought of Suzanna. The room was a mess. Rumpled blankets and sheets were pushed back on the double bed and paper covered just about every surface of the room higher than the floor. An expandable folder, with more papers peeking out the top, sat on the small round table in the corner. The front window curtain was closed, and notes were pinned all over it in a crude timeline with string connecting some of them.

Toni closed the door and hurried over to the table. She picked an armful of papers up off two of the chairs and stood there looking around for a second, before dumping them on one of the pillows on the bed.

"Tea or coffee?" she asked, peering closely at the thermostat on the wall and turning on the heater. "Are you cold? I'm cold."

"Tea, please, black," Samantha said, sitting down. She was starting to shiver as her waning adrenaline stopped masking just how wet she was.

Neither of them said anything until Toni put the two cups of tea on the table.

"Damn," Toni said as her cup sloshed a muddy puddle onto a piece of paper. She rubbed her forearm over the paper to dry it, smearing the scrawling cursive handwriting.

"Alright, what have you got?" Samantha said. "We're under time constraints here, especially if what you said is true."

"Oh, it's true," Toni said. She leaned over the table and moved some papers around, uncovering four photos of young girls.

Samantha stared at them, tentatively putting her hand out and touching them. All four looked similar to her and Suzanna, just younger. They all had long, dark hair, petite facial features, dark eyes. They all looked happy, which was disconcerting.

She looked at Toni, who was still standing, and gestured to the pictures. "Tell me about them."

Toni sat down, picked up one photo, and looked at it as she spoke. "This is Michelle Donovan. Michelle was just six years old when she disappeared from a local swimming pool in Toowoomba, Queensland, in 1976. Some witnesses say they saw her talking to a man, but their description was very generic – brown eyes, short dark hair, close cropped beard. She's never been found."

She put Michelle down and picked up another photo. "Isabelle Bradford. Eight years old, last seen at the local show in Gawler, South Australia, 1978. Seen in the company of a man of similar generic description to Michelle's case. Isabelle didn't seem distressed; witnesses say it looked like she knew this man. Never found."

She put Isabelle next to Michelle and picked up the next photo. "Allison Brooke. Ten years old, disappeared walking home from school in Braidwood, New South Wales, 1980. She'd been held back for an hour in detention, so she missed the school bus and had to walk. No witnesses, no clues, never heard from again."

Isabelle was placed next to Allison, and Toni picked up the last photo. "Audrey Lowe. Eleven years old, just two weeks before her twelfth birthday. Disappeared from her backyard in Albany, Western Australia, 1982. These are the ones I know about. There could be more."

They sat in silence, staring at the photos. Toni looked at Samantha and seemed about to say something but then didn't.

"They were all born in 1970, including Suzanna," Samantha stated. "And they all look similar. If you blur your eyes when you look at the pictures, they could be the same girl, just a couple of years older each time. Is that why you think they're connected?"

Toni nodded. "Yes, I'm glad you see it, too. But the age progression is unusual. From what I've read, serial offenders generally have a 'type'. So, they'll generally target girls, or boys, that are around the same age, not such a wide range as six to fourteen."

Samantha closed her eyes, then opened them again to stare at Toni, taking a deep breath. "Do you think he's killing them?"

Toni looked at Suzanna with sympathy. "I do," she admitted.

"Have you taken all this to the police?" Samantha asked, gesturing around the room.

Toni gave an unamused laugh. "The police aren't interested because, as I said, it's across jurisdictions and they don't like that. I spoke to cops in New South

Wales and Western Australia, but they dismissed it as pure conjecture. They said I was trying to build a story out of straws."

"What do *you* get out of this?" Samantha asked, standing up and going to look at the timeline pinned to the curtain. "Is it just a story to you?"

"Well, I'd be lying if I said it wouldn't be good for my career," Toni said, staying seated. "A story like this can open up so many doors. You're only fourteen, so you wouldn't understand how hard it is for a female journalist, a *young* female journalist, to be taken seriously in this country. In the world."

"You'd be surprised at what I know," Samantha said drily, turning to look at her.

"Hopefully, by the time you're old enough to work, this country – and the world – will be less misogynistic," Toni said, leaning back in her chair. She held her arms out. "I want to be one of the women leading the way, kicking those old white guys in the 'nads while they're looking the other way. I want to prove that women can do investigative journalism just as well, if not better, than them. I don't want to be stuck writing about local shows and grocery specials and hairstyle trends. I'm going to be a trailblazer and, if I can stop any more girls from being taken, and bring some closure to their families, then that's the cherry on the top."

Samantha looked at her. She racked her brain, but she couldn't remember any media story or theory about Suzanna's disappearance being linked to other missing girls, let alone a serial killer, and she didn't recognize the name Toni Clayton. She, again, missed the Internet where she could have just googled her name. Last time around, Toni must have either given up on the story, and her women-empowerment dreams, or something had happened to her, so her story never got out. Or, the variables Samantha had introduced this time around had led to Toni being here.

"I appreciate your honesty," Samantha said. "Believe me, in the future, it will get somewhat better, but there'll always be misogyny. What does your editor think about this? Who do you work for?"

"I'm currently freelance. I'm doing this on my own time and coin, making a small income writing about pet shows, fashion and frocks, and those local shows and grocery specials I already mentioned."

Samantha went and sat back down. She looked at the photos again. "Why do you think this man works at the school?"

"Why do you?"

"OK, what I'm going to tell you stays between us for now. You do not include any of it in your investigative piece without my permission. And I want to read your article before you make it public. If I insist on changes, you have to agree."

Toni hesitated. "You seem a lot older than fourteen." When Samantha said nothing, Toni nodded. "Agreed."

Toni sat back, tapping her pen on the table as she thought. "It's got to be someone local. It has to be, right? Because they had access to the school and to your locker over several weeks, at least, if not months. Can you remember what the notes said?"

"Oh, I remember every single word," Samantha said. "As I said, the originals disappeared with Suzanna, but I wrote out copies and gave them to Detective White. He pretty well dismissed them as irrelevant, but I don't believe that. I believe this man recognised that I was vulnerable and manipulated my emotions, then took Suzanna, thinking she was me."

"It's possible that Suzanna's still alive," Toni said. "But I'm not sure how long he holds them before he kills them. Or what he wants with them in the first place."

"I'm sure she's still alive, for now," Samantha said taking a deep breath before pointing her mind at the problem again. "Why were you at the school today? What did you hope to find?"

"I was going to the administration office to see who'd started working there in the last two years. As much as it creeps me out to think that a teacher could be doing this, that's the way I'm leaning. It could be a janitor or admin staff, I guess, but my gut tells me it's a teacher, someone who knew these girls, someone who knew you. I was hoping to find records of someone who'd moved here from Western Australia after Audrey Lowe disappeared, or with a history of working at schools in the other areas the girls went missing from. Do you know of any teachers, or anyone else, really, who's moved here in the last couple of years?"

"Most places around here have a high turnover of staff, including the schools, the hospital, and even the churches," Suzanna said. "People are always moving in and moving out. They think moving out of the city is an adventure, an opportunity to downsize and slow down. But once they discover the lack of amenities in a small town like this, and just how boring it can be, they change their minds pretty quick and high tail it back to the big city."

"How about new teachers at the high school?"

"I only started there last year, so I don't know who was there two years ago and who wasn't," Samantha replied. A sudden thought occurred to her. "Do you think it's one of my *actual* teachers?"

"Maybe. Probably," said Toni. "How many male teachers do you have?"

"Just about all my teachers this year are men," Samantha said. "And the school principal, Mr Wilde. But I think he's been there for years, at least he looks like he has."

"Did you have different ones last year? Can you give me a list?"

Samantha took a piece of paper and a pen from Toni.

1984

Physical Education – Mr Garrison

History – Mr Beresford

Maths – Mr Dunlop

Science – Mr Blackwell

Art – Mr Hawkins

Drama – Mr Lawrence

Languages (German) – Mr Noll

Agriculture – Mr Pennington

1983

History – Mr Beresford

Maths – Mr Dunlop

Science – Mr Humphries

Languages (German) – Mr Noll

Geography – Mr Ashe

Samantha looked at Toni. "Why wouldn't I recognise the handwriting if it was one of my teachers? They've been writing on the blackboard and marking my assignments and tests. It's hard to disguise your handwriting."

"People's writing varies depending on *what* they're writing, what they're writing *on*, and what they're writing *with*. Writing on a chalk board is different to writing on paper. Writing with a biro is different to writing with a felt tip. Teachers tend to scribble using a red Texta when grading papers or assignments because they often have to do it on their own time and, when you've read basically the same thing thirty or so times, you just want to get it over and done with."

"Sounds like you've done it before?" said Samantha, raising her eyebrows.

"I thought I wanted to be a teacher when I first left school," said Toni with a smile. "A lot of kids think that because, by the time they leave school after twelve years or so, teachers have been their main role models, which makes it an easy occupation choice. A short stint of teacher training quickly made me realise it wasn't for me, which is when I switched to journalism. I assume the notes he wrote were neat, unhurried?"

"They were. Neat cursive handwriting done with a fine biro. Not a smudge or a crooked line anywhere."

Toni took Samantha's list, folded it, and put it in her pocket. "OK, it's a start. Let's go back to the school and see if we can find out when these guys arrived. I'll drive."

24

Connections

Mon, 26 March 1984 – Samantha

SAMANTHA SAT STIFFLY IN the passenger seat as Toni drove back to the school, an awkward silence permeating the car like a bad smell. Toni kept glancing at Samantha and going to speak but changing her mind.

The rain had eased off, with only the odd sprinkle hitting the windscreen now, which was a good thing because the windscreen wipers in the old Toyota only worked sporadically. They'd reluctantly do a slow, uncoordinated sweep, squeaking up and back, then sit unmoving for several seconds as if gathering strength, then lumber upwards again for the next pass.

Toni glanced at Samantha again, took a deep breath, and looked back at the road. "How's your mum doing?"

Samantha stared ahead. "Not well."

"I'm sorry," Toni said with another glance. "It's not unusual, though. Mothers of missing persons often struggle to cope. I'm not saying fathers and siblings don't also, but mothers seem to be hit particularly hard by the loss of a child."

When Suzanna didn't say anything, Toni took the hint, and they drove the rest of the way in silence.

It was after 8 PM by the time they got back to the school. It was still quiet, but this time there were a couple of cars in the carpark, one of them a marked police car.

Toni drove past, did a u-turn, and pulled up alongside the gutter on the other side of the street. She turned off the headlights and the motor, and they sat, watching the front of the school.

The lights were on in some of the classrooms that faced the road. Senior Constable Atkins and Mr Wilde, the school principal, stood silhouetted in the white light that glared through the open front doors.

"OK, we need a plan B," Toni said after a few minutes.

Samantha sighed, thinking as she watched Mr Wilde shake his head and wave his hands around as he spoke to the young constable.

"Dad might know of anyone who moved to Miranda Springs in the last couple of years," she said. "He owns a local mechanics, and most people take their cars there for servicing."

She wasn't sure she wanted her father to know about the potential that Suzanna had been taken by a serial killer, but she couldn't think of any other way forward right now. And how fair was it to him not to tell him?

Toni looked at her. "OK, good plan." She kept looking at Samantha. "You're a lot more mature than you look, you know? If I didn't know better, I'd swear you were a lot older than fourteen."

"What can I say?" Samantha said, putting her seatbelt back on. "I grew up fast."

Samantha directed Toni around to the back lane. The lane was only as wide as one car, and Toni struggled to keep the car straight in the slimy mud, bouncing once off a thick wooden gate post like a dodgem car. She parked the car next to the Buchanan's back gate, blocking the lane for anyone else.

"I'm surprised the vultures out the front haven't found this entrance yet," Samantha commented as they went through the back gate and up the back steps of the house.

Toni just grimaced and followed Samantha through the back door into the kitchen, wincing as the screen door banged closed behind her.

"Please, sit," Samantha said, gesturing to the table. "I'll go find Dad."

She found him sitting alone on the couch in the dark in the living room. The front window curtains were still open, and he was staring out at the empty street.

"I think they've all gone for the night," he said, looking up at her with a tired smile. "The motel and the pub must be having their best nights ever."

"Mum still asleep?" she asked, sitting next to him.

"Yep. She woke up while I was at the press conference, and the young police lady had a bit of a hard time trying to keep her in the house. She kept going out and trying to see along the street, expecting to see Suzanna walking home. She's asleep again now."

Samantha sighed. "How did the press conference go?"

"You were right," he said, taking her hand and just holding it while he looked at her. "Mum would not have handled it. The questions those people threw at me ... I barely held it together. Detective White was disappointed that it was only me there. He thought the plea for the cameras would have been more emotionally effective if we'd all been there. Families apparently make better news than just one solitary father, but I did what I could. I don't know what else to do, Sammie. What do we do now? Where do we go from here?"

Samantha leaned over, put her arms around him, and let him weep quietly into her shoulder. She saw Toni standing in the doorway and mouthed, "Give us a second."

Toni went back to the kitchen to wait.

Samantha's father finally leaned back and pushed a strand of hair off her face. "What about you? Did you find anything?"

"Come into the kitchen," Samantha said, standing up and holding her hand out. "There's someone you need to meet."

Samantha introduced Dad to Toni and put the kettle on. On the way over from the school, she and Toni had discussed how much to tell him, and Samantha decided it wasn't fair not to tell him everything. Secrets hadn't worked out so well for her the first time around. This time she wanted to be as upfront as possible.

He listened closely, not saying a word, as Toni told him about her research and about Michelle Donovan, Isabelle Bradford, Allison Brooke, and Audrey Lowe.

"We need to take this to Detective White," he said after Toni finished talking. "The police have the resources to track this man down."

"That's all well and good," said Samantha. "I agree, but the police Toni's already spoken to aren't interested because all the cases happened in different states and the girls were all different ages when they disappeared. We can't wait for the Victorian police to faff around trying to get the other states to join the party. We need to act on this now. There's a good chance Suzanna's still alive. We just need to work out where she is and bring her home."

"What do you need from me?" her father asked.

"We think this man might work at the school or have some connection to the school. Do you know of anyone who moved to Miranda Springs within the last couple of years? Who might have come from Western Australia? Audrey Lowe was the last one to go missing, and she disappeared from Albany. Maybe you worked on someone's car, and they mentioned they'd come from over that way or their logbook showed they'd been there?"

Her father sat back and watched his fingers drumming on the table as he often did when he was thinking.

Toni pulled out the list of male teachers Samantha had given her. "Any of these?"

He looked at the list, then at Samantha, then back at the list. "You think it's a teacher? One of *your* teachers?"

"There's a good chance it is," said Toni. "The girls were all taken with no fuss, which implies, to me, that they knew this man and they were comfortable with him. A teacher has an authority that kids find hard not to be intimidated by. It's also not that hard to get a job as a teacher, especially in smaller towns, like this."

"One day, schools will properly vet anyone who's going to be around children," Samantha said. "It's just a pity that doesn't happen now."

Toni looked at her and raised an eyebrow but then turned back to Samantha's father. He stood up and retrieved a pen from a drawer. They watched him circle five names.

History – Mr Beresford
Drama – Mr Lawrence
Languages (German) – Mr Noll

Agriculture – Mr Pennington
Geography – Mr Ashe

"I know for sure, none of these men lived in town two years ago," he said, putting the pen down. "Although, I don't know where any of them, except Noll, came from. I know Noll had been working in Germany and moved back to Australia in late-1982. I believe this is the first school he's worked at since he came back."

He scanned the list again, picked up the pen, and underlined two more names.

Science – Mr Blackwell
Art – Mr Hawkins

"These two, I'm not sure, but I think they've been here for more than two years. The rest, the ones I didn't circle, they've definitely been here for longer."

They all sat in silence, staring at the names.

"These two – Lawrence and Ashe." Samantha's father said, pointing to their names. "It can't be either of them. They have families. Wives and kids. Ashe's daughter is a couple of years ahead of you in school, Samantha. If you had a daughter, how could you do this to someone else? How would you hide something like this from your family?"

Samantha looked at him, but he continued to stare despondently at the paper. She put her hand over his. "You never know, Dad. People manage to hide a lot of things, unsavoury or not, from their families and friends. I agree that it's more likely to be someone who's single, but we can't just discount people without knowing more about them, without checking them out."

"We should check out these others first, then the ones with the families," Toni said. "Do we know where these men live?"

"Well, I know Mr Beresford," Samantha replied. "He lives just a few houses down on the opposite side of the street from here. It can't be him, though. He's always been nice to me. Last school holidays, I walked his dog for him. I've been in his house, his backyard, his shed. Why wouldn't he have grabbed me then? Why wait until now?"

"Who knows," Toni said. "Maybe it would have been too obvious? Maybe something triggered it after that? Or maybe, it was Suzanna he was after all along? We should start with him, though, since he's so close." She looked at Samantha's father. "Do you have addresses for these other men?"

"Wait a minute," Samantha's father said, shaking his head and standing up. He took a step back and stared at them both. "I'm not comfortable with this. You're a child, Samantha. No matter what you say about the police, they should be the ones questioning these men." He turned to Toni. "And you should know better than to involve a child in something as dangerous as this."

Samantha understood where he was coming from, but she was not going to be passive about Suzanna's disappearance this time. She would not sit around and wait for someone else to do something. She already knew what the outcome of that would be.

He sat down again, and she stood up, pacing around the kitchen as she thought, feeling her father's and Toni's eyes on her.

"OK, we'll talk to Detective White in the morning, tell him what we've got and what we suspect," Samantha conceded. "But if they sit on it, if they don't act straight away, I'm going to check the addresses myself." She held up her hand when she saw the concern as her father went to say something. "I promise I won't put myself in danger, but I can't stand around doing nothing. Doing nothing will mean the difference between finding Suzanna and losing her for good. You need to trust me on this, Dad."

Her father turned in his seat and put a hand on her arm, stopping her. He stood up and put his arms around her. "I do trust you, Sammie, but please, please be careful. Look from a distance and take what you find to Detective White. Don't try to be a hero. There's no place for heroes in this situation."

25

Where

SUZANNA WAS SITTING ON the bed again, bored. She'd slept for ... well, she didn't know how long, but it felt like hours. *Maybe it was days? Was it day or night? How long ago had Saturday night been?*

Her stomach was grumbling and her head hurt, probably from dehydration, so she got up and went into the bathroom. She dumped the small pink toothbrush out of its plastic cup into the basin and used the cup to drink water from the tap.

She stared at her face in the mirror over the basin. A bruise blossomed, red and purple, on her cheek and crept its way upwards, linking itself to the dark circles under her eyes, making it look like she had black eyes. She rubbed her upper arm where he'd gripped her and dragged her from the kitchen to the bedroom, not giving her a chance to get to her feet. A dark bruise with clear fingerprints ran around her whole arm.

The mirror was one of the ones that swung open to reveal a small space with shelves where people often kept medicines. She swung it open, hoping to find painkillers for her headache, but the only things in there were a straight pink comb with strands of dark hair snagged in its teeth and a small piece of paper that had clearly been torn off the top corner of a book. A child's hand had used a blue crayon to write 'MU'. She wondered if it had been going to say Mum and she closed her eyes. *I want my mum.*

She closed the mirror and stared at herself again. Her fear started to turn to anger. How dare he do this to her? It wasn't her fault he'd lost his kid. There was no way she was calling him Dad, and she was not going to answer to the name Michelle. She was not going to deny her own family!

Then she remembered how quickly he changed from nice to nasty and she thought back to when he'd first taken her and some of the words he'd used when he'd told her his story. *Had he done this before? How many girls had he done this to and why hadn't someone stopped him?*

He'd said his kid supposedly died at birth, but there was range of things in this room for a girl of varying ages, not a baby. Some of the clothes had clearly been worn and washed, and there were strands of hair in the brushes, combs, and hair ties. *Where was the girl who'd worn the clothes and snagged her hair and tried to write to her mum?*

Her anger dissipated into despair and the full enormity of her situation became a weight she could no longer carry on her own. She desperately missed her sister, and she collapsed onto the tiled floor, leaned against the wall, and wept until she had no more tears to weep.

After a while, she wiped her eyes, got up, and went back to the bedroom. She walked around, examining every little thing she could find. There had to be something she could use to get out of here or at least defend herself with.

She went through the closets and clothing drawers. She dropped one of the dresses on the floor and struck the back of the dressing table chair with the plastic coat hanger. But the hanger just snapped in two, and she dropped the pieces on the floor.

Next, she rummaged through the small bookcase, but there was nothing useful there, either. Most of the books were too young for her, picture books or chapter books that she'd read years ago or teased Samantha for reading: *Alice's Adventures in Wonderland*, *Little Women*, *The Enchanted Wood*, *Seven Little Australians*, *James and the Giant Peach*.

She went through the three drawers of the dressing table, but the only interesting things she found were a set of twelve colouring pencils, some of them worn right down, and a kid's activity book. She leafed through the book. Most of the dot-to-dots had been done, and about half the pictures had been coloured in, not well, but there were some relatively blank pages where you had to copy a picture in a grid. She missed her sketchbook, but maybe she could use some of these pages in the activity book to draw on.

She sat on the floor beside the bed on the opposite side to the bedroom door. Emptying her mind, she picked a pencil at random and let her hand draw long sweeping lines on the page. She kept picking colour after colour and sketched without thinking.

After a while, she stopped and looked at what she'd drawn, realising it was a picture of the street she lived on, Madison Street. On the street, a girl with long, dark hair walked a small white dog, outlined in black. That was Samantha, walking Mr Beresford's dog. It had to be.

Suzanna started to get excited. She knew where she was. Mr Beresford lived just a few houses down from her, on the opposite side of the street. She was so close to home, but also so far.

The blocks were quite large in this neighbourhood, which could be why no one heard her calling for help. She also wondered if the house had been soundproofed in some way. She hadn't heard the dog barking or any other outside activity, apart from the faint police or ambulance siren she'd heard when she was in the kitchen.

She turned to a new page and sketched what she knew about this house which, admittedly, wasn't much except for the front and, even then, she had to concentrate to jog her memory. She didn't generally take much notice of other people's houses. She drew what she thought the floorplan might be, considering what she'd seen when she'd run from this room earlier, plus what she remembered of the outline of the house. She was fairly sure the room she was in was at the back of the house.

The key rattled in the lock behind her, and she quickly turned and shoved the activity book under the mattress. Grabbing one of the pieces of broken hanger, she stood and backed up until the small of her back pressed against the dressing table chair. She gripped the hanger tightly and held it behind her back with the sharp, broken side out.

"Michelle?" Mr Beresford said softly as he opened the door. "I've brought you something to eat."

Suzanna didn't speak or move as Mr Beresford brought in a tray with a bowl of steaming soup and a couple of slices of white bread. He stood and looked at her like a parent might look at a sick child. He used his foot to push the door closed behind him.

He walked towards her, and she edged around the wall away from him. When he set the tray down on the dressing table, her stomach betrayed her and growled when she smelled the salty chicken noodle soup. *It smells so good.* She had no idea how long it had been since she'd eaten, and she felt both hungry and nauseous at the same time.

He turned to face her, and she moved so the bed was directly behind her. She held the broken plastic clothes hanger out like a knife, and he sighed.

"Still not ready to face the truth?" he said, raising his eyebrows. "I know, it's a lot to deal with. You've had your whole life upended. It's hard to stop believing something you've had reinforced every day for as long as you remember. Believe me, I understand. I truly do."

He held his hands out, palms outwards. "Put that down. I don't want anyone to get hurt."

"Have you seen my face?" Suzanna asked, incredulous. She gestured towards the bruise on her upper arm. "And that? What's that if it's not someone getting hurt?"

"I'm truly sorry that had to happen," he said. "If you just accept what I tell you and do what I say, it doesn't need to happen again."

"I don't believe you," she responded.

He took a step towards her, and she lashed out with the sharp edge of the broken hanger. A red line bubbled up on the back of his right hand, and he pulled his hand back with a sharp hiss.

She rolled backwards over the bed and had the door open before he realised what was happening. This time, she didn't head for the front of the house but, instead, ran through the kitchen/dining room. She'd seen a door off the dining room that, she assumed, led to the laundry, which would surely be where the back door would be.

She heard him not far behind her and she wrenched on the back door, sobbing in relief when it actually opened. She was going home. She was only a few hundred metres away from Mum and Dad and Samantha. She'd see them soon.

26

Mistakes

Tue, 27 March 1984 – Suzanna

SUZANNA RAN OUT ONTO the concrete landing, glancing behind her quickly, then hurried down the concrete steps, watching her footing in the semi-dark of early morning. If she twisted her ankle now, it was all over. She'd probably never get another chance like this.

At the bottom, she finally looked up. Her feet froze. There was a chill in the air, and the bluish-grey hue of the cloudy early morning sky provided enough light for her to see that there were no other houses nearby. Not even the shape of another house in any direction. Her heart dropped as she realised she wasn't where she'd thought she was. She wasn't in the town, at all. She wasn't just a few steps away from Mum and Dad and Samantha. She was in the middle of nowhere.

The grunt Mr Beresford made as he jumped off the back porch kicked her into gear again, and she bolted, feeling his hand brush the collar of her shirt but fail to grab it. She didn't care where she was going, as long as it was away from him. She ran like she'd never run before. She was fit from years of playing school sports, tennis and netball and hockey, and she could hear him breathing heavily as he tried to keep up with her.

The grass was long, and her feet kept slipping on the muddy ground. Adrenaline pumped through her body, and she barely noticed the pebbles and burrs under her bare feet. She hadn't gotten far before her jeans were soaked through, but she didn't care. She just wanted to get as far away from him as possible.

She risked a glance over her shoulder and ran smack bang into a wire fence. The top strand of barbed wire gripped her shirt like talons, then ripped it as she bounced backwards and landed on her backside. He almost caught her, but she scrambled underneath his grasping hands, ducked between the strands of wire. and kept running.

She was in a paddock, and a chestnut horse snorted and shied away from her, the sound of its retreating hoofbeats bringing tears to her eyes again. She kept going.

She glanced behind again and ran headlong into a gorse shrub. She managed to extricate herself and ignored the blood trickling from scratches on her face and arms as she kept running.

Then her foot caught on something, and she tripped. She put her hands out to break her fall but still smacked her nose on the ground and blood gushed over her lips and into her mouth.

Beresford's hand grabbed her arm and squeezed the existing black and purple bruise as he hauled her to her feet.

"You really don't get it, do you, Michelle? See, this is what happens to girls who don't obey their fathers. They get hurt."

Suzanna stared at four small mounds of dirt in a small, cleared area under a large gum tree. A small black and white willy wagtail sat on one of the mounds chittering urgently at her, but she paid it no attention and it flew up to sit in the tree.

"What are they?" she whispered. "Are they graves?"

"They're mistakes," Beresford said curtly as he dragged her away, back towards the house.

27

Frustration

Tue, 27 March 1984 – Samantha

SAMANTHA WAS GOING STIR crazy.

She stalked impatiently around the house, like a hungry tiger. She'd walk into a room, pick things up – knick knacks, framed photos, books, pens – look at them, then put them down again, before continuing her patrol. It was now mid-morning, and Dad had been gone for hours.

Last night, her father had driven Toni back to the motel since her car was stuck in the mud in the back lane. Samantha had stayed home in case her mother woke up.

Toni had shown him her research, strung up and piled up all around her motel room. He'd been impressed and told her he'd get Detective White over there as early as possible in the morning.

This morning, before the media had finished their croissants and lattes and returned to stake their claims on the front lawn, Dad had rung Detective White and explained that they had some information that might be relevant. He'd arranged to meet him at Toni's motel room and left soon after.

It was excruciating, not knowing what was happening. *How did we all survive without instant access to phone calls and messaging?* she wondered, not for the first time. Hanging around here felt like a waste of time, but her mother couldn't be left on her own. Samantha desperately hoped Mum wouldn't wake up because she knew, if she did, her mother would think she was Suzanna, and she couldn't handle that right now.

She eyed the pile of unopened birthday presents that her father had left on one of the armchairs in the lounge room. Before he'd left this morning, he'd suggested she might like to open hers, but she'd declined angrily. How could he even suggest that? She'd open them with Suzanna or not at all. She felt bad about snapping at him. The look in his eyes was heartbreaking when she thought about it now, but she couldn't stop herself at the time.

She heard a car engine and then the garage door squealing open. Pushing the living room curtain aside, she watched her father's car disappear into the garage, barely escaping the cameramen and reporters who surged forwards like a wave at high tide.

Her father exited the garage through the side door, directly into the backyard. By the time he'd reached the back step, Samantha had the back door open.

"Well, what did they say?"

He didn't say anything at first. He walked into the kitchen and went straight to the kettle. He filled it with water, set it to boil, and then turned to look at Samantha.

He sighed as he leaned back against the bench and crossed his arms. "Detective White seemed to take it seriously, but he said he needs to talk with his bosses to get permission to investigate further. It's the cross-jurisdiction thing, like Toni said. Also, he doesn't think Suzanna is being kept nearby."

"Oh, so they've now agreed she hasn't just walked off on her own to smell the roses?" Samantha said sarcastically.

"They're now working on the assumption that Suzanna has been abducted," he said. "But he thinks that, if someone *has* taken her, they've taken her out of the area, possibly even out of the state. It makes more sense than keeping her nearby in a house in town."

"But they aren't going to do anything," Samantha said, more a statement than a question, even though she'd known this was what would happen. "Not even check the houses of those teachers?"

Dad sighed again, turning to get a mug out of the cupboard and a teabag out of the misshapen brown pottery container. He poured boiling water into the mug, carried it over to the table, and sat down.

"They're going to drive by the addresses and see if anything looks amiss or suspicious," he said, jiggling the teabag. He lifted his other hand to silence her as Samantha went to say something. "They can't search the houses or the yards without a warrant, and that takes time to get. Detective White doesn't think there's enough evidence for a judge to give them a warrant, at this point, so they'll have a look first. If they see something, they'll knock on the door and speak to whoever's there. Try to get a sense of what might be going on and maybe get something they can use for a warrant."

"I don't think that whoever has Suzanna is going to be broadcasting it to the street," Samantha said, crossing her arms and staring at him. "Of course, nothing's going to look 'amiss'. Oh, sorry, officer, here I found this fourteen-year-old girl in my basement. Not sure how she got there," she said mockingly. "They'll be wasting their time, and Suzanna's, not to mention tipping the guy off that he's on their radar."

"I don't know what else you want me to do," her father said with a shrug. He sounded tired and Samantha felt bad. She knew how much this was taking out of him. He hadn't slept any more last night than she had. She'd lain there wide awake, listening to him walking around the house in the wee hours of the morning. She'd been tempted to join him, but thought he might need some time to himself and his own thoughts.

They both heard the front door open and stared at each other before rushing out of the kitchen.

By the time they got to the door, Samantha's mother was stepping off the last step of the verandah, heading to the garage. She was dressed in her nightdress, dressing gown thrown haphazardly over the top, with nothing on her feet. She was already being trailed by reporters calling questions to her, each clamouring to be heard over the others.

An older woman, dressed like a gypsy in a long colourful dress and lacy shawl, put her arm around Samantha's mother and handed her a business card just as Samantha's father caught up to her. He pushed the woman away, put his own arm around his wife, and manoeuvred her back towards the front verandah.

She kept trying to turn around, mumbling about having to pick Suzanna up from tennis practice. When she saw Samantha holding the front door open, she stopped fighting and her face lit up.

When she reached the door, she stopped and stroked Samantha's cheek, saying, "Oh, Suzie, you're back? We were so worried about you. Did someone give you a lift home?"

Samantha's smile felt so fake, and she hated herself for it, but she did it anyway and didn't correct her mother before closing the door and blocking the view of the reporters outside. She tried to take the business card from her mother, but she gripped it tightly and wouldn't let it go.

"Come on," her father said gently to her mother. "Let's get you something to eat, hey?"

Once they were all in the kitchen, Samantha switched the kettle on again. Her father sat her mother down at the table and managed to pull the business card from her hand.

"Damn psychics," he said, tossing the crumpled card into the bin. "I don't know how many phone calls I've had from them claiming they know where Suzanna is. They all have different ideas about where Suzanna is and how can they *all* be right? How can any of them know anything?"

He opened the fridge and started pulling out the ingredients for a sandwich.

"I can't hang around here, Dad," Samantha said, heading to the back door. "I'm going to see what Toni's doing."

"Don't go near those teachers' houses, Samantha," he warned. "Don't compromise the police investigation. That's what Detective White was worried about. He also warned us not to go to the media with this speculation as that could also have an adverse effect on the case, not to mention the reputations of those men."

"Whatever," Samantha said, letting the door bang behind her as she ran down the back steps. She needed to talk to Toni and work out what to do from here.

28

Planning

Tue, 27 March 1984 – Samantha

SAMANTHA HEADED OUT THE back gate into the
lane. Toni's car was still there and for a minute
she was tempted to hot-wire it and drive it back to
Toni's motel room. That was just one of the many
unsavoury things she'd learned from one of her exes
who ran a chop shop before he'd been sent away for
car theft. Older cars, like Toni's Toyota, were easier
to steal than the more modern ones, which didn't
technically exist yet in this universe anyway.

But when she caught sight of her fourteen-year-old
face reflected in the driver's side window, she changed
her mind. She couldn't risk getting caught, especially
with the number of police and reporters currently in

town and the hyperfocus on her family. She couldn't bring more hurt and disappointment to her father.

So, she walked.

The back lane came out on a side street, and she walked back up to Madison Street. She checked around the corner. There seemed to be less reporters today, but those that were there were standing around outside her house drinking coffee from paper cups and chatting like they were mingling at a party. None of them saw her.

She deliberately walked the opposite way, towards Mr Beresford's house, even though it was in the wrong direction from the motel. She slowed down when she came to it and turned her head to look at the front of the house.

It was quiet, and there was no car in the carport. Mr Beresford lived alone, so it looked like no one was home.

A police car turned the corner up ahead and cruised towards her, so she moved quickly towards the lone gum tree that sat on the nature strip between the footpath and the road. She ducked down and pretended to tie her shoelace. The police car stopped and idled near her, but she didn't look up. After a second or two, she heard the driver shift gears and the crunch of the tyres as the car moved off again.

She switched feet, untying and retying her other shoelace, turning slightly as she did it so she could keep an eye on the police car. It prowled up to the next intersection, not in any hurry, and turned right. As soon as the car was out of sight, she stood up and studied the house again.

It was a typical 1970s red brick, single storey, dwelling, sitting on a concrete slab. Samantha knew the basic layout of the house; she'd been in there when she was looking after Casper, Mr Beresford's dog, during the school holidays. There was definitely no basement and no attic, so if Suzanna was being held here, she'd have to be in a bedroom around the back.

A low red brick fence marked the front border of the property. The single-car carport was on the right, with two muddy indentations in the grass leading from the road marking out the driveway. The tyre tracks looked relatively fresh, like the car had driven in or out during the rain or not long after it had stopped.

A mailbox teetered on top of the bricks next to a gap in the middle of the front fence. The front yard was mostly grass, although a small garden of colourful blooms – purples, yellows, oranges, whites – nestled against the bottom of the house under the lounge room window.

A line of crazy paving snaked from the mailbox to the front door. Samantha stepped cautiously onto the first paving stone. She stopped, waited, watched, and listened. Nothing.

She took another step and just about jumped out of her skin when Casper suddenly ran around the side of the house, barking and leaping up at the grey wire fence that separated the backyard from the front. The white Maltese terrier yipped excitedly when he saw her, and wiggled his body urgently, pressing up against the gate.

She walked over to him and let herself into the backyard through the gate. No one would question it if they saw her. She'd walked Casper before, so it wasn't unusual for her to be here with him.

"How are you, little guy?" she asked him, patting his head, which seemed to be the driest part of him. She wrinkled her nose at the wet dog smell. "You need a bath, my friend."

Casper might have been wet and filthy, but he was always happy. He danced in circles, excited to have someone pay attention to him. Then, he dashed off with no warning.

Samantha picked up his lead from where it was lying in the mud just inside the gate and hung it over the fence where he wouldn't get caught in it. It was unusual for Mr Beresford to have left Casper's lead there, but maybe he'd been in a hurry and hadn't had time to hang it in the shed in its usual spot.

An unformed thought niggled at her mind, but it was quickly forgotten when Casper returned and tossed a slobbery green tennis ball at her feet. He took a couple of steps back, looking between the ball and her face expectantly. She picked the slimy thing up with her fingertips and tossed it underarm across the yard.

While the dog chased the ball, she walked around to the back of the house and peered in each of the windows. Unfortunately, all the curtains were drawn, so she couldn't see anything. She held her breath and listened, imagining for an instant that Suzanna was in there calling for help but, really, there was nothing.

She went down to the shed that was in the back corner of the yard. The old bent steel door screeched as she shoved it open across the concrete floor. She checked inside. Nothing but gardening tools and dog food.

She sighed and dragged the door closed again. She threw the ball a few more times for Casper, then filled up his water bowl, and headed back out the gate.

Samantha stepped into Toni's motel room and immediately understood why Toni was fuming. There was a lot less paper than there had been yesterday.

"Detective White took most of it," Toni said, stalking around the room and waving her arms around. Her hair was down today and looked as if it hadn't been brushed after a restless night, giving her a bit of a crazy look. "I guess we should be grateful he's taking it seriously, but, come on, man. Why did he have to take it all?"

Samantha sat down and leafed through a notebook that was sitting on the table. A page had been torn out, but she ran her fingertips over the creases on the next page that spelled out the list of teachers she'd written down last night. She, again, lamented the fact that the Internet was not around in 1984.

"One day we'll all have phones small enough to carry in our pockets that will store more information than we could ever need," she said, still staring at the notebook. "And connect us to anyone anywhere in the world. The world wide web will put information at our fingertips. Just about anything you ever wanted to know, and a lot that you didn't, will be available instantly with the push of a button."

Toni stared at her, then sighed and sat on the chair opposite her. "You're a little bit scary sometimes, you know that? You sound so confident when you say things like that."

Samantha tried to smile, but it came out more like a grimace. "If you ever get the chance to buy shares in Apple Computers, Microsoft, or Google, invest as much as you can."

Toni looked around the room again. "Yeah, well, I wish I had one of your magic phones now. Luckily, I've got copies of most of my research in my garage back in Melbourne. It's just really annoying that I'm going to have to go back and make *more* copies because I don't think the police are going to give back what they took."

They sat in silence for a few minutes. Samantha kept running her fingers over the page in the notebook. Toni looked at the curtains where her timeline had been pinned.

Samantha eventually broke the silence. "So, what do we do now?"

Toni took a deep breath and ran her hands through her hair, making more of it stick out. "Your dad was pretty clear that we have to let the police do their thing. He made me promise to keep you out of it. He's worried about you, worried you'll do something to put yourself in danger."

"Beresford's not home," Samantha said, ignoring what Toni had said. It didn't matter what Dad wanted. Toni raised an eyebrow. "I checked it out on my way here. Casper, his dog, is there, but the house is shut up, curtains drawn, no car in the carport."

"He might be downtown doing his shopping, or at the school, or even taking advantage of the week of no classes and taking a mini vacation," Toni suggested. "We can't really read anything into the fact that he's not home. He's only one person on the list. And we still can't be one hundred percent sure it *is* someone on the list."

"I know, it's just that something's niggling at me, but I can't quite grasp it or put it into words." Samantha stood up and started pacing around the room like Toni had been doing earlier. "We know the cops are going to sit on their hands. Suzanna can't wait for them to get permission to even just talk to the other jurisdictions. Just driving past the houses of those teachers isn't going to do shit. We need to find out more about these men. Narrow it down."

Toni tapped a pen on the table as she thought for a few minutes. "OK, I want to go back to Melbourne and do a bit of digging, a bit more research on the names you gave me. I've got resources there that I can't use while I'm out here in the middle of nowhere." She laughed softly. "If only your wide world web was around now."

"I'll come with you." Samantha couldn't sit around waiting for other people to do what she knew needed to be done.

"I don't think you should," Toni said, shaking her head. "I think you should stay here and keep looking around. Go back to the park, go to the school, let people see you so they don't forget Suzanna is still missing. People's memories are short when they're not directly affected and when there's no news. Maybe seeing you will jog someone's memory. Maybe someone saw something, but they've been too scared to go to the police."

That sounded logical to Samantha, and she reluctantly nodded. She knew her father wouldn't agree to her leaving, anyway. "Alright, that sounds fair. If someone saw something, I'll find out about it. But don't be too long. Remember, the longer Suzanna's missing, the less chance of getting her back alive. And she *has* to live, this time around. There can be no other outcome."

Toni wondered about Samantha's choice of words but didn't question them. She did, however, think about them all the way as she drove back to Melbourne. There was definitely more to this fourteen-year-old girl than appeared on the surface, and there were secrets in those hidden depths. Secrets that piqued the interest of Toni's reporter brain.

Samantha grabbed Suzanna's bike from where it was still waiting patiently outside Toni's motel room.

First, she rode to the park, where there were still signs of their broken birthday party. Soggy streamers and paper plates adorned puddles. Rubbery slivers of green, blue, and pink balloons lay trampled into the mud. Food that had been left on the tables had turned to mush in yesterday's rain. A couple of magpies and a crow squabbled over a soggy crust of bread. When they saw her, they put their argument on hold and flew off to sit in a tree, eyeing her suspiciously while they waited for her to leave.

She stared up at a lone pink balloon pulling and yanking and jerking in the wind high up in a gum tree. The balloon desperately reached for freedom, but the branch refused to let go of its string.

"I know how you feel," she murmured.

She sat on the swing where she'd swung next to Tina just a few days ago. *Was it only a few days ago?* She felt like she'd been living this nightmare for years. *Well*, she thought, *in a way I have been.*

The rhythm of the swing, back and forth, back and forth, lulled her and her mind started to wander. She tried to empty her mind, tried not to think of the last few days, but she couldn't help it. The events of Saturday were like an earworm, a snippet of a song she couldn't dislodge. She went over and over what had happened, blaming herself, pinpointing all the times she could have stopped this. She'd thought she was so clever. Clever enough to save Suzanna and catch the perpetrator, but she realised now that she wasn't clever at all. She was just pathetic.

She hated herself for so easily welcoming the depression back into her life, embracing it like a long-lost friend. She'd lived with it for forty years and something that entrenched in your personality was hard to give up, hard to say no to. Depression was addictive, comfortable, like pulling on an old soft jumper on a frosty night, and she hardly noticed when the rain started again. The misty rain let her pretend the water on her face was not coming from within as she blinked it off her eyelashes.

After a while she got up and rode Suzanna's bike over to the playground on the other side of the lake. The police tape was still around it, but it was now broken and flapping uselessly in the breeze.

She swung for a while – she didn't know how long – on the swing Suzanna had last used, but she couldn't feel her sister at all, this time. She tried not to think of the worst outcome, but her depression lovingly stroked her mind, conjuring images of Suzanna lying on the ground, in the ground, under the ground.

She considered giving up again and the depression encouraged it. *There's nothing you can do*, it whispered. *You couldn't stop it the first time. Couldn't stop it the second time. There are no more chances.*

A willy wagtail landed on the swing next to her. It chittered angrily at her, at least it sounded angry, and she took a deep breath.

"You're right," she said, after a while. "I said I was going to stop giving up, so I really need to stop giving up."

She stood up and the bird fluttered onto the ground. It began pecking at things only it could see.

"Good talk," Samantha said and picked Suzanna's bike up off the ground.

She rode through the main street of the town before doubling back to head home in a round about way, going up and down as many streets as she could.

Most people she saw avoided eye contact with her, but she kept her head up and made herself visible, although it went against her natural inclination. She'd never liked being centre of attention, not like Suzanna. But then again, Suzanna always got positive attention, whereas whenever she'd put her own head up – as a teenager, a young woman, or as an older woman – all she'd ever received was negativity. She wondered if it was her own negativity being reflected back at her, or if she just attracted it like iron to a magnet.

It was dark by the time she got home. She rode back past Mr Beresford's house, but his car was still absent. Toni's car was gone from the back lane, so she'd obviously got away alright.

She dropped Suzanna's bike on the grass under the clothesline and ran up the back steps.

"Where have you been?" Dad was sitting at the table, and he stood up as soon as he saw her step through the backdoor into the kitchen. He spoke loudly, not yelling, but louder than normal. He followed her as she headed towards her room. "I was worried. Look, you're soaked through. I think we've got enough on our plates, without worrying about you getting sick on top of it all. That's the last thing we need right now."

"It doesn't matter where I've been," Samantha said, dismissing him with a wave of her hand as she walked down the hallway and up the stairs.

"You haven't been near those teachers' places, have you?" he asked, still following her. "You haven't been conspiring with Toni again? I told her not to involve you. To leave things to the police."

She slammed her bedroom door in his face, then stood and waited. She wrapped her arms around herself, shivering in her wet clothes, and listened to him just standing there.

After a few minutes, he thumped the door with his fist. She jumped. It was something he'd never done before. "You think I don't want to be out there, driving around, trying to find her, every minute of every day?"

he snapped. "You think I'm not going out of my mind hanging around here waiting for news that never comes? We need to be smart about this, Samantha. Let the police do their jobs." She heard him take a couple of deep breaths. "Your mother can't be left alone..." He tapered off and she imagined him leaning forward, resting his forehead on the door.

Samantha closed her eyes and stood with her head bowed until she heard him walk away.

She felt bad for treating him like that. They were all dealing with this in their own way. But she couldn't let him stop her. He might see a fourteen-year-old girl when he looked at her, but that's not what she was. Not really. No one else in her universe was going to find Suzanna, so she had to step up and do it. The cost didn't matter, whether it was her relationship with her father or even her own life, Suzanna *would* come back this time.

She'd apologise tomorrow, or when Suzanna was back. She promised herself there and then that she'd make it right with him.

29

Searching

Wed, 28 March 1984 – Samantha

SAMANTHA WOKE UP ON Wednesday morning feeling relatively refreshed. Her sleep had been unpunctuated by dreams for a change, and she hated herself for that. She didn't deserve to sleep well. She wondered where Suzanna was sleeping and wished she could take her sister's nightmares and make them her own.

"If wishes were horses, beggars would ride," she muttered to herself. She didn't remember where or when she'd heard that saying. Maybe she'd heard it in a song? Maybe she'd heard Nan say it? She was full of adages and proverbs.

She lay on her back, staring at the ceiling and briefly thought of her grandparents. She'd heard Dad on the phone on Sunday night with Grandma. He'd told her not to come down, that there was nothing she could do here. She lived in Rockhampton, Queensland, so it was quite a distance to drive. But she insisted. Samantha knew she wouldn't get here for a couple more days, since she was driving on her own with the caravan. Grandpa had died a few years ago, so Grandma's only company would be her three dogs and two cats, so she would need to stop quite a bit along the way. That's what had happened the first time around, anyway.

Nan and Pop were on a cruise ship, somewhere on the Pacific Ocean. The first time Suzanna had gone missing, they hadn't known about it until they docked back in Sydney a fortnight later. Then, they'd driven straight to Miranda Springs, but there wasn't anything they could do at that point, except provide some relief for Dad and Grandma by looking after Mum.

She turned on her side and looked at the clock on her bedside table: 8:17 AM. She couldn't believe she'd slept so late, and she scrambled out of bed.

The house was quiet, and she found her parents in the living room. She watched them from the doorway. They were sitting together in silence on the couch. The television was on, the laughing hosts of the morning show muted. Dad's hand was on Mum's forearm like he was holding her in place. Arabella was curled up on an armchair but kept her eyes on Mum.

Dad's gaze kept going to the front window, watching the reporters outside, as if the window was the television screen. There were even fewer out there today than yesterday. The news cycle was moving on and no updates meant Suzanna's story was getting boring for them. There were only so many ways they could spin the same information to make it seem as if something interesting or new was happening. The media was ready to move on even though Suzanna had been only missing for a few days.

Every so often, Mum's eyes would flick from the television to the front door. She'd start to rise as if she'd just remembered something, but Dad held on to her forearm, not letting her stand up. Mum would then sit back as if she'd forgotten what she'd been about to do, and her attention would be drawn to the moving colours on the television again.

Samantha made eye contact with her father, and they both tried to smile, each trying to project forgiveness for the night before. She sighed and headed to the kitchen for breakfast before her mother saw her. She couldn't cope this morning with being mistaken for

Suzanna. She wanted to eat because she had a long day planned and wasn't sure when she'd get to eat again.

She poured a bowl of cereal, slopped milk into it, and sat it on the table. She tore a page out of the notebook that they normally used for the shopping list, grabbed a pen, and sat down.

While she ate, she wrote her father a note.

Hi Dad, I'm sorry about last night.

I know you're just worried about me, but I can't sit around waiting for the police to do something. I can't explain how I know, but I do know that if I don't try to find Suzanna, we never will.

Toni's gone back to Melbourne.

I'll be riding around town again today, trying to find a clue or someone who might have seen something who hasn't come forward.

I promise I won't put myself in any danger. Please don't worry about me.

Trust me, please?

Love you, Samantha

She folded the note in half, wrote Dad on it, and left it propped on the placemat where he normally sat.

Then she dumped her empty bowl in the sink and headed out the back door.

The weather was already warming up, promising to be hot, a complete change from the past few days of rain. Although autumn had arrived, summer was not giving in without a fight. The grey clouds had moved on, and a light warm breeze and the bright sun worked together to raise wisps of steam from the ground as it dried out.

Samantha walked Suzanna's bike out the back gate, along the lane, and up to the corner of Madison Street.

She sat on the bike and looked towards Mr Beresford's house. His car – a dark blue Holden Commodore – was in the carport, so he'd obviously come home last night or this morning. She'd worried a bit about Casper being there on his own, thought he might not get fed, but that was one less thing she needed to worry about now.

She was deciding where to go today, when Mr Beresford stepped out of his front door carrying his briefcase. He closed and locked the door then headed to his car. She watched him put his briefcase on the back seat, then get in, and reverse out onto the road. He turned left and drove slowly towards her house.

She stared at him, willing him to look at her, sure that she'd see the truth in his eyes, even from this distance. She saw the moment when his gaze flicked to her, away again, then straight back again. He looked disconcerted while he tried to look at her and watch the road at the same time. He suddenly sped up, almost hitting a cameraman who was not paying attention as he crossed the road from his news van. Mr Beresford turned right at the next intersection and accelerated away.

She pushed off on the bike, standing up and pumping her legs furiously, trying to keep him in sight. A couple of reporters called out to her as she passed, but she ignored them.

Mr Beresford led her to the high school. This morning there were a couple of cars in the carpark, but still no kids. Classes wouldn't start again until next week, and it looked like, as expected, no one had taken up the offer of free counselling.

Samantha stopped across the road, where Toni's car had been parked on Monday, and she sat there watching.

Mr Beresford remained in his car for several minutes, seemingly doing nothing. She wondered if he was going to get out and she thought about approaching him. She was trying to work out what to say when Mr Wilde drove into the carpark and parked next to him. They both got out of their cars, shook hands and said something to each other, laughing as they retrieved their briefcases.

Samantha coasted the bike closer and stopped in the entrance to the carpark. She made sure she could be seen, but neither man looked around as they strode side-by-side up the steps and through the front doors of the school. Was Mr Beresford deliberately not looking at her? And was he keeping Mr Wilde preoccupied so he wouldn't see her either? Maybe she was reading into things that weren't really there?

Nevertheless, she desperately wanted to run after Mr Beresford, tackle him to the ground, and demand to know where he was keeping her sister. But she restrained herself. As Toni had said, he wasn't the only one on the list and confronting him here and now wouldn't serve any purpose. She had this feeling ... but feelings were not enough.

She stayed where she was, just watching the school for about half an hour. When nothing interesting happened – no one came in, and no one went out – she got off the bike and dropped it on the grass next to the carpark entrance.

She walked over to Mr Beresford's car and peered through each of the windows, in turn. There was white dog hair on the back seat and the front passenger seat. The back seat on the lefthand side had a brownish stain that looked like dried blood that someone had tried to wipe off. But it could just as easily have been coffee, as there were a couple of paper coffee cups on the floor. There was nothing definitive in the car to indicate that Suzanna had ever been in it.

Samantha considered breaking into the car and popping the boot. She could do it easily, thanks to the lessons from her chop shop ex. But when she looked around for something to use to jimmy the door lock, she saw Senior Constable Atkins driving towards the school. He turned into the carpark, pulled up next to her, and wound his window down, leaving his engine idling.

"Everything alright?" he asked with a fake smile.

She nodded.

"What are you doing here?" he asked.

"Looking for my sister," she said. "Like you should be."

Senior Constable Atkins smirked. "I still think she'll come back on her own. She probably just got sick of your shit and wanted a break. I saw what White got from that reporter. Come on, a serial offender taking little girls from hick towns like this? Drawing a long bow, that's all I'm saying."

In Samantha's previous life, she'd had to deal with plenty of cops like this, ones who thought they were untouchable and superior to everybody else because of their badge. Back then, she'd avoided confrontation, said 'yes, sir, no, sir, three bags full, sir' and moved on quietly. This time, however, she couldn't help herself and she let her frustration speak for her.

"Is that right?" she said, raising an eyebrow. "Well, I'm sick of *your* shit and nobody cares what *you* think. I think you need to leave the speculation and the real work to the adults in the room. It was pretty clear on the weekend that you were out of your depth and had no idea what to do."

His face turned red, and he pointed at her. "You need to learn to watch your mouth, little missy. You're not too old for a spanking."

"Oh, you want to teach me a lesson?" she taunted, leaning down so she was face-to-face with him. "You'd like that, wouldn't you? Beating up little girls because you don't like to hear the truth about your cowardly incompetent ass. I bet you were a bully at school, too. I bet you became a cop so you could legally keep bullying people because underneath you know you're a pathetic coward who couldn't investigate their way out of a soggy paper bag."

The constable started to open his car door, but just then Mr Wilde came out of the front doors of the school. He trotted down the steps, towards them, and the constable pulled his door closed again.

"Everything OK here?" Mr Wilde asked with a frown. "Samantha, what are you doing here? You should be at home with your family at a time like this."

"Everything's fine, Mr Wilde. I was just leaving." She sent a mocking glance towards the fuming policeman. "Nice talk, Constable. See you around."

She headed over to where she'd left Suzanna's bike, feeling Senior Constable Atkins' glare piercing her back like a knife.

30

Watching

Wed, 28 March 1984 – Samantha

SAMANTHA PEDALLED SLOWLY THROUGH the streets, glancing over her shoulder a few times, just in case the constable decided to teach her a lesson by running her down. But there was no sign of him. *Weak*, she thought.

After a while, she forgot him and rode up and down the streets, again making sure she was seen. She felt like she was wasting time but couldn't think what else to do until she heard from Toni. She sent a mental message to Suzanna. *Just hang on a little bit longer, Suze. I'm coming. It's just taking longer than I expected.*

Like yesterday, people avoided eye contact with her. In her current mood, she found it slightly amusing to greet them loudly and force them to look at her.

Some of them did a double take, obviously thinking she was Suzanna returned from the mysterious hole she'd disappeared into. When they realised it wasn't, they stammered their return hello and hurried on their way.

She didn't bother to greet Becca, Catherine, or Andrew who were all sitting on the kerb outside the milk bar eating Peters Drumstick ice creams. Samantha always liked the original vanilla flavour, while Suzanna always preferred the lemonade-flavoured Icy Poles in summer. Suzanna argued that ice blocks quenched your thirst better than ice cream in the heat. *Maybe she was right?*

Catherine and Becca glared at her as she passed, but Andrew looked embarrassed, or maybe ashamed, as he made quick eye contact, then looked down at his ice cream which was starting to melt and drip down his hand.

Around lunchtime she stopped at the Bluebird Café. She went in and stood for a second looking at who was working behind the counter. It felt odd, almost like a different place, an impersonal place from the future. A place where her mother no longer worked, no longer joked with customers and colleagues, cooked food, or manned the coffee machine.

When Mrs Corcoran spotted her, she immediately came over and started fussing. She sat Samantha down at a table near the front window and insisted that she order whatever she wanted and that she didn't have to pay.

Mrs Corcoran asked if there'd been any news and how her mother was doing. Samantha said Mum was fine, reluctant to tell her the truth: that her mother was a mess and, if they didn't manage to find Suzanna, she'd never be coming back to work.

While Samantha waited for her toasted ham and cheese sandwich and vanilla milkshake, she watched people walk by. Everyone seemed so normal, as if nothing was wrong, like this was just another day in the life. A deep sadness at the unfairness of it all suddenly filled her heart, and she remembered these feelings, remembered how, in another life, she'd brooded on these questions for years. *Why us? Why did this have to happen to my family? Aren't these sorts of things supposed to only happen to other people?*

She'd never worked out the answers, but now she realised the futility of this type of thinking. Truthfully, how could she wish this on anyone else? It *had* happened, fair or not, and now she and her family had to deal with it. Not many people got a second chance at something like this, so she was already ahead on that count. Not that she was doing any better this time around.

She watched Mrs Corcoran set her sandwich and milkshake on the table in front of her, then stand with her hands linked in front of her apron just watching her with a sad smile on her face.

"Thank you," Samantha said staring at the food. She looked up. "You don't have to watch me. I'm fine. I'm not about to disappear."

She realised what she'd said when Mrs Corcoran's cheeks turned bright red.

"Oh, I'm sorry, dear," Mrs Corcoran said, flustered. She unlinked her fingers and her hands jerked like they were controlling a marionette as she stepped back a step. "I don't mean to smother you. I'll just ... go ... and help with the other orders. Take your time, love, and remember you're not paying. Let me know if you want anything else or if there's anything any of us can do for you and your family."

"Thank you," Samantha said again, looking at the food and realising her appetite had deserted her. She picked up half of the sandwich and took a bite. She looked out the window again and chewed slowly. Her taste buds appeared to have left town with her appetite because it tasted like she was eating cardboard.

The bell on the café door jangled and a swish of colour caught Samantha's eye as a woman stepped inside and looked around. It was the psychic who had slipped the business card into Samantha's mother's hand yesterday. When she saw Samantha, she came over and slid into the chair opposite her.

The woman wore the same dress and shawl as the last time Samantha had seen her. She looked like a stereotypical fortune teller from a carnival, a refugee from a horror movie. A red bandanna adorned with white mystical symbols held the woman's greying shoulder-length hair off her face. Her gold hooped earrings were large, thin, and round, dangling almost down to her shoulders.

"Whatever you're selling, I'm not buying," Samantha said drily, taking another tasteless bite out of her sandwich. She looked out the window again.

"You have the strangest aura," the woman said. "It's mostly an ash grey, a colour I've never seen in an aura before. It roils like storm clouds, and every so often, other colours – blue, purple, red, black, white – flash through like lightning strikes."

Samantha looked back at the woman and studied her face. It was hard to tell her age. She could be anywhere from forty to seventy. Thick makeup accentuated her tanned face, filling in the myriad creases and wrinkles which were still obvious up close. Red rouge marked her cheek bones and bright red lipstick made her full lips look as if they were bursting with blood. Mascara blobbed on her eyelashes, dark grey eyeshadow swept across her eyelids. Despite the horror movie vibe, her hazel eyes looked kind and intelligent.

"I see Death watching you," the woman said, tilting her head slightly.

"Believe me, I've seen Death too, and there are worse things to worry about. Death and I are practically mates, now," Samantha said, putting down her sandwich. She licked melted butter off her fingers and pointed to her temple. "You'd be surprised what's going on in here, in my universe."

"I can see that you've recently been on a trip. A boat or a bus or..." The woman hesitated, looking Samantha up and down before continuing to speak. "A train?" She pointed to her own temple. "You'd be surprised what goes on in here, in *my* universe."

They sat and contemplated each other for a few minutes without speaking.

"What do you want?" Samantha asked, breaking the silence. "I don't have any money."

"Well, if you're not going to eat that…" the woman said, pointing to the other half of Samantha's sandwich.

Samantha pushed the plate over to her and the woman delicately picked up the sandwich. She started to pull it apart with her fingertips, placing each piece into her mouth carefully to avoid smearing her lipstick.

"I don't believe in psychics," Samantha said, sipping her milkshake as she watched the woman eat. Out of the corner of her eye, she could see Mrs Corcoran frowning and contemplating whether to come over.

"What *do* you believe?" the woman asked. "What do you have faith in?"

"I have faith in myself," Samantha said. "I believe what I can see. When I can't see something, I believe incontrovertible evidence. And, in all my years, I haven't seen any that confirms the existence of the special powers that people like you claim to have."

"People like me?" the woman said, raising her eyebrows. "In 'all your years'? How old are you? Fourteen? What 'special powers' have I claimed to have?"

Samantha slurped the last of her milkshake loudly, not looking away from the woman. "Why are you here? You gave your card to my mother because she's vulnerable, right now. And vulnerable people don't always think clearly. They grasp at straws, but those straws come at a cost and don't always hold up."

"I only want to help," the woman said, wiping her hands on a paper serviette. "I'm not asking for money. I'm not asking for anything – well, except for this sandwich." She smiled. "I've seen some things that might help you find your sister."

"Might?"

"Yes," the woman said. "My faith says I need to tell you what my cards are telling me that you need to know. What you choose to do with my words after that is completely up to you."

Samantha turned her attention back to the people walking by the window. She wondered what forces had been at work to bring this woman's universe bumping up against her own. Was it random or was there a reason? From what she'd seen on the Ash Train, she suspected it was the former. *What have I got to lose?*

She turned back to the woman and saw that she'd laid out three tarot cards side-by-side on the table between them. Reaching out, Samantha touched the first card, Judgement, and experienced a small electric shock jolt through her fingertip. She quickly withdrew her hand.

"OK, tell me what you need to tell me. But make it quick. Time's ticking."

"I did a past, present, future reading for you." The woman pointed to the Judgement card. "This one represents the past and says you're not who you used to be. That you need to forgive yourself and work to fulfil your higher purpose. I think there's something deeply spiritual going on here." She stared at Samantha as if waiting for her to speak.

Samantha sighed. That wasn't anything new. "Aren't I supposed to shuffle the cards and draw them? Isn't that how tarot cards work?"

"I did it for you because my dreams told me not to wait," the woman said matter-of-factly. She tapped on the next card, the Ace of Wands. "This one represents the present and is telling you to trust your gut and maintain your momentum. Don't stop now."

"Hmm, OK," Samantha said, reaching out and almost, but not quite, touching the card. "And the third?" She pointed to the Knight of Swords. "I assume that's the future card?"

"Correct," the woman said. "This one says you're going to take bold action, but it might be risky. If you move too fast without a plan, you might not end up with the outcome you desire. The Knight of Swords says precision matters, not speed. So, while time is running out for your sister, you need to be smart about how you use that time."

"And how does any of this help me find my sister?" Samantha said, watching Catherine, Becca, and Andrew walk past on the other side of the street. "It sounds more like a pep talk full of vague language rather than specifics or details that I can use. Now, if you give me an address or a name or even a general location that *will* actually help me find her, *that* would be useful. Is she even still in the state?"

The woman sighed and gathered up the cards, disappearing them somewhere under her shawl like a magician. She put her hand over Samantha's hand, and it felt warm and sincere. The woman closed her eyes, and Samantha watched her eyelids move as if the woman was in REM sleep, like she was dreaming.

"She's not nearby, but she's also not too far away. I see pink. And other girls that look a bit like you, only younger, but I'm not sure if those girls are with her physically or only in spirit. They keep urging her to run, but I don't think she can hear them." She shook her head. "No, I don't think they can help her." The woman opened her eyes. "Your sister is still alive ... for now. But time is running out. He's starting to get confused, and when he's confused, he gets angry. And when he get angry, he gets ... violent."

Samantha stood up, yanking her hand out from under this woman's hand. She knew it was irrational, but she was angry and blaming this woman for not telling her anything beneficial. "I *know* I'm running out of time. You don't need to tell me that. What I do need you to tell me is *what do I do now? Right now! This instant!*"

The woman also stood up, and Samantha saw Mrs Corcoran coming over with concern on her face.

"Go back to the park," the woman said, pulling the café door open, jangling the bell. "There's something there that you need to find."

31

Witnesses

Wed, 28 March 1984 – Samantha

SAMANTHA RODE SUZANNA'S BIKE as fast as she could back to the park.

She stalked around the picnic grounds where they'd had the party. She looked under tables, in the bathroom, through the carpark, even kicking at bushes and digging through the rubbish bins. But there was nothing there that she hadn't already seen. No clues, no nothing. Just the sad remains of a birthday party gone wrong. A birthday party that should never have been.

The sound of people arguing drifted in on the breeze. Samantha stood and cocked her head, trying to work out where the voices were coming from. When she realised that they were coming from across the lake, she jumped back on the bike and headed around to the playground where Suzanna had disappeared from.

She got there and found Becca and Andrew yelling at each other. Catherine stood next to Becca, glaring at Andrew, obviously backing Becca's side of the argument.

"We can't," Becca yelled. "We'll get in trouble. My father can NOT know what we were doing."

"We have to," Andrew yelled back. "What if it helps find her?"

Catherine switched her glare to Samantha as Samantha coasted to a stop and let the bike fall to the ground. "Oh great, now look who's here."

Samantha ignored Catherine and looked from Becca to Andrew. "What's going on? Do you know something about Suzanna?"

Becca said, "No."

Andrew said, "Maybe."

Andrew continued speaking as Becca threw her hands up and turned away. "On Saturday night, Becca and I snuck away from the party. We were under some trees, over there." He pointed. "We saw a dark coloured car pull into the carpark here. It parked up the back, where it couldn't be seen, and shortly after that a man and a small white dog came from that direction. We couldn't see his face, it was too dark, but he just looked like someone taking his dog for a walk. He set off that way." Andrew pointed along the lakeshore away from where the party had been held over the other side.

"What the fuck! What time was this?" Samantha demanded.

"Not long before Suzanna came over here," he said. He indicated between himself and Becca. "We saw Suzanna walking along the footpath, heading this way, when we were heading back. She didn't see us in the dark, but the way she was moving ... she looked pissed about something."

"Why didn't you tell the police?" Samantha couldn't believe this. "You're supposed to be Suzanna's friends."

"Why do you think?" Becca snapped. "If my dad finds out that Andrew and I were out here alone, he'll be livid. I'll be lucky to be allowed out of the house again before I turn twenty-one."

"What the fuck were you doing over here anyway?" Samantha turned away, then turned back as it dawned on her. "Oh."

The looks on their faces said everything. Becca's father was the local deacon in the Anglican Church, and he would not be happy to know that his fourteen-year-old daughter had been in the dark alone with a boy.

Samantha pointed at Andrew. "I always thought you liked Suzanna."

Andrew looked down. "I did ... do ... but she didn't ... doesn't ... seem to like me in the same way."

"Seriously?" Becca screeched, stepping forward with her fists clenched at her sides. She got right up in Andrew's face. "I'm second best? That's not what you told me all those times you were feeling me up."

"Piece of shit." Catherine spat on the ground at Andrew's feet. She gripped Becca's arm and pulled her away. She jabbed her finger at Samantha as if it was a knife. "And you. This is all your fault. If you'd gone missing, nobody would have cared. No one would have even noticed. Even your own parents preferred Suzanna over you. Why don't you do us all a favour and disappear yourself!"

Samantha stared at Catherine and Becca as they walked away, arms around each other. Catherine glanced back a couple of times, once yelling to Andrew, "You'd better not say anything, Andrew, or you'll be sorry."

"I'm already sorry," Andrew murmured to Samantha. "I know we should have said something, but those two were adamant. I was too weak to fight with them until I saw you riding around today on Suzanna's bike. You looked so sad, but determined, too, you know? It really brought home to me how much I miss her. I want to help find her."

"What sort of car was it?" Samantha asked numbly, still watching the two girls go.

"It was too dark to properly tell, but I think it was a dark blue sedan, like a Holden or a Ford or something."

Mr Beresford drove a dark blue car. And he had a small white dog. Two pieces of the puzzle that hadn't come out the first time. Things might have turned out very different if Suzanna's three supposed friends weren't so gutless, thought Samantha in disgust.

It had to be Beresford, but she still didn't think it would be enough for the police. She had to talk to Toni, find out what she'd found out. And they needed a plan. The psychic was right about that.

"You have to go and tell the police," Samantha said, turning to Andrew. "That's how you help. Go and tell Detective White what you saw. Don't worry about Becca or Catherine. What are they gonna do? They're fourteen years old, for god's sake. Becca's dad will get over it."

"OK, sure, you're absolutely right," Andrew said with an attempt at a smile. "Will you come with me?"

"No, I can't," Samantha said, already heading towards the bike. "I've got something else I need to do."

Samantha rode home past the school, but Mr Beresford's car was no longer in the carpark. She also rode past his house on her way home, but his car wasn't there, either.

She dropped the bike on the ground in the backyard, ran up the back steps, and through the back door. She dug the Melbourne phone number Toni had given her out of her pocket, went to the phone in the hallway, and dialled.

"Come on, come on," she muttered, listening to the ringing on the other end of the phone.

"Who are you calling?" Dad asked, walking up behind her and making her jump.

"Toni," Samantha said distractedly. "I need to talk to her."

"I thought you said she'd gone back to Melbourne," he said.

"She has, but I need to talk to her," Samantha repeated.

Toni finally answered, out of breath, as if she'd run to answer the phone. "Hello?"

"Toni, it's me, Samantha." She rushed on. "It's got to be him. It's got to be. Some kids saw a car like his and a dog like his at the park not long before Suzanna went missing. They were too scared to come forward sooner because they thought they'd get in trouble. Also, when he saw me today, he was totally freaked out."

"Who?" her father asked, frowning. "What are you talking about?"

"Yeah, well, I've found out some stuff, too," Toni said. "I was going to ring you later, but I think I've pretty well narrowed it down to him, too. I've got an address for his ex-wife. I'm going to talk to her tomorrow morning. Then, I'll come back there."

"I want to be there when you talk to her," Samantha said. "I want to hear first-hand what she says." She looked at her watch. "There's a bus that comes through here about six in the morning." *At least it used to*, she thought, *or will*. In her last go round at this life, after she'd moved to Melbourne, she'd always bussed it both ways when she visited Miranda Springs. Presumably the timetable wouldn't have changed that much. "It goes to Melbourne via a bit of a roundabout route, but it gets in around nine. Can you pick me up at the bus station?"

"Absolutely," Toni said. "But..."

Samantha's father slammed his hand down on the phone, cutting off the call. "You're not going anywhere, Samantha. I've told you to leave this to the police."

"I'm not a child, Dad," Samantha said, pushing his hand off the phone and starting to dial again.

"Yes, you are, Samantha," he replied, grabbing the receiver out of her hand and pushing her away from the phone. "You're fourteen years old. You *are* a child, you're *my* child. I'm the parent and you don't just get to do what you want. You are not going to Melbourne on a bus on your own. I will not give you money for a bus ticket. You'll stay right here, in this house, and let the police do what they're paid to do."

Samantha closed her eyes for a second. She hated arguing with her father. She understood his concerns, but he wasn't going to stop her. He just had to think he'd done so.

"OK, whatever" she said, putting her hands up and shaking her head. "I give up. You're right. We'll totally get Suzanna back by just sitting around here twiddling our thumbs. She'll come back, alive and well, and everything will be hunky dory."

At that, she walked to her room and closed the door, not looking back at him.

"I'm sorry, Dad," she said quietly as she sat on the edge of her bed. "But I'll be on that bus tomorrow morning, one way or another, whether you like it or not. Suzanna is coming home this time. You can quote me on that."

It was midnight and the house was quiet.

Samantha knew her parents had gone to bed. They'd all had a silent dinner, then she'd gone back to her room while her parents watched television for a while. She'd heard her father walk her mother along the hallway to their room a couple of hours ago.

She lay in bed trying to work out how to pay for the bus ticket tomorrow. She didn't even know how much money she needed. If she had a mobile phone with a banking app or a credit card, she could have bought the bus ticket online. But that option was way in the future and no use to her now.

Do I steal money from Mum's purse? It was the only thing she could think of, but it didn't feel right. In her old life, she'd done worse, but in this life, she wasn't yet at that desperation point. *Second chances are meant to make you a better person, aren't they?*

She slipped out of bed and went to Suzanna's room to think. She lay on top of Suzanna's bed and stared at the ceiling. The main curtains were open, and moonlight shone through the sheer curtains that sat within the window frame, making patterns on the wall as it illuminated the spaces in the lacy fabric.

Help me, Suzanna, she thought. *Help me, help you.*

She wasn't aware that she'd dozed off until she suddenly jerked awake. She was lying on her side and the first thing she saw when she opened her eyes was Suzanna's Concert Fund.

She got up and tipped the coins and notes from the jar onto the bed. Counting the money, she thought there should be enough for a one-way bus ticket. Possibly not for an adult, but she wasn't an adult at the moment, as her father kept reminding her.

She headed back to her room, switched her bedside lamp on, and got dressed. She pulled everything out of her school backpack, dumping it all on her desk, and tried to decide what she needed to take with her.

A three-hour bus trip would be boring, so she threw in a couple of novels, a notebook, and some pens. At the last minute, she also threw in a sketchbook, even though she was nowhere near Suzanna's level at drawing.

According to her clock, it was 3:27 AM, so she sat on her bed and watched the minutes tick by. At one point she got up and put on the silver necklace, bracelet, and earrings that her mother had given her. Then she sat back down and ran her hands over the charms while she waited.

At 4:04 AM, she heard Dad walking down the hallway, so she switched off the lamp, slipped under the covers, and faced the wall. She heard him open her door, the bottom of it scraping across the carpet. He stood there for a couple of minutes, then she heard the door close again.

She turned over and watched the clock. At 5:30 AM she got up, grabbed her backpack, and headed out the back door, closing it as quietly as she could.

32

Angry

Thu, 29 March 1984 – Suzanna

SUZANNA WAS SCARED. SHE sat on the floor next to the bed and dashed the prickling tears out of the corners of her eyes.

She had no idea how long she'd been here – *was it day or night?* – but she was hungry and she wanted her mother, her father, her sister. She'd had no food, hadn't even seen Mr Beresford, since her escape attempt. She had to keep using the toothbrush cup in the bathroom for drinking water, although dehydration and stress contributed to the headache pounding away behind her eyes.

She was pretty sure Mr Beresford had left yesterday for a few hours. She'd tried to get the bedroom door open but couldn't get the lock to give. Then, she'd moved to the boarded-up window, trying to kick out the corrugated iron, but that didn't work either. After that, she'd scrabbled desperately at some of the screws in the tin, but the only thing she managed to do was rip off half a fingernail and bleed all over her shirt.

She knew when he'd come back, because he slammed the front door, then walked around the house, hitting the walls and talking to himself. He stopped outside her door, thumped on it with his fist, but didn't come in.

She couldn't stop thinking about the four graves out there in the paddock. What did he mean by calling them 'mistakes'? Would she become the fifth mistake? The more she tried not to think about it, the more she felt the dirt pressing down on her, immobilising her muscles, creeping into her eyes and nose and mouth, blocking her airways, slowly suffocating her until she became one with the earth, and one with those other girls she was sure were buried there.

To try to make herself think of something else, she pulled out the activity book she'd hidden under the mattress. She tried to clear her mind, and just draw, but when she opened her eyes, she saw that she'd drawn five mounds of dirt side-by-side in amongst a sea of long grass. Each of the mounds had a cross, like a grave marker, but no names or words adorned them. Out of each mound of dirt, arms reached out and clasped the hands of the ones coming out of the next one.

She heard the door being unlocked. Glancing at the open bathroom door, she contemplated running into there, but there was no lock on that door, so it wouldn't help. Instead, she crouched down lower, keeping the bed between her and the door.

She peered over the edge of the bed and watched Mr Beresford open the door. He bent down and put a tray of food on the floor just inside the room. Her stomach betrayed her with a loud growl, but she stayed where she was. He stood up and pushed the tray forward with his foot as if he was reluctant to fully enter the room.

He looked around the room, and the look he gave her when he saw her hiding behind the bed took her breath away, like the imaginary dirt in the imaginary grave she'd just been thinking about.

She tried not to move at all, remembering the time she and her friends had run across a paddock unaware there was a massive bull in there. When the bull had noticed them, it had snorted loudly and started to paw the ground. They were still a long way from the fence and Andrew had yelled at them all to stop. Stop moving. Any movement might mean the bull would chase them down and gore them, toss them like a rag doll, and stomp on them until they were bloodied and broken. Once they'd stopped moving, the bull had quickly lost interest and ambled away. After that, Andrew had motioned for them to edge slowly toward the fence in silence. Every time the bull looked around, they'd all become motionless statues again. Finally, they'd all scrambled through the barbed wire fence – Suzanna remembered ripping a hole in her shirt and scraping a bloody line down her back. Once through, they all collapsed on the ground, hugging each other and laughing in relief that they were all safe. She'd given the bull the finger as they walked away.

The look on Mr Beresford's face matched the one she remembered on the bull's face that day. He took a breath and seemed like he was about to say something, but then he withdrew from the room without a word, closing and locking the door behind him.

Suzanna waited for a few minutes and, when she was sure he wasn't coming back straight away, she hurried over to the food. She hated herself, berated herself for being weak, as she gobbled down the toasted ham and cheese sandwich, then drank tomato soup from the bowl, not bothering with a spoon.

It wasn't until after she'd finished, when she started to feel drowsy, that she thought to wonder if he'd put something in the food.

33

Melbourne

Thu, 29 March 1984 – Samantha

SAMANTHA BOUGHT THE BUS ticket with no problems. The woman behind the ticket desk looked bored and handed over the ticket without even looking at her. No one seemed at all concerned about a fourteen-year-old girl travelling alone.

While she waited for the bus to arrive, she used the payphone to make a collect call to Toni. She didn't tell Toni that her father had forbidden her to make this trip. After the abrupt end to yesterday's phone call, and the timing of this one, she knew Toni suspected that was the case, but she didn't ask. Toni said she'd be waiting when the bus got in and that the ex-Mrs Beresford had agreed to meet them at around 11 AM at her home.

The bus rattled to a stop on Main Street at 6:04 AM. Samantha was the only one boarding in Miranda Springs, and she walked down the aisle, trying to decide where to sit. There were five other people already on the bus. A young woman sat in the middle of the back seat nursing a baby. A woman sat about a quarter of the way down on the right, with a girl of about eight asleep with her head in her lap. An older man sitting near the front on the left, kept up a constant stream of chatter with the driver.

She chose a window seat, about halfway down on the left, and put her backpack on the seat next to her. As the bus lurched away from the bus station, she pulled the window blind up. At first, all she saw was the white fog and the grasping shadows she'd seen out the Ash Train window. But then she blinked and the fog changed into normal early morning mist and, as they drove, the scenery gradually morphed into forests, fields, and towns marching by.

After a while, she pulled out the sketchbook and a pen and experimented by drawing a few lines, trying to remember how Suzanna had done it. But it wasn't long before her eyelids grew heavy. She'd barely slept the night before and the swaying of the bus and the sound of the tyres thrumming along the road made her drowsy. She eventually let her eyes drift closed.

She awoke with a fright when the bus stopped abruptly. She opened her eyes, blinking at the light, and realised that the bus must have stopped a few more times while she was sleeping because it was now almost three-quarters full. No one had sat beside her, though, because her backpack was still taking up the seat.

A couple of people stood up and shuffled down the aisle to the front doors. She checked her watch – almost 8:45 AM – so she was almost there. The sketchbook had slipped off her lap onto the floor, under the seat in front of her. She quickly retrieved it as the doors swooshed closed, almost catching the bottom of the last departing passenger's coat, and the bus lurched off again.

She stared at the drawing on the open page of the sketchbook, not sure what she was looking at. She didn't remember drawing anything. Then the lines turned into what looked like graves, five of them. Crosses marked each mound of dirt, and the whole lot seemed to be surrounded by long grass. The odd thing about the picture was the arms pushing out of each mound, each one holding hands with the ones on either side of them. The one on the end had a bracelet with charms on it: a cat, a sunflower, a castle, a leaf, and an 'S'.

The style was Suzanna's, and she wondered if Suzanna had guided her hand while she'd slept. She reached out her mind and tried to feel Suzanna, but there was nothing. Like the phone line had been cut. This picture felt like a premonition, though. A message meant to spur her on and she spent the rest of the bus ride trying to mentally hurry it up as they travelled through the outer Melbourne suburbs, heading for the inner city.

As soon as the bus pulled up and before the driver had even turned the engine off, most of the passengers stood up, grabbing their belongings. They pushed and elbowed each other as if it was a contest to see who could get off first. Samantha sat and waited impatiently with her backpack on her lap.

It was 9:32 AM by the time she finally stepped down off the last step of the bus. She was the last passenger off, and the bus driver alighted behind her, closing the doors behind himself.

She stood and looked around. Melbourne's city centre looked a lot different to what she remembered from her previous life, but the people were essentially the same.

Cars were parked along the street and trams rattled past. Office workers scurried along, seemingly having somewhere important to be. Other people weren't in any hurry at all, strolling along like tourists, looking in shop windows, or sitting in cafés sipping tea or coffee. *The only things missing from this picture*, thought Samantha wryly, *are the mobile phones in every hand and the people speaking loudly into their phones making sure everybody around them knows how important they are.*

Then there was the third type of person. Mostly men, these were the people Samantha knew the best. Not actual individuals, but she recognised and empathised with the despair and downtrodden countenance of people with nowhere to be and no way of getting there. These people looked like they hadn't slept properly for years and hadn't washed in months. They wore dirty trousers and ragged shirts or jumpers with gaping holes. Some looked lost, as if their minds were elsewhere or nowhere at all.

A couple of men with long, shaggy beards and dark rings around their eyes begged the passing office workers for money: *one coin, surely you can spare one coin?* The office workers' eyes slid over them, around them, through them, unseeing and unmoved as they hurried past. She watched two policemen saunter up and move the beggars on, displaying their truncheons to forestall any argument.

She sighed, then saw Toni's fountain ponytail bobbing above the crowd like a dolphin riding the waves.

When Toni reached her, she hugged her, then leaned back, still holding Samantha's arms as she looked her up and down. "You're not supposed to be here, are you?"

Samantha didn't respond, just indicated for her to lead the way.

Toni's car was parked a couple of blocks away, and they started walking. They passed a small café that was doing a great trade in take away coffee and Toni suggested they stop for breakfast.

"It's about a thirty-minute drive to Brunswick in the traffic at this time of the day," Toni reasoned. "So, we've got about an hour to kill before we leave. I assume you haven't eaten this morning?"

Samantha wanted to go straight there, but understood they'd be too early, so they went into the café and sat down. A waitress took their order, then they sat and talked while they waited.

"Tell me about this woman we're seeing this morning," Samantha said, running her hands over the red and black tablecloth, smoothing out the wrinkles.

"Her name is Margaret," Toni said. "She was married to Beresford for nine years, from 1966 to 1975. After they divorced, she reverted back to her original surname of Watford."

"Why did they divorce?"

"I'm not sure, but she sounded odd and a bit evasive on the phone when I asked. We'll ask her when we see her. But, what about you? What did those kids say?"

Samantha explained what Andrew had told her, what he and Becca had seen. She stopped talking when the waitress brought their food and drinks, then continued after she left.

"I told him to tell Detective White, which I assume he did. He wanted me to go with him, but I wanted to check out Beresford's house again on my way home," she said. "He wasn't home," she added.

Toni stirred her coffee and watched the milk swirl and eddy as she thought. "Your dad told you not to go near him." she finally said, raising her eyes and looking at Samantha. "And I have to agree with him. If he's our man, then he's dangerous. You could be putting yourself and your sister's life in danger if he knows you're watching him. Promise me you won't go anywhere near him alone. If you can't promise me that, I'll put you straight back on the bus."

Samantha rolled her eyes. "Really? Don't start trying to boss me around. I'm finding Suzanna this time, with or without your help."

Toni paused as she raised a slice of toast to her mouth and regarded Samantha. "I've noticed you say 'this time' a couple of times when you've talked about Suzanna's disappearance. What do you mean by that? 'This time'?"

Samantha kept eating, hoping her silence would move Toni on from this line of questioning.

But Toni persisted. "Has she disappeared before? Is there more to this story than you've told me, or even the police?"

Samantha finished eating and sipped at her cup of tea. She sighed and looked at Toni. "You wouldn't believe me if I told you."

"Try me."

"Would you believe me if I told you I'm actually a fifty-four-year-old woman in a fourteen-year-old body? That I've already lived this scenario once? That I died in 2024 never knowing what happened to my sister? That I was given the chance to time travel back to change the outcome of Suzanna's story?"

"Probably not," Toni said. "But it sounds like a good movie."

"Told you you wouldn't believe me," Samantha said, putting her teacup down with a clink. She checked her watch and stood up. "Anyway, it's time to go."

Toni paid for their breakfast and led Samantha to her old blue Toyota which was parked down the street a little way from where they were.

They drove in silence, both thinking about what Samantha had said.

34

Ex

Thu, 29 March 1984 – Samantha

TONI PARKED OUTSIDE A Federation-style house on a residential street crowded with similar houses in varying conditions. The street had a mixture of neat, well cared for homes, and others that needed work to fix overgrown lawns and scruffy gardens, peeling paint, rusty roofs, and warped floorboards on front verandahs.

The ex-Mrs Beresford's house was one of the neat ones. The cream-coloured weatherboard walls looked like they'd recently been painted, as did the dark brown window frames. Neither the tin roof nor the bullnose verandah showed any signs of rust or wear. In fact, the roof was shiny and clean, as if it had recently been cleaned or maybe even replaced.

The house was almost the full width of the block, so the neighbouring houses were quite close. The block had no driveway, and Samantha thought there was probably an external lane for access to the rear of the property.

The small front lawn was cut short, and a small, half-grown deciduous tree spread out in the middle just starting to lose its leaves. Flowers bloomed along the front border of the property, just inside the wood and wire fence next to the footpath. Pink and white roses grew on both sides of the red brick path that led from the front gate to the front door.

Toni and Samantha let themselves in through the small wire gate and walked the gauntlet through the thorny rose bushes to the front door. Toni rang the bell, and it was only a few seconds before the door opened.

Margaret Watford was small and neat, just like her house and garden. She was pretty and looked to be in her late-thirties or early-forties. Her wavy brown hair curled at the bottom, just touching her petite shoulders. Her hazel eyes twinkled, and her heart-shaped lips, naturally turning up at the corners, made it look like she was always smiling. From her clothing choice – a dark blue woollen skirt that reached to mid-calf, a light blue blouse, covered by a white knitted vest, and flat, sensible brown shoes – and the way she moved, Samantha pegged her as either a primary school teacher or a librarian.

"Oh, I thought there'd be only one of you," Margaret said.

"Yeah, sorry about that," Toni said. "I'm looking after my sister today. I'm Toni and this is Samantha. I hope you don't mind?"

"No, no, that's perfectly alright," Margaret said, holding the door open and ushering them inside. "You have to look after family, don't you?"

Toni and Samantha smiled at Margaret as they entered the house, then waited in the hallway while she closed and locked the door behind them. The narrow hallway was dark with the front door closed. The house had a faint sweet smell, one that Samantha associated with her Grandma's house after she'd been baking.

Margaret pointed to an open door on the left. "Just down there. On the left. I thought we'd talk in the lounge room, if that's OK with you?"

They both nodded and walked ahead of Margaret to the doorway she'd indicated. There was a closed door on the right, almost opposite the lounge room door, and Samantha thought that must be a bedroom if she remembered rightly from when she'd lived in similar places to this.

Toni and Samantha went into the lounge room, and Margaret stayed in the doorway. She pointed down the hallway. "I've just made a pot of tea and some biscuits. Sit down, girls, and I'll just fetch them."

The room was on the small side, but cosy. Puffy cushions were strategically arranged, as if by an interior decorator, on the floral two-seater couch that took up most of the back wall and on the matching armchair beside it.

Wooden bookcases, overflowing with books, lined one wall. A boxy television sat on top of a small wooden cupboard in the corner near the door. Polished wooden floorboards could be seen around the edges of the room, while a rectangular short-pile cream-coloured rug sat under an oval glass coffee table in the centre.

The room was dim, even with a small amount of daylight coming through the two tall windows at the front. The floral curtains on both windows were pulled back, exposing another layer of sheer lacy drapes underneath which dulled the light somewhat.

Samantha and Toni edged past the coffee table and sat on the couch.

"What have you told her about why we're here?" Samantha asked, keeping her voice low.

"Not much," said Toni. "Certainly not what we suspect him of doing. I spun her a line about writing a story about marriage and divorce. What causes friction in a marriage, what changes lead to a couple deciding they don't love each other anymore, how they move on with their lives afterwards."

Toni stopped speaking as Margaret bustled back into the room carrying a tray. The large white china teapot sported a blue knitted tea cosy and was accompanied by teacups and saucers with English hunting scenes on them, and a plate piled high with obviously home-made Anzac biscuits.

She put the tray on the coffee table and pulled the armchair around, so she was facing Toni and Samantha. Leaning forward, she daintily poured three cups of tea, then sat back and smiled.

"Thank you for seeing us, Miss Watford," Toni said, pulling out a notebook and a pen from her bag. She leaned back on the couch and set her notebook on her lap. She made a show of looking around the room. "This is a beautiful home. You obviously put a lot of work into it."

"Thank you, but please call me Margaret," Margaret said, sipping her tea and picking up a biscuit. "I am very proud of my little piece of Australia here and I'm glad to be of help. Now, what do you want to know? Please, drink and help yourself to a biscuit or two while we talk."

Samantha picked up one of the Anzac biscuits and bit into it, savouring the oaty texture and the sweetness that flooded her tongue and made her mouth water. It was exactly how she always liked them, how her grandmother always made them: soft on the inside, but crunchy on the outside. It had been so long since she'd had home-made food like this, she'd forgotten how delicious it could be. She reached for another one.

"Can you start by telling us a bit about yourself, Margaret?" Toni said. "I know you were a primary school teacher and your ex-husband is a high school teacher. What do you do now?"

Margaret sighed, leaned forward and put her teacup on the saucer. "I still teach, but not on a permanent basis, now. I fill-in when teachers call in sick or take leave."

"Do you get much work?" Toni asked, jotting words down in her notebook while looking at Margaret. She looked like she'd interviewed plenty of people like this before.

"Oh, there's plenty of work. So much that I can pick and choose where and when I work." Margaret's expression turned serious as she seemed mesmerised by Toni's hand scribbling on the paper. "You know, the low pay that teachers get doesn't come close to compensating for the stress of looking after other people's kids all day. Sometimes it feels like you're a quasi-parent or a glorified babysitter. And, at the same time, you have to try to make them learn enough so they have a chance at becoming competent adults. It's no wonder so many teachers end up with all sorts of mental and physical problems. It's not like an office job, is it, where you can take a day off and just pick up where you left off when you come back. Someone has to be in that classroom every single day. You should consider doing an article about that some day."

They sat in silence for a couple of minutes while Toni finished writing her notes.

"I'm sorry if that sounded a bit harsh, Samantha," Margaret said, looking at Samantha. "You look like you must be in high school? How old are you? Fifteen, sixteen?"

"I've just turned fourteen," Samantha said. "And what you said makes perfect sense. I've seen what schoolkids can be like and it's certainly not pretty at times. I don't envy you your job, that's for sure. I don't think I could do it."

Toni got Margaret's attention again, trying to get the conversation back on track. "I understand your ex-husband was also a teacher, Margaret. How did you meet?"

"Oh, that was such a long time ago. We lived quite close to each other and actually went through primary and high school together. I was a year behind Mark."

"So, you were high school sweethearts?"

"No, no, nothing like that. We knew each other at school but never really interacted. After I left school, I became a primary school teacher. I like teaching general subjects to kids whose minds are still open. I've found that by the time a lot of them get to high school, they've absorbed much of their own families' biases and outlooks and are less receptive to other points of view."

"And Mark?"

It felt weird, and slightly wrong, to Samantha to hear Mr Beresford referred to by his first name. She'd always been taught that people in positions of authority were always referred to by their title and surname as a gesture of respect. You only got to use someone's first name if they were a close friend or if they were subordinate to you, which teachers never were.

"Mark was fascinated by history. I always thought he should have been a historian, working for a university, but he came from a working-class family. They didn't have a lot of money, and they talked down on higher education, said it was the working man who kept the country running. To them, academics were people who might know things but couldn't actually do anything useful. Mark ended up becoming a high school history teacher."

"How did you end up married then, if you never dated in high school?"

"A few years after we'd left school, we both attended a seminar here in Melbourne. Gosh, it was so long ago, I can't even remember what it was about. But Mark recognised me from school, and he asked me out. I didn't know anyone else there, so I said yes and, well, it went from there. We were married in 1966."

Margaret got up and went to a bookcase, returning with a photo album. She put it on the coffee table and turned pages until she came to a wedding photo. She turned the album around and pointed to the photo. "That's us."

"You look so happy," Toni said, reaching out and almost, but not quite, touching the photo. "I understand you and Mark divorced in 1975? Can you tell me a bit about that? What happened?"

Margaret frowned and took a deep breath. She closed her eyes for a few seconds, looking as if she was trying to draw on some inner strength, then opened them again.

"Are you married?" she asked Toni. "Children?"

"No, I'm not," Toni said. "Married to my job, maybe, but no, I've never been married, and I have no children." She turned to Samantha, nudged her, and winked. "Except for my sister here."

Samantha just looked at her with no amusement, then looked back at Margaret.

"Well, dear," said Margaret. "When you get married, you'll find that everyone around you expects to hear baby news very soon after the event. I would have been happy to wait, but Mark wanted a baby, and wanted one 'now'. Against my better judgement, I let him convince me that I wanted a baby 'right now', too. That our lives would never be complete without our own children to carry on our legacies.

"He was ecstatic when I told him I was pregnant. I insisted I could keep working, at least until I started to show, and he agreed, albeit reluctantly. You have no idea how devastated we were when I miscarried at around the three-month mark."

"I'm so sorry," Toni murmured.

Margaret took a breath and continued. "Mark convinced me to quit my job when I got pregnant the second time. But it wasn't that, because I lost the second baby around the same three-month timeframe. He blamed my work for the miscarriages. And me, I guess, even though he never outright said it ... although his mother was never shy in blaming me out loud. Over the next few years, I lost another three babies. Five babies all up. I just couldn't keep doing it, so I said enough was enough."

"Did he hit you? Was he violent?" blurted Samantha.

Margaret looked at Samantha and paused a beat before answering. "He was never physically violent to me. It was more like an emotional control that I can see now when I look back on those years. It wasn't something I saw when I was living it."

"So, why did you divorce?" asked Toni. "Was it because he wanted to keep trying and you didn't?"

Margaret turned her attention back to Toni. "Maybe that was part of it, eventually. But not the whole story." She put her cup back on the saucer and leaned back in her chair. "I suggested adoption, but Mark was dead set against it. He was adamant that any child he was going to put time and money into would have to be his.

"Then, I found out I was pregnant again, for the sixth time. This time, I spent most of the pregnancy in hospital, which wasn't much fun, I can tell you that. But we were both ecstatic when we passed that cursed three-month mark. Our little Michelle managed to hang on – or I hung on to her – for eight months before neither of us could hang on any longer."

"Where is Michelle now?" asked Toni, thinking of Michelle Donovan, the first girl she'd identified as having been abducted. *Was the name a coincidence?*

"Our Michelle was stillborn," Margaret said with a sigh.

"Oh, I'm so sorry," Samantha and Toni murmured at the same time.

Margaret looked sad, but Samantha thought she also looked like it was something she'd come to terms with, that she had cried all the tears for her daughter that she was going to.

Margaret looked at Samantha with a slight smile. "Michelle would have been fourteen this year, the same age as you, you know. You look a little bit like Mark's side of the family."

"But you and Mark stayed together for another five years?" Toni asked. "What went wrong?"

Margaret leaned forward and studied Toni's face before she answered. "I haven't ever told anyone about this. Before I continue, I need to know that nothing you write will identify me or Mark. Neither his nor my family knows exactly what happened, why we separated."

"I promise," Toni said, holding her hand up as if she was in a court of law. "I'll use fake names and there will be no identifying information in anything I publish."

"Will I be able to see your story before it's published?" Margaret asked. "It's not that I don't trust you, but I've seen what the media does and how it twists people's words to fit their own agenda. What if I'm not happy with what you write?"

"It will be a few months down the track. You're the first one I've interviewed, so I'm still trying to get a feel for the angle of the story," Toni said. "The article will go through several rounds of editing before it's published. I'll make sure you see it with enough time for you to give me feedback. I can't promise to agree to all the changes you might ask for, but I promise to carefully consider them, along with my editor." She moved her hand, making a cross symbol over her chest. "I promise, cross my heart and hope to die, that you will not be identifiable in anything I write or publish."

Margaret poured herself a second cup of tea while she thought about it. She either didn't notice, or chose to ignore, the fact that Toni had only included her in that last promise, not her ex-husband. She turned and looked out the front window, sipping her tea, before turning back and meeting Toni's gaze. "OK, that sounds fair. Maybe I'm naïve, but I do believe you're sincere."

Toni nodded and indicated for her to continue her tale.

35

Paranoia

Thu, 29 March 1984 – Samantha

"LOSING MICHELLE, ESPECIALLY AFTER carrying her for that long, was absolutely devastating," Margaret said. "For both Mark and me. While I'd been in hospital, he'd spent his time (when he wasn't working or visiting me) fitting out a room in our house as a nursery. Michelle's very own room."

"This house?" Samantha asked, looking around the lounge room. She hadn't noticed any sign of a male living here, but they had been divorced for almost ten years now so that wouldn't be unusual.

"No, we were living in Bendigo, then. Mark liked working in smaller towns – said the kids were more receptive, less hostile, than kids he'd taught in the bigger cities. We travelled around a bit, working in even smaller towns, before we settled in Bendigo a couple of years after we married."

Samantha nodded.

"Anyway, I didn't see this nursery of his until I got home, after they finally discharged me from hospital. My god, you should have seen how pink and girly it was. Just being in the room, you felt like you'd eaten too much dessert.

"That room became one that I couldn't enter – it made me feel sick and was a reminder of what we'd lost. But Mark started to spend a lot of time in there. I sometimes stood just outside the door and listened to him talking to her. It seemed odd, but I understood. We were both grieving and that was just how Mark coped, how he could feel close to our lost little girl. But he would never accompany me to the cemetery to visit Michelle's grave. He attended the funeral, but that was the only time he ever saw her grave, at least to my knowledge."

Margaret went quiet for a few minutes and closed her eyes. Samantha could almost see the memories flitting past behind this woman's eyelids, just like her own had done outside the Ash Train window.

A Siamese cat padded silently into the room and jumped nimbly up onto Margaret's lap. Margaret's hand began stroking the cat, like it was an automatic calming ritual, drawing out rumbling purrs as the cat curled up and settled in. Samantha thought of Arabella at home, who did the same for her and her family. Cats always seemed to be able to read moods and offer comfort when it was needed.

Margaret took a deep breath and opened her eyes again. She watched her hand stroking the cat as she continued her tale.

"Mark and I bumbled through the next three years or so, each of us living in our own world. We grew apart and started living separate lives, albeit in the same house. I went back to work, and Mark did too after a bit of a break.

"We both immersed ourselves in our jobs, and I worked hard in our garden on weekends. For me, not having something to occupy my mind, and my hands, meant I'd brood and think dark thoughts. I suspect it was the same for Mark, but I couldn't live like that so I always had to have something to do.

"After a while, I'm not sure how long, Mark moved the cot out of the pink room and into the garage. He put a single bed in the room and started sleeping in there. I'd made it clear that I was not going to put myself through another pregnancy. I accepted at that point that I just wasn't meant to be a mother, and I wanted to get on with my life.

"Then, sometime in early 1973, around what would have been Michelle's third birthday, Mark started to become … paranoid, I guess you could say. He read something, I'm not sure where, but he got it into his head that Michelle hadn't died at all, but that the medical staff had taken her and given her to another family. His own family was also a bit odd, and they fuelled his belief even as I tried to dampen it.

"We used to walk to work together in the mornings, even though we barely spoke except about the most mundane things. My primary school was just a couple of blocks away, then his high school was a bit further on.

"I started to notice Mark watching some of the mothers at my school in the mornings. They were dropping off their older kids but also had younger kids with them. There was one girl in particular, with longish dark hair and green eyes. Very pretty little thing. She would have been about three – so, the same age Michelle would have been."

Margaret's attention was still on her hand stroking the cat on her lap and she didn't notice Samantha and Toni glance at each other.

"He started to become fixated on this girl, and it made me uncomfortable, the way he'd watch her and the look he'd get on his face. One morning, he tried to speak to this girl, grabbed her arm and pulled her towards him, but the mother made him let go and told him to leave her daughter alone or she'd call the police.

"That night I listened to him talking to himself in the pink room, saying 'it's you, I know it's you'. I pushed open the door and told him in no uncertain terms that our daughter – our Michelle – was dead. That girl he'd been looking at was not her. It *couldn't* have been her. I knew that family and I knew the girl was theirs, not ours."

"How did he take that?" asked Toni, frowning.

"Not well, at first," Margaret said, looking at her. "He was angry for a while, ranted a bit about how we'd been manipulated into thinking our Michelle was gone, when they'd obviously sold her to someone else. He raved about a conspiracy amongst the hospital staff to steal and sell babies. When I wouldn't believe him, he slammed his fist through the plaster on the wall beside the door."

"You said he wasn't violent," Samantha reminded her.

Margaret sighed. "He was always quick tempered. He could change from calm to angry in a heartbeat, and vice versa. But he never once touched me, and I never felt like I was in any danger from him, even then," she said. "By the morning he'd calmed down and he seemed to accept what I was saying about that little girl. Everything appeared to go back to normal, except that I insisted, then, on driving to work. I would drive him to his school and drop him off, return to mine, work the day, then pick him up in the afternoon.

"He seemed OK for about a year, before I noticed him looking at little girls again. In the supermarket, at the park, in shopping centres, on the street. He always watched the dark-haired ones, the ones who were about the same age that our Michelle would have been, and he'd get this weird calculating look in his eyes.

"At night, I'd hear him mumbling to himself in his pink room and I worried. I won't lie. I worried about those girls, and I worried about him. I told him he needed to see a psychiatrist so he could come to terms with Michelle's death and get some closure. Surprisingly, he actually agreed."

"What year was this?" Toni asked.

"1974," Margaret replied. "The psychiatrist sessions seemed to go well. Mark settled down and seemed to be almost back to normal, although he still refused to visit Michelle's grave. He said he didn't need to because she was always in his heart and she would always know he loved her."

"Is it possible that he wouldn't visit the grave because he didn't think she was in there?" asked Samantha.

Margaret looked at her thoughtfully. "Maybe. I never considered that, but it's possible."

"Were you too far apart by that point to reconcile?" asked Toni. "Whose idea was it to divorce? Yours or his?"

"It was my idea," Margaret said with a sigh. "In early 75, I found some photographs he'd cut out of a newspaper. They were grainy but were clearly of young girls. I confronted him and he yelled at me. I said he needed to go back to the psychiatrist, but he said he didn't need to. That he knew the truth.

"I didn't know that he'd been on medication and that he'd stopped taking it. I'm ashamed to say that I gave him an ultimatum. Either he go back and sort himself out or I'd leave. Needless to say, I ended up leaving."

"Weren't you worried he'd try something with a young girl? Take her, for example?" Toni said with a frown. "It doesn't sound like I'd want him anywhere near a daughter of mine."

"I spoke to his psychiatrist about that," Margaret said softly, looking down at her hands. "He was the one who told me Mark was on medication. He was positive that Mark would do nothing but watch from a distance. He was adamant that Mark would never approach the girls, not like the first one. Said he'd bet his degree on it, and I could only believe him. He was the expert, after all.

"So, I packed my bag and went home to Mum. I told my parents we'd been arguing for a while and that I couldn't live with him any longer. I don't know what he told his parents, but they never particularly like me anyway, so I doubt they had any problem with it."

"How did Mark take it when you left?" Toni asked.

"As far as I know, he was fine with it. When I spoke to him on the phone, he seemed calm and quite normal, but he never tried to convince me to come back. He also never again mentioned his theory about what had happened to Michelle. I thought he must have gone back to his psychiatrist and must be taking his medication again. That, or his mother and stepfather had persuaded him he was better off without me. It wasn't until after I moved out that I realised how much strain I'd been under, living with him like that, walking on eggshells all the time.

"I met him at a café a few months later to tell him I wanted a divorce, and he agreed readily enough. The divorce was amicable. We agreed to sell the house and split our assets fifty-fifty. What neither of us wanted, we sold or gave away. The house sold very quickly. He said he was going to move up north, somewhere in Queensland, for a new start. He joked about chasing the sun. As far as I know, that's what he did. And I moved here, and that was that. Here we are. Me talking to you."

The three of them sat in silence, listening to a grandfather clock somewhere else in the house ticking loudly. The clock had chimed the hour a couple of times since they'd been talking, and Samantha was surprised to see that it was almost 2 PM when she checked her watch.

"That's some story," Toni said, looking at Margaret. She seemed to suddenly remember her cover story about why she and Samantha were there. "How has your divorce affected you, Margaret? Have you had other relationships since?"

"I've been on my own now for almost ten years," Margaret said with a smile. "And to be honest, it's been the best ten years of my life. I own my own house, I work my own hours, I do what I want when I want. There've been a couple of men, but nothing serious enough for me to consider giving up my freedom again." She raised her eyebrows as she looked at Samantha, then back at Toni. "Don't let anyone tell you that a woman needs a man or a partner of any kind. It's just not true."

"Do you keep in touch with Mark?" Toni asked. "Do you know what's become of him?"

"No, I've never felt the urge to contact him or track him down. There's nothing I have to say to him," Margaret said. The cat jumped down from her lap onto the floor, and Margaret watched it start licking its paws and rubbing them over its ears. "I did see, in the newspaper, that his stepfather died a few months after we divorced and that his mother died not long after that. Those were no losses to society, let me tell you. I assume Mark inherited their property. He had a lot of cousins and uncles and aunts, even two stepbrothers, but his mother doted on him. I can't imagine that she wouldn't have made sure he got everything."

Toni and Samantha exchanged a look.

"Where was this?" Samantha asked. "I thought you said you both grew up near each other. I just assumed you were in a city, or a town at least."

"Yes, that was before Mark's mother remarried, though," Margaret said. "We both grew up in Shepparton. Mark's father died in the war – World War 2," she clarified. "I'm not sure which campaign he was in, but Mark was born after he shipped out, so father and son never met. I often wondered if that was why his mother was as protective of Mark as she was. I guess I shouldn't speak ill of the woman. She was a single mother at a time when single mothers were looked down on. She had an on-again-off-again relationship with Mark's father's best friend while Mark was growing up. They got married not long after Mark moved to Melbourne to get his teaching degree.

"I don't think she was the sort of person who could live on her own. Mark's stepfather had around a hundred acres in the middle of nowhere, and she moved out there with him. I couldn't even tell you what they did with the land. The few times we visited, they made it very clear they didn't like me, and I was happy every time that place was in the rearview mirror again. His stepfather was weird; in fact, his whole family was weird. Not very bright, but full of opinions. And if you didn't agree with those opinions, well, let's just say it wasn't pleasant."

Samantha was just about to ask Margaret for the address of the property, when Toni put her hand on her forearm and shook her head slightly.

"Do you have photos of the property?" Toni asked, pointing to the photo album.

"Well, now you're asking something," Margaret said. She sat and thought for a minute, before turning the photo album back to face herself. "I'm pretty sure there are some in here, taken when we visited one Christmas." She smiled wryly at Toni and Samantha. "It's been a long time since I walked down memory lane with these photos. I don't do it very often. These are mostly memories I'd rather forget. Although the times weren't all bad, I suppose."

She turned page after page, until finally stopping at a photo of an old weatherboard house with several people sitting on the verandah scowling at the camera. She tapped a fingertip on it. "This is it. Happy looking bunch, aren't they?"

"Would you mind if I have a closer look?" Toni asked.

Margaret pulled the photo out of the album and gave it to Toni. Toni studied it, then turned it over. A date, several names, and an address had been written in blue biro on the back. Toni passed the photo to Samantha.

"Which one is Mark's mother?" Samantha asked Margaret, distracting her so Toni could jot the address down in her notebook without being too obvious about it.

Margaret pointed to a stern woman sitting in a rocking chair. Her long dark hair, streaked with grey, was braided into a single braid and pulled forward over her shoulder. Her mouth was a thin line that looked like it had lost the ability to smile, if indeed it had ever been able to. Maybe she was looking into the sun, but Samantha thought the woman's narrowed eyes were studying the person on the other side of the camera, boring directly into his or her soul and keeping notes on what she saw there.

Samantha shivered involuntarily, then handed the photo back. Margaret slotted it back into place in the album.

"I feel like Mark would have sold the property if he did inherit it," Margaret mused, turning the page and showing them a couple more photos.

In one, an old wooden barn leaned precariously to the left. It looked like it would take only the slightest touch for it to collapse into a heap. The trees near it also leaned in the same direction, as if the wind had bullied them, holding them down as they struggled to grow.

Another photo showed a paddock of long grass behind a barbed wire fence. Two horses and a handful of kangaroos grazed peacefully, locked in time in the photo for all eternity.

"History was his passion. He was never interested in farming, and he didn't like his stepfather or his stepbrothers. He told me once that, when he was a kid, he was scared of them. To be honest, he was still scared of his stepfather as an adult. He certainly wouldn't stand up to him, or his mother, even when they treated me like something that needed to be scraped off your shoe before you tracked it through the house.

"When he was growing up, Mark and his mother used to sometimes stay there on weekends and during school holidays. This was before they married, before Mark left for Melbourne. Mark said he always locked his bedroom door whenever he stayed there, even though it used to drive his mother mad when she'd go to wake him in the mornings."

Margaret seemed lost in her memories as she flipped through a few more pages of the photo album. "I do hope he's OK," she murmured to herself.

Toni and Samantha looked at each other, a silent signal passing between them. Toni closed her notebook and slipped it and her pen back into her bag. They both stood up.

"Thank you, Margaret," Toni said. "Thank you for being so honest with us and telling us your story. I'm sure it must have been hard for you, dredging up these memories after all this time."

Margaret remained seated for a few seconds, before she closed the photo album and stood up. She smiled at them both. "Thank you for listening to me. It's been surprisingly cathartic, telling someone the real truth of what happened. I probably should have done it a long time ago."

"Thank you for the tea and biscuits," Samantha said. "They were delicious."

"You're quite welcome, both of you," Margaret said. She pulled the chair she'd been sitting in out of the way so they could get by.

They followed her down the dark hallway, back to the front door. They all exchanged pleasantries again, and Margaret watched them from the doorway until they were about to get into Toni's car. Then, she waved and closed the door, disappearing back into her own life.

"That's got to be where he's holding her," Samantha said, sliding into the front passenger seat. She pulled the seatbelt across. "That's where we go next."

36

Options

Thu, 29 March 1984 – Samantha

THEY SAT OUTSIDE MARGARET'S house for a few minutes, discussing their options. Toni wanted to call Detective White and let him know what they'd discovered. Samantha wanted to drive directly to the address Toni had written in her notebook.

"We have to let the police know," Toni reasoned. "We don't even know exactly where this property is."

"I don't recognise the property name, Cloudridge, but it's got to be close to Miranda Springs," Samantha said, urgently. Once again, she missed the convenience of a mobile phone, being able to put a destination in and have instant directions. "The fact that he has a house in town but keeps coming and going, means it can't be that far away. Just head in that direction and we'll buy a road atlas or a map on the way."

Toni started the car, then turned to Samantha. "Why would he have a house in town if his property isn't that far away, though? That doesn't make sense to me."

Samantha shrugged. "Maybe he stays in town during the week because it's close to the school? If the property is an hour, an hour and a half drive away, maybe he doesn't want to drive that far to and from every day?"

"A lot of people have a longer commute than that," Toni mused. She sat there thinking.

"Or maybe he doesn't want anyone to know about this property," Samantha said. "Doesn't want random people dropping in at random times and finding random children there."

Toni nodded, then thought of something else. "Why didn't your dad know about this property? He thought Beresford moved to Miranda Springs in the last couple of years. It sounds as if Beresford's stepfather owned it for years, so he might be considered a local, if it is near Miranda Springs. I'd think your dad would know if the Beresfords had been around the area for so long."

"I don't know," Samantha conceded. She stared out the window at Margaret Watford's house. Something jogged her memory, and she clicked her fingers. "She said his mother remarried, so his stepfather would have had a different name. That's why Dad wouldn't have known or connected Beresford with his stepfather's property."

Toni looked at her and scrambled out of the car, leaving it running. She ran back to Margaret's front door and knocked. Samantha watched them talk to each other. Margaret closed her door again and Toni ran back to the car, sliding smoothly into the driver's seat.

"Anderson," she said, breathing deeply. "The stepfather's name was Anderson."

"Doesn't sound familiar," Samantha said, shaking her head and frowning. "But I'm not an expert on local families."

"We have to at least go back to my place and pick up my notes," Toni said, pulling out from the kerb. "I'll call Detective White from there and fill him in. In all good conscience, I can't not let him know. His people are closer, anyway, and could get there well before us. Not to mention how dangerous this might be."

"If he takes it seriously," Samantha said, not at all sure that he would.

Toni pulled into the driveway of a small red brick house. Samantha wasn't sure what suburb they were in, but she thought it was inner west Melbourne, so maybe Footscray or somewhere bordering that.

The house was a little rundown, the lawn needed mowing, and there wasn't really any garden to speak of. It was completely opposite to Margaret Watford's tidy place and there was an air of neglect hanging over it, as if the occupant either didn't care or wasn't there enough to bother with regular cleaning or maintenance.

Toni turned the car off, and got out, not bothering to close the car door. A mid-sized black and white speckled dog, of no obvious breed, pushed through the bent backyard gate. It bounced happily beside Toni who patted it as she walked quickly along the cracked concrete path to the front door.

Samantha struggled for a second with her seatbelt, then got out of the car and followed Toni.

The front door was already unlocked. Toni held the door open, waiting for Samantha, and the dog slipped inside before them.

Just inside the door was a small wooden telephone seat, a type of vintage furniture Samantha hadn't seen in a very long time. It had a cushioned seat on one end, and a drawer and table on the other. On the table sat a white bowl and a chunky ivory-coloured rotary telephone.

Toni tossed her keys into the bowl and picked up the phone receiver. She dug Detective White's business card out of her pocket and dialled. She smiled at the dog, who was sitting by her leg looking lovingly up at her.

"Come on, come on," she said, returning her attention to the phone. She slammed the receiver back down. "No one's answering."

"Everything all right, love," an older woman asked, appearing at the end of the hallway. She was almost the spitting image of Toni, just twenty or so years older.

"Yeah, Mum," Toni said, turning to her. She pointed her thumb over her shoulder at Samantha. "This is Samantha. I'll be away again for a few days. Can you please give us a hand with some boxes?"

Samantha was surprised to learn that Toni lived with her mother. For some reason, she'd assumed Toni lived on her own.

"It's nice to meet you, Samantha," Toni's mother said, her eyes crinkling at the corners as she smiled. "Of course I can help."

The three of them loaded boxes of paper from the garage into the boot and back seat of the old Toyota. The dog followed Toni in and out of the garage a couple of times, but lost interest when it realised that she was not going to play. It disappeared around the back of the house before they were finished.

When the last box was loaded, they went back into the house and Toni retrieved a road atlas from her room. When she got to the front door, she tried phoning Detective White again, but there was still no answer.

She looked at Samantha. "I guess we try to contact him again somewhere along the way."

Samantha nodded, eager to be going.

Toni's mother followed them out to the car and Toni kissed her on the cheek and hugged her. "Thanks, Mum. I'm not sure how long I'll be this time, but I'll call you."

Toni's mother smiled and waved as they backed out into the street. Toni beeped the horn once and the dog barrelled around the corner of the house. It barked as it chased the car partway down the street before giving up and trotting home, looking very pleased with itself.

"I suppose your magic future phone would have directed us straight to Cloudridge, since it knows everything with the push of a button," Toni said, trying to keep her eyes on the road and fumble a cassette tape into the car's player at the same time.

"Yes, it would." Samantha held onto her seat with one hand and the road atlas in her lap with the other. "And you wouldn't need cassette tapes. You'd have unlimited music on your phone, and you could play it wirelessly through your car stereo. And you could have phoned Detective White while you drive, although you'd need a hands-free kit for that to be legal."

Toni glanced down at the tape player, pushed the cassette in with a click, and the car drifted towards the gravel on the side of the road. She yanked the wheel to get the car back into the middle of the lane and Cindi Lauper started singing loudly about how girls just want to have fun.

"I'm looking forward to your future," Toni said, glancing at Samantha, then back at the road. "It sounds like it has a lot going for it."

"Yeah, well, there's good stuff and there's bad stuff," Samantha said, letting go of the seat and staring at the road atlas in her lap.

"There always is, isn't there?" Toni commented as she pulled into a small service station on the outskirts of Melbourne. The sun was setting in the distance, making the shadows grow longer and the light dimmer.

Toni topped up the petrol and, when she emerged from paying for the fuel, she had an armful of potato chips and chocolate bars. She dumped them on the back seat, then headed to the payphone to ring Detective White again.

While she did this, Samantha switched the internal light on in the car and studied the road atlas. It looked like Cloudridge was about an hour and a half drive east from Miranda Springs, and about two hours from where they were now. The property itself wasn't shown on the map, but they had the road name, and she could deduce approximately where it was from the closest major highway. Once they turned off the highway, they'd have to drive through some hilly, forested country, through a small town that was most likely just a grouping of a few houses, then over some dirt roads. She just hoped the property would have its name on the driveway, otherwise they'd be guessing at which driveway to take.

"Still no luck," Toni said, getting back in the car. "I don't understand why Detective White gives out this number if no one's going to answer it." She sighed and looked at Samantha. "Worked out where we're going?"

Samantha didn't acknowledge her for a moment as she continued to tear small strips of paper from a notebook, bookmarking the route over several of the pages of the map. Once she was done, Toni took the road atlas and flipped backwards and forwards across the pages, following the planned route with her fingertip.

"We need to get going," Samantha said, taking the road atlas back. "It's already getting late, and dark. We need to get Suzanna out of there sooner rather than later."

Hang in there, Suze, she thought, playing with the bracelet on her wrist. She projected her thoughts outward, hoping they would somehow cross the barrier between her universe and Suzanna's. *I'm coming to get you.*

37

Chase

Thu, 29 March 1984 – Samantha

AROUND 10 PM, SAMANTHA admitted they were lost. She wasn't sure when they'd taken a wrong turn, but they'd been backtracking and trying different roads now for at least an hour and hadn't come across any more road signs that would help pinpoint where they were on the map.

They were currently on a steep single lane dirt road, surrounded by thick forest on both sides. The road snaked, twisting left and right around sharp bends. On the left side of the road, the ground fell sharply away. On the right, the trees marched steadily uphill reaching for the sky. They hadn't seen any sign of civilization for at least an hour. Nothing looked familiar and it didn't help that the left headlight of the old Toyota had flickered out about half an hour ago as they drove across some particularly rough corrugations on the road.

"We need to get back to that town – Stonecastle Creek – and work out exactly where we are," Toni said, stopping the car. "We're not helping anyone by driving around half-blind in the dark."

"OK, what do we do?" Samantha asked, turning the interior light on. She'd been using a small torch she'd found in the glovebox to try to follow the map, but the batteries were almost dead and having to switch back and forth between the pages of the atlas had made the route more difficult to follow.

Toni leaned over and studied the map for a few minutes. She pointed at a dotted line that indicated a dirt road. "I think we're somewhere along here. We shouldn't have taken that last turn. We head back there and keep backtracking until we get back to that town. I think that's where we took a wrong turn. Maybe we can knock on a door and get directions from there."

Samantha switched off the interior light while Toni turned the car around. What should have been a three-point turn ended up more like a six-point turn on the narrow road. As they were heading back the way they'd come, heavy droplets of rain started to plunk onto the windscreen, becoming a torrent in a short time.

Toni sighed. "Of course, what else should I expect? Someone up there's not making this easy for us."

She turned the windscreen wipers on, but they worked reluctantly, only occasionally thumping up and back, and definitely not as a team. She leaned forward, trying to gauge where the edges of the road were so she could keep the car in the middle.

She glanced across at Samantha, then back to the road as a patch of sticky mud grabbed the tyres and tried to pull the car to the left. "You said you died in 2024. How did you die and how did you end up back here in 1984 as a fourteen-year-old again?"

"I thought you said you wouldn't believe me if I told you that," Samantha said, staring listlessly out the window at the dark. Her whole body was telling her to just give up. After all, it was what she was good at. The thought of throwing up her hands and walking away felt comfortable and familiar. She tried to quash the depression by thinking of Suzanna and the last time she'd seen her. She told herself she wouldn't be giving up on herself, but on Suzanna, which was out of the question.

"Indulge me," Toni said, fighting the wheel again. "Tell me a story to keep me focussed."

"What do you believe happens when you die?" Samantha asked, turning to watch Toni.

Toni blinked and thought for a second. "I really don't know. My parents belong to the Anglican Church, so my brother and I were brought up the same way. We went to Sunday School every week, observed all the appropriate religious rituals and listened to bible stories. Mum believes in Heaven and Hell. I'm not so sure. I guess I'm inclined to hedge my bets and be good, just in case."

"Interesting," said Samantha. "To answer your question, I don't know exactly how I died and I don't think it matters that much. Dead is dead."

"Did you just not remember or is your death something that gets wiped from your mind after you're gone?" mused Toni. "But obviously death wasn't the end for you if you're back here now?"

"The last thing I remember was sitting in my mother's house all alone after her funeral. Everyone I ever cared about was gone. Then I woke up on a train. The Ash Train."

"A train? That's weird."

"You're telling me. I didn't know what was going on and no one else in the carriage would tell me. I found out later that if you've only lived one life, you don't know what the Ash Train is when you wake up there."

"That implies you can live more than one life. That implies reincarnation."

"Yes. It turns out, when you die, you end up on the Ash Train. You're given two chances at judgement in the first carriage. I don't know if the questions the Ash Man asks are the same for everyone. I think they're tailored to each individual, but I don't know that for sure."

"So, this Ash Man ... he judges your life?"

"Yes and no. Technically, you judge yourself. He just asks the questions and has the power to turn you into a pile of ash if you're not facing the real truth and taking responsibility for your life and how you lived. If you pass the Ash Man, you move onto the second carriage. There you choose rebirth or eternal afterlife. If you choose rebirth, you start a new life from scratch, with no memories of any previous lives. If you choose afterlife, well, what you get depends on what you believe should be your eternity. It could come from your religion – so Heaven or Hell or something in between – or something else, like complete nothingness."

They drove in silence for a while, both thinking about Samantha's story.

"So, how did you..." Toni started to ask, but she suddenly swung the car sideways left, turning onto a narrow bitumen road and stopping. "I think this is the way back to the town. What about you? What do you think?"

"I guess," said Samantha. "I'm obviously crap at navigation, so trust your gut. If you think we go this way, then go this way."

Toni pushed Cindi Lauper back into the cassette player and hummed along to the songs as they drove. About thirty minutes later, the sign for Stonecastle Creek loomed out of the dark like a phantom. The town was just a small gathering of houses on each side of the road, more a hamlet than a town.

Toni parked in front of a tiny community hall. The rain had eased off, and they both got out and stretched their backs and legs. Even though it was so late, the house across the road had an outside light on.

"Wait here. I'll go and ask for directions," Toni said.

She was just about to step onto the road, when a pair of headlights on high beam appeared over a small rise, lighting up the road. Toni stepped backwards as the car barrelled past, not slowing down at all.

"HEY!" Samantha yelled. She grabbed Toni's sleeve. "That's him. That's Beresford!"

"Are you sure?" Toni questioned. "How can you tell? I couldn't see anything. The lights blinded me."

"I know his car and that was definitely it. I don't know if he saw me, but we need to follow him," Samantha said, running back to her side of the car.

Samantha automatically pulled her seatbelt on, while Toni slipped into the driver's seat and cranked the engine.

They backed out onto the road and headed back the way they'd just come from. Toni floored the accelerator, making the Toyota's fan belt scream as if it was being murdered. The rain started falling again, although it was more of a drizzle this time. Just enough to keep everything damp and to need to ask the clunky windscreen wipers to reluctantly do their job again.

Samantha thought they were going to lose him. He'd been moving pretty fast through the small town, and he sped up once he was through it. He obviously knew the roads around here better than they did, and a mantra went through Samantha's head, over and over. *I'm coming, Suze. Just hold tight.*

"What are we going to do when we catch him? What's the plan?" Toni asked as they flew down the wet road. The panels of the old Toyota sounded like they were going to drop off when the wheels clanked across some major potholes.

"We'll just have to wing it," Samantha said, leaning forward to try to spot Mr Beresford's car. "We just need to catch him first."

About twenty minutes later, she spotted the Holden Commodore near the end of the bitumen road and saw him turn right. "There," she yelled, pointing. "He's on the dirt road we were just on."

The back wheels of the Toyota slid precariously on the muddy dirt road as Toni yanked the wheel to the right at the end of the bitumen, barely slowing down. The car fishtailed wildly and she overcompensated, struggling to make it go straight again. The tyres slipped and struggled with the muddy road but eventually the car jolted forward again as it regained its grip.

The Commodore easily pulled away from them, and they lost sight of it as the road started to wind up the hill ahead. Toni kept her foot to the floor and flung the Toyota wildly around the bends. Samantha held on to her seatbelt with one hand and put her other hand on the dashboard to steady herself. *Please, don't let anyone else be coming the other way*, she thought.

Samantha was vaguely aware of a dark shadow sitting unmoving as they passed an almost invisible driveway on the left. High beam headlights suddenly sprang to life and a car pulled out onto the road behind them, quickly gaining on them.

Samantha twisted around in her seat. "It's Beresford!"

"He must have seen us following, and hid and waited," Toni said. She eased her foot off the accelerator a bit, holding one hand up to shield her eyes from the blinding light in the rearview mirror.

But the Commodore did not slow down. Toni and Samantha were flung forward as the Commodore slammed into the back of the Toyota. Samantha's seatbelt locked in place, but Toni, who wasn't wearing her seatbelt, smacked her nose on the steering wheel.

"I think I broke my nose," she said, sitting back up with blood gushing down over her mouth and chin.

The Toyota jolted forward again as the Commodore rammed them a second time.

Toni put her foot down again, but the car behind easily matched their speed. She navigated successfully around a few more bends, then, as they headed into a sharper one, the Commodore hit them again, slightly off to the side and with more force. Toni's hands came off the wheel for a second and the Toyota spun sideways out of control on the wet road. The Commodore slammed into their side, and Samantha felt the Toyota tip and flip as they careened over the left edge of the road. The car rolled several times down the hill before coming to rest the right way up, the driver's side of the car bent around a tree.

38

Keep Going

Fri, 30 March 1984 – Samantha

SAMANTHA WASN'T SURE IF she lost consciousness, but she suddenly became aware of the grinding, clanking noise of the windscreen wipers, and the plink-plink of dripping water. Her chest ached where the seatbelt crossed it, her shoulders were stiff, and her neck hurt like she'd slept on it wrong. Her tongue stung and she tasted the iron tang of blood as she swallowed, trying to soothe her parched throat.

"Toni?" she croaked. There was no answer. "Toni?"

It was pitch black, and she couldn't see a thing. She put her hand up and felt the roof of the car just centimetres above the top of her head now.

She fought with the seatbelt but couldn't get it to unlatch. Feeling in front of her, she hit the glove box with her fist, and it dropped open onto her knees. She pulled out the torch she'd been using earlier to read the maps and switched it on. The feeble light put out by the dying batteries was just enough to see that the driver's seat was empty – Toni wasn't there – and that side of the car was bent around a large tree trunk. Toni hadn't been wearing her seatbelt, so Samantha assumed she'd been thrown out as the car rolled.

She reached as far into the glove box as she could and rummaged around until she found the small penknife she'd seen in there earlier. She used it to saw at the seatbelt strap across her chest until the fibres gave way and she fell forward. She pulled her legs up, through the lap strap, and fought to open her door, but it wouldn't budge. Lying on her back, she brought her legs up, and kicked and kicked at the twisted door until it squealed open enough for her to get out.

"TONI!" she called, sweeping the torch from side to side, but there was barely enough light to see her own feet, let alone someone else. She was disoriented at first, and she stood for a second trying to get the fog in her mind to disperse. She realised they'd rolled down the hill, so she started heading up the slope, following the path of destruction.

The Toyota's boot had come open as the car rolled, liberating the boxes they'd stowed in there back in Melbourne. Paper was strewn like giant confetti across the ground and Samantha almost tripped over the car's front bumper, which had given up its feeble grip halfway down the hill.

When she found Toni, Toni was standing upright in front of a tree looking back up the slope towards the road.

"You scared me," Samantha said, moving closer. "I thought you were hurt. Why didn't you answer me?"

The torchlight flickered, threatening to go out, but it was enough to illuminate the branch that skewered Toni's chest and the blood running down her legs, pooling beneath her. All the fight went out of Samantha.

"Oh my god, oh my god, Toni, I'm so sorry for getting you into this," Samantha sobbed, leaning forward, her hands fluttering uselessly like they wanted to do something, but they didn't know what. She shakily felt for a pulse but couldn't find one. Her self-hatred rose up again. "I'm so fucking useless. Not only did I not save Suzanna, but I killed you, too. I might as well just give up now. I'm no good to anyone. I don't know why I thought I could make a difference to anything. Oh god,

I'm so tired. Tired of everything going wrong all the time. Tired of trying and trying and just spinning my wheels, going nowhere. Fuck this! Fuck the Ash Train! Fuck everything!"

She collapsed onto the wet ground next to Toni's body and wept. Wept for Suzanna, wept for Toni, wept for herself, for being such a waste of space. She didn't deserve to live while all these people who were better than her died. What had made her think she could make a difference a second time around?

At some point, she lay down, curled up into a small ball, not caring about the dampness seeping into her clothing. She was bone-crushingly tired, and she fell asleep. At first, she slept like the dead. No dreams, just nothingness that she wasn't aware of.

"Get up!" Suzanna berated her. "You promised you wouldn't give up on me!"

"Let me sleep," Samantha mumbled. "I'm so tired."

"No," Suzanna said firmly. "You need to keep going. You're so close."

"I can't, I'm too tired," Samantha said, rolling onto her back.

"Don't let me have died for nothing!" Toni admonished, flicking water at Samantha's face.

Samantha gave in, the dream voices fading as she opened her eyes. She was shivering and a drop of cold water splashed onto her forehead, and another. She tried to work out where she was.

She looked up and, in the dim morning light, saw Toni's white face and the tree branch poking through her chest like the monster in *Alien* frozen in time. The events of the night came flooding back. She scrambled to her feet and backed away from Toni's body.

She imagined that she saw Toni's eyes flicker open and thought she heard her hiss, repeating what she'd said in her dream. "This is not about you, Samantha. Don't let me have died for nothing. Now get going!"

She blinked but Toni was still in the same position, still pinned to the tree, still dead, not in a state to be able to say anything. Still, the message was clear.

Samantha turned and scrambled up the hill back to the dirt road. She looked left, then right, trying to decide which way to go. Opposite where their car had left the road, she saw a narrow dirt road, almost hidden among the foliage. There was no road sign, no property signs, just a couple of mailboxes.

Remembering the maps she'd pored over yesterday, she was pretty sure this wasn't the road to Cloudridge, but she headed along the road, anyway. It first went up through the trees, then angled down and around, out of the forest, and came out into a valley of brown grass.

Just past the tree line, she came across an old car with rusted holes in some of the panels. It was parked at the junction of the first driveway and the road. She knew that, even though they were not old enough to have a licence, some of the farm kids she'd gone to school with drove old cars like this from their property to the main road to catch the school bus.

The door wasn't locked – why would you bother in a such a remote place – so she opened it and got in. There were no keys, but there was a screwdriver jammed into the ignition. She turned it, and the car jerked roughly into life. The engine missed a few beats, so she revved it a few times, which smoothed it out. She was grateful that she'd learned to drive a manual car, when the world seemed to be moving more towards automatics. It had been a little while since she'd driven, though, and she winced at the crunching noise of the gears as she tried to coordinate the clutch and the accelerator. Luckily, the skill came back quickly as she headed out onto the road.

She drove back up to the main road and turned right to continue up the hill in the direction they'd been heading last night. Mr Beresford had been heading this way, so they had been right when they'd thought they were wrong. There was only one set of tyre tracks on the dirt ahead of her. They had to be his.

As she drove, her mind wandered and she thought about what the psychic had told her. *Was that only a couple of days ago?* The woman had said it was risky to move fast without a plan, and she'd been right. They'd had no plan and now Toni was dead.

Tears threatened to spill, and she angrily dashed them away. She imagined Toni waking up on the Ash Train. She had no doubt that Toni would make it through to the second carriage and wondered what choice she would make.

She crested a hill and the forest on the right-hand side of the road grew sparser, until it petered out into paddocks of wiry brown and yellow grass stretching as far as she could see. Dots of brown and white showed this was sheep country. It looked to be an extension of the valley she'd seen earlier, where she'd got the car.

The tyre tracks she was following turned right at a crossroads, onto another unsignposted dirt road. About ten minutes down the road, the tyre tracks turned into a driveway on the left. A boxy mailbox had the name Anderson scrawled on it in what looked like black texta. A small blue and white sign, scratched and weather-worn, was wired onto the closed metal gate: Cloudridge.

She pulled up in front of the gate and let out a breath she hadn't even realised she was holding.

39

Hiding

Fri, 30 March 1984 – Suzanna

SUZANNA WAS HIDING IN the closet, behind a curtain of dresses. She'd broken another coat hanger and clutched it so hard her hands had turned white and were starting to cramp.

The last few days – at least she thought it had been days – Mr Beresford only come into the room a few times, bringing food on a tray, leaving it on the floor near the door and taking the previous one.

She hid behind the bed whenever she heard the key in the lock. She watched his face in the dressing table mirror, saw him frown and narrow his eyes as he looked at her reflection, both of them locking eyes. He would then tilt his head as if confused, but he didn't speak to her at all before he left again.

She'd been bored and spent most of her time sketching in the activity book. She drew her family: Mum, Dad, Samantha, even Arabella, and talked to them as if they were here with her. She drew some of her friends from school and had whole conversations with them. About what? She had no idea. She just rambled.

Other pages in the activity book now held nightmare pictures of monsters and darkness and blood ... so much blood. She wasn't sure why; that was just what came out sometimes when her mind wandered too far into the abyss.

When she wasn't drawing, she slept. She only slept lightly, though, ready to wake at an instant, jumping at any creak or groan as the house settled through outside temperature changes. She was petrified of what he might do to her if her eyes were closed for too long.

Occasionally, after she ate, she'd walk around the whole room, checking the door, which was always locked, and pushing on the corrugated iron behind the empty window frame and curtain. Once she tried to kick the iron off, but it didn't budge. She didn't even make a dent, just hurt her foot. She'd expected Mr Beresford to come in at the first kick, yelling at her to stop, but he didn't, which made her think he sometimes left the house. She wondered where he went. She kicked the iron a few more times, before giving up.

Then, last night – she thought it was night, that was what her body was telling her – she'd heard him stomping around the house. He'd hit the wall once and swore. A couple of times, he'd paused outside her room, but he hadn't come in.

Then, a little while ago – she thought it was morning again – she'd heard him stop again outside her door. She stood by the door and put her ear against it. He was breathing heavily and muttering to himself. They both stood like that for quite some time before the key rattled in the lock. This time, she bolted and hid in the closet, pulling the dresses in front of her like a curtain.

She heard him walk into the room and close the door behind himself. She held her breath as if he'd be able to hear her breathing even behind the closet door and the dresses.

"Where are you?" he called. "I think I've made a mistake. I believe you've been telling me the truth, Suzanna. Let me take you home. Let me correct my mistake."

Suzanna stayed quiet. She didn't believe him. She'd seen what he did with his 'mistakes'.

She heard him slam open the bathroom door, making it bounce off the doorstop. She considered running and trying to get out of the room, but he was too quick. She heard him walk over to the bed and she assumed he was checking under it. He sighed in frustration.

The closet door suddenly flung open, and he reached in, pulling her out by the arm. She dropped the broken coat hanger and scratched at his arms, drawing blood in a couple of places.

"Let me go!" she screamed, slapping at the hand he had clamped around her upper arm.

Suddenly, he stopped moving and cocked his head, listening to something. He pushed her onto the bed and practically ran to the door, slamming and locking it as he left.

A car horn started blaring outside. Someone was here!

40

Found

SAMANTHA LEFT THE FRONT gate open and drove towards the house. She could see it at the end of the short driveway. It was definitely the old weatherboard place she'd seen in Margaret's photos.

Mr Beresford's car was parked on a dirt patch in front of the house, about where the photographer must have been standing to take Margaret's photo. The rocking chair his mother had been sitting on was in the same place as in the photo, to the left of the front door. Even without her on it, the chair looked like it disapproved of everything it could see. The steps and some of the floorboards of the verandah were twisted and warped. The doorframe and window frames were weatherworn and grey. The whole place looked solid but shabby, in need of a good paint and a lot of maintenance.

The falling-down shed she'd seen in the photos was to the right of the house, but it had finally succumbed to gravity and was now just a tumbled heap of weathered grey boards. The wind-swept trees from the photo still stood, although they were little more than skeletal branches now. Next to the shed pile were some wood and metal sheep yards that must have been just out of shot when the photo had been taken. They looked like they hadn't been used for a very long time.

Samantha stopped the car behind Beresford's, her front bumper almost touching his back bumper. She sat for a second. She still had no plan. Without thinking, she leaned on the horn.

Casper bolted around the side of the house and jumped up on the car door, yipping happily.

A couple of seconds later, Mr Beresford stepped out of the house onto the verandah. He left the front door slightly ajar, but the screen door wheezed slowly closed behind him, not quite shutting completely. He moved to stand near the top step, shading his eyes from the glare of the sun as it rose over the rim of the valley behind her.

She let up on the horn and got out of the car, not taking her eyes off him. She ignored Casper who was now wriggling around her legs, trying to get her attention.

They stood there staring each other down for what felt, to Samantha, like an eternity. Her universe seemed to slow right down, everything moving at a snail's pace including the blood and adrenaline pumping through her body and the thoughts crowding her mind.

Suddenly, Suzanna's voice pierced the silence. "HELP ME! PLEASE, HELP ME! I WANT TO GO HOME!"

Samantha jerked into action and started to run towards the house, almost tripping over Casper who thought she was playing. "I'M HERE, SUZE," she yelled.

Mr Beresford ran down the steps and, at the bottom, grabbed Samantha's wrist as she tried to push past him. He squeezed tightly as confusion spread across his face, before it morphed into a look of vindication.

"I knew it," he said, pulling her close so they were almost nose to nose. "I did make a mistake, dammit."

She twisted her wrist so that it pushed against his thumb – the weak point their self-defence instructor had taught them about – and forced him to relinquish his grip. In her fifty-four years, that was the one thing she'd always remembered from those lessons … and used often against abusive exes, cops, and anyone else who grabbed her like that.

She brought both hands up and shoved his chest hard, making him stumble backwards off balance. Casper was right behind his legs, and he fell over him, landing on his back. Casper yelped and ran off around the side of the house.

She ran up the steps and yanked the screen door open. "WHERE ARE YOU, SUZE?"

"SAMANTHA?" Suzanna yelled back, banging on the bedroom door. "I'M IN A BEDROOM NEAR THE BACK OF THE HOUSE."

Samantha ran through the archway, into the lounge room. She turned right into a hallway, then left, running down to the end to a closed door. She tried to turn the handle. It jiggled but wouldn't move. She rammed her shoulder into the locked door, but the door wouldn't budge. She ignored the pain that flared in her shoulder as the move aggravated the damage caused by Toni's car rolling down the hill. She leaned back and kicked at the door just below the handle, and again, but it still wouldn't budge. *It looked so easy in the movies.*

She'd forgotten about Mr Beresford in her rush to get to Suzanna, and she wasn't prepared for the huge shove he gave her. She slammed into the wall, her head bouncing off it and she collapsed onto the floor. Her head spun as her mind tried to make sense of what had just happened.

He grabbed her by the hair and yanked her to her feet. She put her hands up to protect herself and felt a chunk of hair from the top of her head rip out of her scalp. He pushed her backwards into the wall again and she felt a stinging slap across her right cheek.

"STOP! STOP, NOW!" Mr Beresford yelled, banging the back of her head into the wall again and again.

He finally let go of her and started to turn away, before suddenly spinning back and slamming his fist into the wall beside her head, leaving a hole in the plaster.

"Now look what you made me do," he said, throwing his hands up, half turning away again before turning back and leaning in to glare at her.

"What's going on?" Suzanna called, banging on the other side of the door with her fists and kicking it with her feet. "Don't you hurt my sister, you bastard!"

"Shut up. Shut up. Let me think, why won't you?" Mr Beresford banged his fist several times on the door, emphasising each phrase. He ran his hands through his hair and stared at Samantha.

Samantha hated the whimpering sound that came from her throat, but she couldn't help it as she cowered away from him. She remembered this noise well – and this feeling – from her past life, when boyfriends would come home drunk, spoiling for a fight. They'd tell her she was weak, especially if she cried, and that this was all her fault. She'd quickly learnt to agree and to suppress the tears until later. But she always *had* been weak, so she'd always figured it wasn't much of a stretch.

"Please," Samantha said in a rush, holding out her hands in a placating gesture. She was breathing heavily and trying to think through the nausea and dizziness that was flooding her body. "Please let Suzanna go. You can have me. I'm the one you want. Please, let her go. I'll do anything you say."

He stood there glaring at her for a few more seconds before grabbing her hair on the top of her head again. She put her hands over his, trying to prevent any more hair being ripped out. He dragged her to the locked door and held her firmly as he fumbled in his pocket for the key. He dropped it once, forcing her to bend down with him when he leaned down to pick it up.

He unlocked the door, pushed it open, and shoved her inside. She stumbled and fell, knocking some books off a bookshelf, as he pulled the door closed again. She heard the key turn and heard him muttering to himself as he walked away. "A mistake. A mistake. Another damn mistake."

"Samantha?" Suzanna whispered, kneeling by her sister.

Suzanna helped Samantha up and they threw their arms around each other. They stood there crying into each other's shoulder for what seemed like a very long time. After a while, they moved to sit side-by-side on the edge of the bed holding hands.

"Are you alright?" Suzanna asked, studying Samantha's face. Her hand hovered but didn't touch her sister's red cheek and the bruising that was starting to appear around her right eye.

"I'm fine," Samantha said, feeling her stinging scalp where the hair had been ripped out. She looked at the dark circles around Suzanna's eyes and the bruise on her cheek. "Are you alright? What's he done to you?"

"I'm OK," Suzanna said and they both sat in silence again just looking at each other, grateful to be together again.

After a while, Samantha looked around at the room. "Well, she was right," she said. She tried to smile, but her lips wouldn't move in the right direction.

"Who was right?" Suzanna asked.

"The psychic," Samantha said with a sigh. "She said she saw pink and that you were not nearby, but not too far away. We're about an hour and a half from Miranda Springs."

"What's going on, Sammie," Suzanna asked, standing up and facing her sister. "Where are the police? Where's Dad, Mum? They are coming, aren't they? You didn't come here alone? Please, tell me you didn't come here alone."

Samantha didn't understand where all the tears were coming from as more started to roll down her cheeks when she thought of Toni. Toni, all alone out there in the forest. Toni, who didn't deserve any of this, who should never have been a part of this.

"I'm such a fuck up," she whispered. "I didn't start out alone, but..."

She couldn't continue and Suzanna pulled her face into her shoulder and held her while she cried until she was empty again.

41

Confession

Fri, 30 March 1984 – Samantha

THEY WERE STANDING IN the bathroom. Samantha winced as Suzanna dabbed a wet face washer over her eyes, cleaning off the tears and dirt and blood as gently as she could.

Samantha looked at herself in the mirror over the basin. Her ribs hurt when she took a deep breath. She lifted her shirt and her reflection displayed a massive purple bruise from her shoulder diagonally down to her hip, and across her stomach. *To be honest*, she thought, *this isn't the worst I've ever looked.*

"You're not a fuck up," Suzanna said, continuing their conversation from before.

"Yes, I am," Samantha replied, tucking her shirt in again. She sighed. "You don't know the half of it. I don't know why I ever thought I could make a difference. I was useless the first time, and twice as useless the second. If I was a pile of ashes, I couldn't hurt anyone else. That's what I should have chosen."

"I don't know what you mean," Suzanna said with a frown. She put the back of her hand on Samantha's forehead, checking for a temperature. "I'm worried you might have a concussion from him slamming your head into the wall like that."

They went back into the bedroom. Suzanna sat on the dressing table chair, while Samantha sat on the edge of the bed.

"You found the notes, didn't you?" Samantha asked.

"Yes," Suzanna replied. "They fell out of your bag when I knocked it onto the ground. I wasn't snooping, I promise. But you can't have honestly believed them? You're the smart one of the two of us. I thought they were a prank that someone was going to use to embarrass you in front of everyone, either at the party or at school."

Samantha looked down at her hands, then made herself look back at her sister's face. "I'm ashamed to say I did believe them. I really thought someone was finally seeing *me*. Seeing me for who I am. Before the notes, I felt so invisible, like people only saw me as a pale reflection of you. Just a sad imitation that would never be as good as the original. I tried to fool myself into believing that it didn't matter that everyone loved you and forgot about me. I'd just work hard and get a better job, make something of myself that would make them finally *have* to see me. But it did matter. And look at where it got us."

Suzanna moved to sit beside Samantha and put her arms around her. Samantha rested her head on Suzanna's shoulder.

"I'm so sorry you had to think like that," Suzanna said. "I'm such an idiot, such a bad sister. I should have known how you were feeling and I should have done something about it."

Samantha lifted her head and looked at her sister. "How did he make you go with him? I've always wondered that. You were always so strong, I couldn't work out how someone could snatch you up and disappear you like that."

"The last note said to meet him at the playground on the other side of the lake at 9 PM. Obviously, it was meant to get you on your own."

"I never saw that note," Samantha said, shaking her head. "I was waiting all night for him to contact me, either with a note or in person, but he never did. Then

Tina arrived and I forgot all about him." She suddenly remembered something. "Hang on, he spoke to me earlier when I was with Mum. He picked my bag up off the ground. He must have slipped the note in there then."

"I thought it was a prank," Suzanna said, moving back to the dressing table chair. "I was just going to give 'your secret admirer' a piece of my mind. I actually wondered if it might have been one of my friends. I wouldn't put it past Catherine to do something like that, thinking it would be funny. She can be a real bitch, sometimes. But I didn't think I was in any danger. Anyway, I was sitting on the swing, and his dog ran up to me."

"Casper?"

"If that's his name, yes. The little white one. His lead was dragging behind him and Mr Beresford called out to me, asking me to grab it. He thought I was you and I didn't tell him I wasn't. Anyway, he ended up dropping the dog's lead again, and the dog ran off to the carpark. He asked if I could catch him, so I followed the dog to a car. Mr Beresford was right behind me, and I didn't even know until he grabbed me."

"Didn't you fight him?"

"Of course, I fought. I gave him a fantastic bloody nose, but he held my mouth and nose closed so I couldn't breathe, and I passed out. Next thing I knew, I woke up in this god-awful pink room."

Suzanna didn't tell Samantha about Mr Beresford changing her clothes while she was unconscious. That was something no one else needed to know right now.

Samantha went to say something, but Suzanna put up her hand. "OK, your turn. What day is it? How long have I been here?"

"It's Friday," Samantha said. "It's been nearly a week."

"Fill me in what happened after he took me," Suzanna said. "What happened to you? Why do you look like you've been through the wringer? Not all of those bruises are from him, are they? Tell me everything, right from the start."

"Well, that's the thing," Samantha said, looking down at her hands. "There are technically two starts. You're going to think I'm nuts."

"I won't think you're crazy, I promise," Suzanna said, shaking her head. "Come on, Sams, just tell me what's going on. Why are you here alone? Why are you here at all?"

Samantha took a deep breath which reminded her painfully of her injured ribs. She pushed Toni's memory away for the moment and started talking. It was like a floodgate had opened and all the words gushed and tumbled over each other as they forced their way out through the small opening.

As she was talking, she remembered how it had felt, doing this same thing with the Ash Man beside her, watching her life play out on the foggy screen outside the Ash Train window.

Samantha told Suzanna about the first time she went missing, how they never found her, not even a clue. How their family had barely it held together, everyone always conscious of the Suzanna-shaped hole in their lives. How Dad was the glue that tried to fix what was broken but the glue never really held for long. How Mum had never lost hope; how she always believed Suzanna was coming home. How her own life had spiralled out of control, how she'd given up, and given up, and given up. How she'd taken no responsibility for any of the crap she'd endured, any of the awful things she'd done just to get by.

She reached the Ash Train part of her story.

"So, you died? In 2024?" Suzanna interrupted. "How?"

"I don't remember. The Ash Man said he could show me, but I chose not to see it. It wouldn't have mattered anyway. After the initial shock, I realised I had nothing to live for anyway. Anyone I ever cared about was gone, so I might as well be gone, too."

"So, everyone ends up on this Ash Train when they die?"

"I assume so. At least, that was the implication."

"That's a hell of a lot of people. It doesn't sound very practical."

"Yeah, well, I just know what I experienced and what I was told."

Samantha told Suzanna about the second carriage and the choices she was given. "So, you see, this is the second time around for me. They said I could have one second chance. Only one. That if I couldn't do what I was trying to do, there would be no more chances."

"So, wait, wait," Suzanna said, holding up her hand. "So, last Saturday, on our birthday, you woke up as your fourteen-year-old self, knowing what was going to happen?" She looked thoughtful. "That's why you were clinging to me like a grass seed on a sock and acting so weird. Weirder than normal, anyway."

"Correct," Samantha confirmed. "I knew what was going to happen and nothing I did changed the outcome. I thought I was so clever that I could stop you from being taken and catch him at the same time. But I'm not clever. I should have realised that. You were still taken and I didn't stop anything."

"But you're here now," Suzanna said. "So, you did change things. You said the first time around, no one ever found me." She shuddered, thinking of the four mounds in the paddock and how it would feel to be the fifth. "How did you find me?"

When Samantha told her about the other missing children – Michelle Donovan, Isabelle Bradford, Allison Brooke, Audrey Lowe – Suzanna nodded and took a deep breath. She felt so sorry that no one had come to save any of them before they'd been declared 'mistakes'.

Suzanna kept nodding as Samantha explained what Margaret Watford had said. About the miscarriages, about Michelle, about his belief that his little girl was not dead.

"He told me that, too," she murmured. "He kept calling me Michelle and wanted me to call him Dad."

Samantha cried again when she told her sister about how he'd run Toni's car off the road, about how she'd woken up and found Toni, pale and dead.

"She sounds like a fantastic person, someone I would have liked," Suzanna said, leaning forward and holding Samantha's hand.

"You really would have," Samantha agreed through her tears. "She was tough, just like you. She was going to set the world on fire, trailblazing the way for girls like us. But instead that monster extinguished her flame."

When Samantha stopped talking, they both sat there in silence for a while. They could hear Mr Beresford roaming around the house, slamming doors and stomping his way from room to room. A couple of times he thumped his fist on their door, but he didn't come in.

"Does anyone know you're here?" Suzanna asked quietly. "Anyone at all?"

Samantha looked down at her hands in her lap. They reminded her of how the people had sat on the Ash Train, waiting their turn at judgement. Her shoulders slumped, all the fight and all the hope gone out of her.

"No," she whispered.

42

Together

SAMANTHA AND SUZANNA CURLED up together on the bed. After a while, Samantha fell asleep, but Suzanna lay awake, thinking about Samantha's story. It sounded incredible, like something out of a movie, but she didn't doubt her sister in the slightest. Samantha was smart, so if anyone could have worked out how to time travel, it was her.

It was weird to think of Samantha being fifty-four years old, though. That sounded so *old*, and Suzanna wondered if she would ever reach that age. And if she did, what would she be like? She hoped she wouldn't be as jaded and worn-down as Samantha seemed to be. She loved her twin, but she couldn't imagine living like that.

A sense of guilt, heavier than gravity, suddenly overwhelmed her, pressing her into the mattress. Samantha's life *had* turned out awful the first time around and it was her fault, Suzanna's. She realised now that she should have spoken to her sister about the notes, rather than storming off to be the hero coming to the rescue of the poor defenceless maiden.

She'd always underestimated Samantha, always thought that she wasn't tough. Now, she realised how wrong she was. How tough did you have to be to do the things Samantha said she'd done? How tough did you have to be to do the impossible and negotiate a second chance to right a wrong? *Pretty damn tough and pretty damn smart*, she thought with pride.

She thought about how, the first time around, Mr Beresford must have killed her and buried her next to those other girls: Michelle, Isabelle, Allison, Audrey. She allocated them a special place in her memory and told herself she would never forget their names and she'd make sure no one else forgot them, either. She wondered if he'd taken any more girls after her. *How many graves were in that paddock while Samantha lived her wretched life the first time around?*

How had he done it? Did he strangle them? Shoot them? Stab them? Drown them? Bury them alive? How long did it take to die? She found herself, not for the first time, struggling to breathe as imaginary dirt filled her nose and mouth, covered her eyes, pressed her body down, down, down into the ground.

Suzanna's own breathing slowed to match Samantha's regular rhythm, making her drowsy. She eventually fell asleep too, the warmth of her sister's body seeping into her own. The events of the day turned into muddled, confusing dreams.

When Suzanna awoke, she was alone on the bed. She sat up quickly, calling out for Samantha, irrationally scared that she'd dreamt her sister being here.

"I'm here," Samantha said, walking out of the bathroom.

"What time is it?" Suzanna asked with relief.

Samantha looked at her watch. "Almost 6:30 AM."

Suzanna leaned back against the headboard of the bed and adjusted the time on her own watch. She wound it up and felt an absurd burst of joy to see the hands ticking their way around and around the watch face again. "It's so good knowing the time again. It makes me feel a bit more human. A little less lost."

"I told you you should have got one with a battery," Samantha said. "That way you don't have to remember to wind it up all the time."

"But I like this one," Suzanna said defensively. "It was Grandpa's and it reminds me of him."

Samantha sat on the dressing table chair and picked up the activity book Suzanna had been drawing in. She flipped through it, stopping at the picture of the graves with the joined hands. She showed Suzanna. "I've seen this before."

Suzanna raised her eyebrows in an unspoken question.

"When I was on the bus to Melbourne, I fell asleep with a sketchbook on my lap. When I woke up, it was on the floor, but when I picked it up, the picture I assume I drew was almost identical to this. I don't remember drawing it, and I'm not good at it, like you."

"Must be that twin connection," Suzanna said with a smile.

"Oh, yeah, that reminds me," Samantha said. "I'm sorry but I had to use your concert fund money to buy my bus ticket. I'll pay you back as soon as I can."

"Don't worry about it," Suzanna said with a smile. The smile disappeared quickly, though, as the reality of their situation crashed back over her like a king tide. "How are we getting out of this, Sams? Where do we go from here? How do we make sure we get to that concert?"

"I'm not sure we *can* get out of this," Samantha replied, putting the activity book back on the dressing table. She looked at herself in the mirror, then at her sister's reflection. "Everything I've tried has just cascaded into worse and worse outcomes." Tears came to her eyes again. "Toni's dead because of me. If I'd listened to her and waited until we could talk to Detective White, we would have all been home safe now, having dinner and fighting over what to watch on TV. But, no, I needed to be the hero and now we're both trapped here with a madman and no way out."

Suzanna could almost see the darkness of her sister's depression surrounding her head, clouding her mind, telling her just to give up. Why bother when everything always went so wrong?

"Why are you blaming yourself?" Suzanna said. "I'm as much to blame, if not more. I should have talked to you, been a better sister. If *I* hadn't wanted to be the hero, none of this would have happened."

"That's not true," Samantha said, vehemently shaking her head. "Every single bit of this is my fault, both the first time and this second one. I thought I was so smart, Suzanna. But I'm not. I'm just a pathetic excuse for a human being. Don't you dare try to take the blame for this."

"Stop it, as someone recently told us," Suzanna said, standing up and moving to stand behind Samantha. She picked up the hairbrush, pulled her sister's hair back, and started to brush it, with long, slow strokes. She worked through some of the tangles, gently pulling them apart with her fingers. "We're both here now, and we're unstoppable together. We *have to* get out of this. I have a life to live, and you have a second life to live. Now, think. You're the smart one and you have a lot more life experience than me, old girl. Look around and think. What do you see that I don't?"

Samantha stood up and wandered around the room while Suzanna sat on the dressing table chair and watched. She stopped at the window frame and tested the iron sheet that was nailed on from the other side. It didn't move, didn't even bend, when she pushed on it. She didn't want to try kicking it, didn't want to risk Mr Beresford coming back. Her body had taken as much of a beating as it could handle for now.

She turned around and contemplated the rest of the room. She completely understood why Margaret Watford had said the pinkness of the room her husband had decorated made her feel sick, like she'd gorged on cake at a birthday party. The colour certainly didn't help her own nausea and she could almost feel the diabetes seeping into her skin every second she had her eyes open.

She'd left the light on in the bathroom, and a harsh light illuminated a rectangle of floor in front of the bathroom door. The glow-in-the-dark stars and planets sprinkled across the ceiling were fading, needing a recharge.

Her eyes roamed over the books that were still on the floor near the bookcase where they'd fallen when Mr Beresford had shoved her into the room. The dim blue glow of the night light reminded her of nights long ago when she'd been unable to sleep and instead lay there doomscrolling on her phone.

She stared at the main bedroom door, specifically at the door handle. She walked over to the door, switched on the main room light, and jiggled the handle. She knew how to pick a lock. But what could she use? She shoved her hands in her jeans pockets to think, and her eyes widened as her knuckles banged against the small penknife she'd put in there after she'd cut the seatbelt off in the car. She'd forgotten about that.

She pulled the knife out and knelt down. Inserting the small blade into the keyhole as far as it would go, she felt it hit the back of the lock. Then she turned it, applying light pressure as she rocked the blade up and down. When the pins didn't disengage, she pulled the knife out, took a deep breath, then tried again with slightly more force. This time, she felt the lock give. She turned the handle and the door opened with a slight creak.

Suzanna jumped to her feet and came over to the door. "Hidden talents, sis," she said, clapping Samantha on the back.

"Yeah, you don't want to know why I learnt how to do that," Samantha said, slipping the penknife back into her pocket.

Samantha stepped quietly out of the bedroom, holding her hand up to stop Suzanna from following straight away. The house was dark. She held her breath and listened. The only thing she heard was the hum of the fridge in the kitchen and snoring coming from the bedroom at the front of the house.

She put a finger to her lips, warning Suzanna to be quiet as she gestured to her to step out of the room. They crept down the hallway. The door of the front bedroom was open, and Samantha took a hesitant step into the room.

Mr Beresford was fully dressed, lying on his back on top of the doona on a double bed. His eyes were closed and his mouth was open. A framed black and white picture of his mother, frowning at the camera, sat on the bedside table. Even in death, she kept a stern watch over her son as he slept.

Samantha's hand went to her pocket as a foolish urge rose in her brain, telling her to rush in and stab, stab, stab the penknife into his throat. She *wasn't* weak and she desperately wanted him to know that. She wanted to see the realisation in his eyes as his soul left his body. She wondered how he would go with the Ash Man, what questions he'd have to answer. *What would his story be and what choices would he get, if any?*

She felt Suzanna grip her sleeve and let her pull her back out of the room.

They went to the front door, but the handle was locked and the three deadlocks had been engaged. The keys were nowhere in sight. Suzanna picked up the telephone receiver and listened, but the line was dead. She dragged open the small drawer of the telephone table, wincing as it jiggled up and down, causing the pens inside to roll and clank. She rummaged as quietly as she could through it, but the deadlock keys weren't there. She looked at Samantha and shook her head.

Samantha leaned in and whispered in her ear. "The knife won't fit in these locks. Is there a back door?"

Suzanna nodded and led her sister through the dining/kitchen area, through the laundry, to the back door. It, too, was locked, but it was only one handle, similar to the one that had been on the pink bedroom. No deadlocks.

While Samantha picked the lock, Suzanna went back into the kitchen. She opened cupboards as quietly as she could, searching for something she could use as a weapon. She found a knife block under the sink. She assumed Mr Beresford had hidden it there so none of the girls would find it if they somehow escaped.

She was on her knees, head and shoulders into the cupboard, when she heard Samantha open the door and hiss at her to come on.

She pulled a long, thin knife out of the knife block, and was backing out of the cupboard when the dog started barking.

43

Escape

Sat, 31 March 1984 – Samantha

SAMANTHA STOOD ON THE concrete landing in the early morning light. She was holding the back door open, waiting for Suzanna.

The sun was already rising, providing a distinct glow in the east. The sky was grey, but the clouds were high and it didn't feel like it was going to rain. Samantha took deep breaths in the clean crisp air and, even though her ribs hurt, it felt so good, like that first breath you take after swimming underwater for longer than is comfortable, pushing yourself to the limit.

Casper suddenly bounded up to her, barking happily. He started to run up and down the back steps.

A loud crash came from the front bedroom, then footsteps ran down the hallway, followed by swearing as Mr Beresford discovered the open door of the pink bedroom.

"What were you doing?" Samantha snapped as Suzanna ran through the doorway.

Suzanna held up the knife. "Getting this. I'm not going back in that room."

Samantha shook her head and followed Suzanna down the steps. When Suzanna hit the ground, she winced and Samantha noticed she didn't have any shoes on, just a pair of pink socks. *Oh well, too late now.* Hopefully it wouldn't slow her down.

She put her hand on Suzanna's shoulder and pointed to the end of the house. "Round the front. The car I came in is there."

Casper ran with them around the house to the old car, which was still where she'd left it nose-to-tail with Mr Beresford's car. Samantha yanked open the driver's side door and slid in, while Suzanna went around and got in the other side. Casper disappeared back around the side of the house.

'Shit, shit, shit!" Samantha yelled, slamming her hand against the steering wheel in frustration when she discovered the screwdriver was no longer in the ignition. She looked up and saw Mr Beresford come running around the side of the house. Casper was now snapping at his heels. "We're going to have to run. I don't have time to fuck around trying to hot-wire it."

She got out and noticed that both tyres on her side were flat, so there was no way she'd be driving it any distance anyway. The tyres had been slashed, so she assumed Mr Beresford had been thorough and had done the same to the two on the other side.

"This way," she yelled, taking off down the driveway. Maybe if they could get to the road, someone might come along and this could all be over.

"We should split up," Suzanna called. "He can't chase us both."

"No," Samantha said, stopping and turning around. "We need to stick together."

But Suzanna kept running. Casper followed her, loving this game, as she disappeared around the other side of the house. Samantha saw Mr Beresford hesitate when he reached the cars. He looked at her, then looked in the direction Suzanna had gone.

"I'M THE ONE YOU WANT, YOU IDIOT!" she called, waving her arms in the air. "I know where you live," she added with a smirk. "I know all about you. Margaret told me everything."

At the mention of Margaret's name, he frowned and took a step in her direction, and she turned and started running down the driveway again.

She was about halfway to the front gate, and extremely out of breath, when she heard a car start. She glanced back over her shoulder and saw his car moving forward. He turned in a tight circle, then he floored the accelerator, gravel spraying out from the tyres as he headed straight for her.

She turned and started running again, but she knew she wouldn't make it to the road. She could hear the car right behind her now, jouncing through potholes and thrumming over the corrugations in the dirt, and she had no doubt that he'd run her down with no hesitation. She suddenly threw herself sideways, rolling in a way that would have made her self-defence teacher proud, and came back to her feet, facing back towards the house. She took off again.

It took him a couple of seconds to turn around, but it gave her time to decide to head for the pile of boards that used to be a shed. She pumped her legs and arms, running faster than she'd ever run before. She was almost there, air burning in her lungs and a stitch cramping in her side with every breath ... she was going to make it. Until the front of the car slammed into her lower back, sending her flying. Rusty nails and long splinters dragged long bloody gashes, embedding themselves in her arms and chest as her body skidded across the top of the ancient pile of wood. She came to a rest near the other side of the jumble of boards.

Groaning, she rolled off, landing on her knees, immediately feeling the dew soaking through her jeans. She threw up and tried to stand, but her legs were too shaky, so she remained on her hands and knees.

She heard him turn the engine off and fling the car door open.

"Now what?" he asked moving around to her side of the pile. He stood over her like a triumphant gladiator. "You think you're so clever, don't you? But you're not. You're just a weak little girl. You can't get away."

"You don't know what I can and can't do," she said, turning her head and squinting up at him. "You don't get to tell me what to do."

"Look around," he said, holding his arms out and turning in a circle, before looking back down at her. "Where are you going to go? I'll deal with you, and I'll deal with your sister. I admit that I made a mistake. If there's one thing my mother taught me, it's to own your mistakes, take responsibility, and fix them yourself."

He leaned down and grabbed her by the hair, pulling her to her feet. Her right ankle was swelling. She thought it might be broken, so she tried not to put any weight on it.

He pulled her face close to his and leered at her. "It's a shame. You were so much like her, well, how she would be now. I would have been proud to call you my daughter and teach you the things you need to know to get by in this world. But not now. Now I see how useless you really are. My Michelle will be nothing like you."

Samantha spat a bloody gob of phlegm in his face. "Michelle is dead, you moron. The only ones she's like now are the girls you've killed: Michelle Donovan, Isabelle Bradford, Allison Brooke, Audrey Lowe. All of them, Michelle included, nothing but bones and memories. If Michelle knew what you've done in her name, she'd be disgusted. She wouldn't want anything to do with you."

He shook her violently and slapped her face over and over, punctuating his words with each slap. "You don't know anything. You keep Michelle's name out of your filthy mouth."

"I know more than you think," Samantha said. She was dizzy and she tasted the iron tang of blood as she swallowed. "What are you going to do when Margaret finds out what you've done? She's going to be devastated that she didn't do something about you when she had the chance."

"Margaret gave up any rights in relation to me when she divorced me," he said coldly. "How she feels is none of my concern. I should have listened to my mother when she said Margaret wasn't good enough for me."

"You're a real mummy's boy, aren't you?" Samantha sneered. "Did you play Mummy Says instead of Simon Says as a kid? Did you imagine Mummy when you were knocking up Margaret all those times?"

"You can keep my mother out of your filthy mouth, too," he growled. Then he punched her.

Samantha's head snapped backwards and everything went black. She didn't feel him toss her over his shoulder in a fireman's carry position and start walking towards the paddock.

44

Fixing Mistakes

Sat, 31 March 1984 – Suzanna

SUZANNA RAN AROUND THE house, heading the same way she'd run days ago when she'd first tried to escape. *How many days ago was that?* Her legs were stiff and she was silently berating herself for not putting shoes on. She hadn't bothered for the last few days because there was no point to shoes when you're confined to one room in a house. Shoes were really only useful outside.

She ran gingerly. Her socks had amassed a mighty collection of grass seeds and were soaked through from the morning dew. She felt every little pebble and burr she stepped on; it felt like stepping on blunted thumbtacks. There seemed to be a *lot* of them, and her feet were managing to find every single one.

Casper was running with her, loping easily along beside her. She stopped near a rusty old swing set with one single swing and a double where a kid sits on either end. One of the metal arms had broken off the single swing, and the faded orange plastic seat rested forlornly on the ground on that side. *How many of the other girls swung here*? she wondered briefly.

She heard a car start and the crunch of gravel under the tyres as it took off in a hurry. She turned around, expecting to see it hurtling round the corner of the house, but it didn't. *He must be chasing Samantha*, she thought with dismay. Even though it had been her idea to split up, she was regretting it now. She'd assumed he'd chase *her*, since she was closer. Then Samantha could have made it to the road and gone for help.

She started back the way she'd come, then saw Samantha running flat out on the other side of the house. She was heading for a heap of old boards near some metal yards. Mr Beresford's car was very close behind her and he wasn't slowing down.

Suzanna decided to head for the back paddock, then angle across and meet Samantha on the other side of the pile. They could hide in the long grass of the paddock and make their way around to the main road together.

"SAMANTHA," Suzanna screamed as she ran. "HEAD FOR THE PADDOCK."

Samantha gave no indication that she'd heard her, and Suzanna put her head down and ran, Casper bounding happily alongside her. She watched her feet, the pain from the rocks forgotten as she concentrated on not tripping over a mound of dirt or a dip or a dog. The wind swooshing in her ears made it hard to hear and she didn't hear the thump as the car slammed into Samantha, knocking her flying across the boards.

She remembered the wire fence at the last minute and ducked between two strands of wire, awkwardly ending up on her hands and knees. The knife she'd forgotten she was carrying bounced away. She looked up as the same chestnut horse she'd frightened the last time she did this snorted and galloped away. Casper abandoned her to chase this more interesting game.

She picked up the knife and moved as stealthily as she could towards Samantha, keeping low in the long grass. She couldn't hear the car anymore. She could hear voices, although she couldn't make out what was being said. All she focussed on was that Samantha was still alive.

The voices stopped suddenly and Suzanna stopped moving. She tried to breathe quietly, just listening, ignoring the shaky complaint from her thighs about being in a squat position for too long. She put her head up, and her heart missed a beat when she saw Mr Beresford heading towards her. He had Samantha slung over his shoulders and she wasn't moving.

She's not dead, Suzanna told herself ducking down again and moving as quietly as she could out of his way. *I'd know if she was dead.*

As he passed her, she heard him muttering, 'Filthy little bitch. I should have seen it. All you are is a mistake, and I know how to deal with mistakes. First, I'll deal with you, then I'll deal with the other mistake."

Suzanna followed him quietly. She had to suppress the urge to rise up out of the long grass like a savage and plunge the knife she was holding up to the hilt into his back. But she knew she needed to pick her moment and, while he was carrying Samantha like that, this wasn't it.

She knew where he was heading.

When she reached the clearing, Suzanna crept around and stood behind the gum tree that oversaw the impromptu graveyard. The trunk was large enough that she didn't think he'd see her, although she still stayed low, hunched down close to the ground.

Mr Beresford stood beside a fifth grave. *He must have dug it yesterday for me*, Suzanna realised. *He was about to kill me yesterday when Samantha turned up.*

He was breathing heavily from carrying the dead weight of Samantha's limp body all that way. The grave was shallow and empty, and a long-handled shovel lay on top of the dirt that was piled up next to the hole.

He turned sideways and shrugged Samantha off his shoulders. Suzanna winced as Samantha's body landed with a thump on her back in the grave.

"Here's one I prepared earlier," Mr Beresford chuckled. "Sorry, but you'll have to share. I hope you don't mind. It might be a little cosy, though. I thought I was only cleaning up one mistake, not twin mistakes, so it's not as deep as it should be."

Casper suddenly decided to return to the humans and see what he was missing out on. He ran out of the long grass behind Suzanna and jumped up against her back with a small yip. She grunted in surprise and the dog ran over to Mr Beresford.

"See, this is what happens to mistakes," Mr Beresford said, leaning down to pat Casper. He stood up again and spoke, still looking at Samantha's lifeless body. "I know you're there, Suzanna. You might as well come out."

Suzanna stepped out from behind the tree. She clutched the knife tightly and held it out in front of her. "Get away from her."

Mr Beresford sighed condescendingly as he turned to look at her, but he didn't move away. "You're as dumb as her, aren't you? Must run in the family." He gestured to the grave. "She's dead. You should have run while you had the chance. Now what are you going to do? Stab me? Good luck with that. You're just a little girl. You're no match for me. Or will you run? Where are you going to run to? You won't get far."

"She's not dead," Suzanna whispered, her eyes drawn to Samantha.

Despite the scratches, the splinters, and the bruises, Samantha's whole body was relaxed, all the tension completely gone out of her muscles. She looked peaceful. She could have been asleep.

Suzanna stared at her until she thought she saw Samantha's chest rise slightly. But maybe she imagined it because she couldn't imagine a world without her sister. Tears filled her eyes as she thought about how Samantha had lived a whole life without *her*. She couldn't do that. She'd always thought she was the strong twin, but now she understood how wrong she was. It had always been Samantha.

"Even in the classroom, you always thought you were better than everyone else, didn't you?" Mr Beresford said, startling her out of her thoughts. He was looking at her like he was appraising a cut of meat in the butcher shop. "Bossing people around. Always thinking the rules didn't apply to you. I don't know how I ever thought you were my daughter. I wouldn't *want* you for a daughter."

"Well, I don't want *you* for a father, so that makes us even," she responded, glancing between Samantha and him. "I pity any child of yours and I'm glad they all died, especially Michelle. It was a mercy for them to never have to know you."

Mr Beresford's face went dark as if storm clouds had just rolled in. "Give me the knife," he suddenly demanded, using his authoritative teacher voice and holding out his hand.

"No," she said, advancing towards him, gripping the knife hilt so hard her hand turned white.

"You always were stubborn, weren't you?" he said taking a step towards her.

"I still am," she said, taking a step to the side, making him turn to face her.

He suddenly lashed out with his leg, kicking the knife out of her hand. It landed in the dirt, just near the edge of the cleared area, half in and half out of the grass. The shock kept her motionless for a second, which was all the time he needed to step up to her, clamp a hand on her wrist, and twist it up behind her back.

Pain blazed through Suzanna's shoulder as she struggled to get away, but he was too strong.

"Not as tough as you thought you were, little girl?" he sneered.

He forced her to walk with him. He stopped twisting her arm but kept hold of her wrist as he bent to pick up the knife. She twisted her own wrist against his thumb, and suddenly she was free. She backed away, keeping her eyes on him.

"Not as smart as you think you are, old man?" she taunted him.

Without warning, he lunged forward and lashed out with the knife. Instinctively she stepped back, but she wasn't quick enough. Her eyes went wide and she brought her hands up to her throat where she felt a stinging sensation, then a warm sticky liquid trickling over her fingers. She fell to her knees in shock as he watched her with a smirk on his face.

"Little girls shouldn't play with knives," he said, standing over her. "Now, watch how we deal with mistakes."

"NO FUCKING WAY," Samantha shouted, climbing out of the grave behind him like an avenging angel. "YOU DON'T KILL MY SISTER ON MY WATCH, YOU BASTARD."

She leapt onto his back screaming like a banshee. "Now I'm going to deal with *my* mistake," she yelled, wrapping her legs around his middle. She clawed at his eyes with one hand, while her other hand stabbed the penknife again and again into the side of his neck.

Blood spurted and ran down his collar as he staggered around, trying to throw her off. Suzanna put her hands up, thinking they were going to fall on her, but Samantha's shifting weight caused them to move away from her and into the long grass.

Mr Beresford stumbled over Casper, who yelped and bolted away. The momentum caused Samantha to tumble forward, over Mr Beresford's shoulder, bringing them both down. He landed on top of her and Suzanna heard him grunt in satisfaction. He stood up, holding his hand to his neck, trying to stem the flow of blood that was pumping from several wounds.

"This time, stay dead, you bitch," he spat and kicked her in the side.

"NOOOO!" Suzanna howled when she saw the kitchen knife buried in her sister's stomach.

She threw herself at Mr Beresford, lashing out wildly, punching, kicking, forcing him away from Samantha. He was unprepared for the ferocity of her attack, and he backed further into the long grass that surrounded the little clearing.

Suzanna was so enraged she barely saw the slight movement just behind him on the ground, but her brain saw it. Australian country kids were brought up to be aware of where they were stepping, especially in long grass. The large brown snake was almost the same colour as the dirt and dried grass and at least a metre and a half long. Instinctively she stepped back and she watched the snake sink its fangs deep into Mr Beresford's calf. The snake hung on for a minute or so as Mr Beresford screamed and batted at it, trying to make it let go, then it dropped to the ground and slithered silently away.

Mr Beresford crawled away, clawing his way across the ground until he reached the tree. He pulled himself up, so he was sitting with his back against the trunk. He was whimpering and wheezing and the blood started to pump faster from his neck as the snake venom worked its way through his system, affecting his blood's ability to clot.

Suzanna moved around to the other side of the grave and picked up the long-handled shovel. She walked up to Mr Beresford, and he looked up at her weakly. "You won't be doing this to any other girls," she said. Then, she swung the shovel with all her strength. "That's my mistake dealt with," she said, dropping the shovel. "There'll be no more mistakes today."

Suzanna turned to Samantha. She looked at the knife in Samantha's stomach. There was no way she could remove it without causing her sister to bleed out faster. But, if she didn't do anything, she would bleed out anyway.

Torn, she knelt by Samantha's side and stroked her forehead, tears rolling down her cheeks. "What do I do, Sammie? Tell me what to do."

45

Promises

SAMANTHA WONDERED IF IT was weird that the warm blood pooling beneath her felt kind of nice, comforting even. She felt no pain, just free and light, as if her addiction to her depression had finally been conquered, the heavy darkness that had weighed her down her whole life banished forever. She opened her eyes and smiled at her sister.

Suzanna knelt by Samantha, then moved so she was sitting with Samantha's head in her lap.

"Go back to the house and see if the phone is really dead," Samantha said. "If he's just unplugged it, you can plug it back in. If not, take his car. The keys are in it. I think it's an automatic, so 'R' for reverse, 'D' for drive. Accelerator on the right, brake on the left."

She closed her eyes and the smile stayed on her lips. "Remember when Dad used to sit one of us on his knee when we were little and let us steer on the dirt road when we took the rubbish to the tip?" She opened her eyes again. "Just do that. Drive to the next property and phone home. That's all you have to do."

"I'm not going without you," Suzanna said, shaking her head. "That's not happening."

"You *are* going without me," Samantha said, still looking at her sister. Casper lay down beside her and snuggled up close. She absentmindedly stroked his fur as she closed her eyes again. "You're going to live. I know I'm not. I had my chance. I had *two* chances. I didn't go through all this for the both of us to die."

Suzanna kept shaking her head, not willing to accept that her sister was not going home with her.

"I see myself in you, like I'm looking at a reflection," Samantha said softly, reaching up and pushing a strand of hair off her sister's cheek. "I often wondered if I was the reflection, though. Earlier, when I said people thought I was just a pale imitation of you, well, by 'people', that includes me. I thought that. You were always more real than I was, the one everyone loves."

"That's not true. I love you!" Suzanna sobbed, stroking her sister's hair. "You can't die, Sammie. You can't leave me alone. How am I supposed to live a whole life without you?"

"You'll do a way better job than I did without you," Samantha said. She ran a finger over the cut on Suzanna's neck, smearing the blood like she was fingerpainting. "I thought he'd slashed your throat." She'd acted without thinking when she'd seen Suzanna holding her throat and the blood on her hands. All that blood. But Suzanna must have moved quick enough that the blade just caught the surface of the skin. "I thought I'd fucked up royally again. You're going to have an awesome scar, sis. Every time you see it in the mirror, think of me."

"I won't need to see a scar to think of you," Suzanna said, still stroking Samantha's hair. "I'll think of you every minute of every day."

"No, you won't," Samantha said. "You might think that now, but life will start up again for you and you'll have other things to think of. Think of it as a new beginning. Please live your life ... for both of us. Don't do what I did the first time around. Don't waste the wonder. If you remember to look, you'll see the wonder, and me, reflected in every leaf, every flower, every butterfly, every animal, every raindrop, every moment, every universe."

Neither of them said anything for a few minutes. The only sound was the rustle of grass as a light breeze moved through. Samantha was vaguely aware that Mr Beresford had now stopped making any noise. *Good*, she thought. *Have a great time with the Ash Man, you bastard.*

Samantha kept smiling as she looked at Suzanna, remembering their lives together, much like she had on the Ash Train. She filled her memory with her beautiful twin. Her sister had her whole life ahead of her and she knew it was going to be as beautiful as she was. "You know, sis, maybe it would have worked out differently if I'd stepped up the first time around. Maybe we both could have lived? But then, maybe we're so awesome that there's only room for one of our universes at a time. This time, it's your turn."

"It's not fair," Suzanna sobbed. "Why can't we both live? Why does it have to be one or the other?"

"Life's not fair," Samantha said, closing her eyes. "It's just the way it is. Random things happen – that's the nature of universes, apparently. We all make our choices, every second of every day. Some of them we regret, but hopefully most of them we won't. If we're smart, or lucky, the non-regrets will outnumber the regrets, and the regrets won't grow into beasts we can't let go of." She took a deep breath. This time it hurt, but she didn't mind the pain. "All we can do is do what we think is right at the time. And this time around, I regret nothing, whether the Ash Man believes that or not. I believe it with all my heart."

The breeze picked up, whisking away the sound of Suzanna's despair. The sun moved out from behind the clouds and shone its warming rays on the world. A magpie in a nearby gum tree chortled. A vivid green and yellow grasshopper leapt high and landed on the tip of a swaying blade of grass. The chestnut horse that had run from Suzanna earlier edged closer, snuffling quietly, curious as to why these people were lying about in its paddock.

Samantha took a shaky breath and Casper moved, draping his head over her thigh. She rested her hand on his head. "Please take care of Casper. None of this is his fault."

Suzanna couldn't speak, but she nodded through her tears.

Samantha opened her eyes one last time, smiling up at her sister. "Remember what we promised Dad? Promise *me* you'll do what you want to do, not what other people tell you to do. Make things happen *for* you, don't just let them happen to you. Promise *me* you'll live happy ... for me, for both of us. Promise me you won't waste the wonder."

"I promise, Sammie. I promise with my heart and soul. Always and forever."

46

The Ash Train

Samantha

THE SWAY OF THE Ash Train woke Samantha, and she looked around.

She was near the front of the carriage this time. The piles of ashes were on different seats from last time she'd been here, but everything else was pretty much the same.

She turned and smiled at the people behind her. They all looked worried and were all sitting in the same posture she remembered from the first time she'd caught this train: straight backed, knees together, hands clasped on their thighs.

She turned to face the front again and thought about the last week. She wondered how she could be both sad and happy at the same time.

She was sad that she and Toni had both died, but happy that Suzanna had lived, which was the most important thing. Suzanna now had the chance to live the life she was supposed to have lived in the previous timeline, albeit without her sister. She knew Suzanna wouldn't waste her life like she herself had the first time around.

She wondered how Mum and Dad would cope with her death. At least they'd have closure this time, so there was a good chance they could get on with their lives this time around, too, rather than being stuck in limbo with their wheels turning but going nowhere like last time.

From experience, she knew that a missing person always leaves a hole in a family, but the fact that they knew she was dead would help them move on. At least they wouldn't be looking for her every time they walked down the street. Mum wouldn't need to insist the door remained unlocked and the porch light on forever, and they could even consider moving away from unpleasant memories. Although, they would also not want to forget the good memories, so maybe they would stay?

Her family would have a proper grave to visit to reinforce that their daughter, and sister, was not coming home this time.

She, again, wondered how Toni had got on with the Ash Man and what choice she'd made between afterlife and rebirth. She still had no doubt that Toni would have reached the second carriage. *Toni would choose rebirth*, she thought, nodding to herself. Toni seemed like someone who loved life and would want another chance to make her mark on other universes.

She thought briefly about Margaret Watford, the ex-Mrs Beresford. *What would she be like when she found out what her ex-husband had done?* She suspected Margaret would be crushed when she found out. *Would she be able to forgive herself for not doing something all those years ago? Something that might have stopped him or at least warned people about him?* Hopefully, she would be able to pick herself up and continue to live life on her own terms. She was a strong lady, and Samantha thought she'd be OK.

Wrapped in the rhythmic sound of the Ash Train as it hurtled along its phantom tracks, Samantha smiled and relaxed for what felt like the first time ever. She leaned back in her seat to wait for the Ash Man.

She'd spend the time contemplating her own choices, not quite sure which way she'd jump this time.

47

Beginnings

Tue, 24 March 1998 – Suzanna

SUZANNA SQUATTED DOWN AND propped a sketch up against her sister's headstone. She rubbed the scar at the base of her neck as she often did when she was thinking. She briefly wondered what happened to the sketches she left here every year but dismissed the thought. It didn't matter.

"Happy birthday, Sammie. I miss you every single day."

Every year for the past fourteen years she had visited Samantha's grave on their birthday and left a sketch showing her sister what had happened in her life over the past twelve months. She would continue to do this for as long as she could. When the time came to meet again, Samantha would know that Suzanna had kept her promises.

The splash of colour from the bouquets of mixed flowers – pinks, whites, blues, oranges – told her that Dad and Mum, and possibly others, had already been here today. A tuft of white dog fur was caught in one of them and she smiled.

Casper and Dad were almost inseparable these days. The dog was still the happiest dog she'd ever known, although he'd slowed down a lot now with age. Casper had helped Dad weather some dark days, gave him a purpose on those days when he'd get lost in his own head. She knew that would make Samantha happy.

She thought of the other girls who hadn't been as lucky as her: Michelle Donovan, Isabelle Bradford, Allison Brooke, and Audrey Lowe. Every year she also made pilgrimages to visit their proper graves. She'd reached out to their families, but she understood why they were reluctant to talk to her, and that was OK. She was a reminder of what they'd lost, but she'd promised never to forget them, and they were never far from her mind.

She leaned on the grey granite headstone for support as she started to stand up, moving a hand to her belly when she felt the baby kick. Michael noticed her hesitation, and he quickly stepped forward and helped her up.

Michael pulled her close and wrapped his arms around her, murmuring, "Be careful, Suze. It's more than just you in there now."

Suzanna smiled up at him, reached up, and stroked his cheek. "I know."

She stayed in his arms for a few more minutes, before reluctantly pulling away. She linked her arm through her husband's arm and looked around at this place of sadness. At the cold hard stones half buried in the cold hard dirt. At the grief-laden people staring teary-eyed at their loved ones' last resting places. At the colourful flowers and mementos, attempts to brighten up this indifferent grey plot of land.

The warmth of the sun on her shoulders, the warmth of the child inside trying out its arms and legs, and the warmth of her husband's love enveloped her like a blanket on a cold winter's night, and she felt guilty for just an instant.

It felt wrong to be so happy, especially in a place like this, but she would keep her promise to Samantha. Always and for ever.

She was still smiling, although tears threatened to spill, as she looked back down at Samantha's grave again. "I might need a bigger sketch each year after this, Sammie, or even a couple of them, to fit all of us in. The next few years are going to be busy, assuming we all survive the arrival of the new millennium in my universe! Wherever you are, whatever choice you made, I hope you're as happy as I am."

She and Michael turned and started walking back to the car.

THE END?

Other Books and Stories by GK Bird

Story collections

Saving the Scarlet Macaw & Other Stories

The Ash Train series

Reflections: Samantha's Story